OHIO DOMINICAN UNIVERSITY
LIBRARY
1216 SUNBURY ROAD
COLUMBUS, OHIO 43219-2099

W9-ASA-244

OHIO
DOMINICAN
UNIVERSITY™

SINCE 1911

Donated by
Floyd Dickman

walk away home

OTHER NOVELS BY PAUL MANY

These Are the Rules
My Life, Take Two

F Many
any, Paul.
alk away home

OCT 2004
Received
Ohio Dominican

walk away home

paul many

walker & company
new york

Copyright © 2002 by Paul Many

All rights reserved. No part of this book may be reproduced or transmitted
in any form or by any means, electronic or mechanical, including
photocopying, recording, or by any information storage and retrieval system,
without permission in writing from the Publisher.

All the characters and events portrayed in this work are fictitious.

First published in the United States of America in 2002 by
Walker Publishing Company, Inc.

Published simultaneously in Canada by Fitzhenry and Whiteside,
Markham, Ontario L3R 4T8

For information about permission to reproduce selections from
this book, write to Permissions, Walker & Company, 435 Hudson Street,
New York, New York 10014

Library of Congress Cataloging-in-Publication Data

Many, Paul.
    Walk away home / Paul Many.
        p. cm.
    Summary: To escape his problems at school and at home,
Nick, who prefers walking to automobile travel, hikes to his aunt's
cabin in hopes of spending the summer there.
    ISBN 0-8027-8828-9
    [1. Coming of age—Fiction. 2. Family problems—Fiction.
3. Aunts—Fiction. 4. Walking—Fiction.] I. Title.
PZ7.M3212 Wal 2002
[Fic]—dc21   2002022964

Visit Walker & Company's Web site at www.walkerbooks.com

BOOK DESIGN BY JENNIFER ÐADDIO

Printed in the United States of America
10 9 8 7 6 5 4 3 2 1

To Linda and Zoe

and the memory
of Aunt Mary

*We should go forth on the
shortest walk ... in the spirit of
undying adventure, never to return.*
—HENRY DAVID THOREAU

Acknowledgments

Thanks to the Power of the Pen team at McCord Jr. High, Toledo, Ohio, for their metaphorical suggestions.

To my editor at Walker & Company, Emily Easton, for keeping me honest.

To my wife, Linda Dove, for keeping me.

chapter 1

SO LEAVE ME ALONE, WILLYA?

I mean, here I am walking off the edge of Buttpimple Nowhere, and this guy comes shuffling up the other side of the road—one arm stuck out, thumb up, the other wrapped around some big green . . . something. Next he's passing me, and of course he's got to wave and it's "Howdy!" and I wave back and not so much as *smile*, but then, of course, he's crossing over.

"Where you headed?" he says. We're walking against traffic, and he keeps looking over his shoulder.

I nod ahead, not wanting to give him much to work with.

"Just quit a job myself," he says. "Changin' tires on trucks." He's shorter than me and has a weaselly look like he just smeared dog crap on somebody's doorknob. "Got on my nerves."

I nod again, taking a quick glance: hair all stringy and blond, T-shirt with the sleeves rolled, dirt-streaked arm wrapped around . . . It's a big blow-up alligator he's got there!

"Guys used to wait till they saw me drinking a coffee or something, and then they'd bust one off the rim. 'BLAM!' Man, I would j-jump. . . ." He pinches out the front of his shirt between two shaky fingers, and there's so many brown stains on it, I thought it was the pattern.

"So it's on to cleaner pastures," he says. "How about you?" He's running along beside me to keep up, scrunching the alligator under his arm. I swear I'm not asking him about it. In fact, I'm not saying *anything*.

He keeps right on going, anyway, just like I was afraid, pouring out his whole miserable history in steam-powered, banjo-backed, three-part harmony, laying on heavy all the "dangers, toils, and snares," he's suffered and how "he don't need no regular job anyways" since he likes "the simple ways." (Since they're more like him, I guess.) Amen.

In spite of myself I'm nodding like one of those bobble-head dolls in the back window of a car—"terminal politeness," my ex-girlfriend called it.

Now, listen; it's not like I hate people, but sometimes you want to be alone. You understand what I'm saying? If I hankered to hunker by the campfire and chew the rag, I would have taken the bus.

You see, it's like this: When you're out walking, you see all this amazing stuff—a tree growing straight from a wall, a store with barrels out front full of live crabs, a path that leads to a pond where you can sit and eat your baloney sandwich and an otter pokes his slick head from the water to take a look at you. One day, I saw the Statue of Liberty going by, lying on the back of a truck!

Not that you need to be by yourself to see all this, but if you're with somebody, they can't leave it alone. They've got to tell you to *look*, when *there* it is. Then they've got to try and figure out what it all *means* ("Can't be the *real* one; wouldn't fit on a truck, never, but I wonder if . . .") and how it got there and where it's coming from and where it's going to and yammer on about it for the next couple of miles until it gets all chewed up and spit out in a wad of ordinary.

"So where *you* running from?" he says.

"What makes you think I'm running?" I say, finally riled.

"Come *on*," he says. "Everybody on the road is running from somewhere."

"Not me," I say.

And technically I am speaking the truth. I am *walking*, and walking is not the same as running; it just puts things on hold for a while. I'd have the whole summer before I'd have to report to Colonel Saltine at the academy and loads of road to figure out all the things Samantha said before *she* walked.

The guy seems to think for a second, but he only seems to, and it's just for a second. "Why, if I wrote down *half* the things I done," he says, and he's off again.

Finally a pickup truck stops. "You boys looking for a ride?" The driver is an old guy with a gray buzz cut. I don't hitch and get carsick anyway, but my newfound friend runs right over and hops right in.

I give the usual thumbs-down, and the driver ("Yeah, bo, suit yerself") peels off and I can see my traveling buddy looking out the back, his rubber alligator sticking out the window, his face all screwed like he can't figure me out.

Join the club.

Like I said, if I wanted to mingle, I would have taken the bus.

My foolishly trusting parents had gone off on their trip the day before, and I had the whole house to myself and all morning to get ready. I loaded my pack with camping gear and road food, draped my bedroll tight around the top, and walked out the front door. I did not break the Prime Directive. I did not look back.

That's the beauty of walking. You don't have to figure out schedules or make reservations. There's no kissing good-bye. It's pure leaving.

When I passed the bus station at the far edge of town, I glanced through the foggy window at all the poor souls sticking to their plastic chairs in that sweat-soaked diesel-smelling purgatory and kept going.

After a while I passed row houses, then houses with their own yards all around, then farms, then woods. Every once in a while, another town would come up, and I'd see all this in reverse—the woods, the farms, the houses, the couple of blocks of streets and storefronts. When I'd get to the crossroads downtown I'd park my pack next to the counter in a diner and have something to eat, people mostly treating me like I was invisible, talking only with waitresses.

"What'll it be, hon?"

I tipped extra when they called me that.

I slept out behind the far outbuildings of farms a couple of nights, the stars like the winking points in some infinite connect-the-dots puzzle. I'd lie awake looking at them, imagining that if I could only draw in all the lines, I'd have a picture of everything.

The towns got smaller and smaller, and it was longer and longer between them. The last town I passed through had one sad-looking diner—the counter guy in his white cap sitting on the curb out front, reading a newspaper—a flea market, and a dusty grocery. Then it, too, played out.

It was starting to get dusky and chilly. I found myself looking closely at houses with For Sale signs, checking for one with no lights. You'd think I'd have learned by now.

Soon I was passing a row of high, overgrown bushes. Through a break I could see a grassy field with a plywood wishing well in the middle, surrounded by a circle of run-down cabins, one with mounds of old scrap metal—bedsprings, farm machinery, a pyramid of rusted milk crates—in the yard around it.

I pulled a wadded-up piece of paper out of my shirt pocket and for the hundredth time read the address in my father's cramped handwriting. It should be right near here, but I saw no signs or mailboxes or anything. Then I realized I was standing between a pair of crooked green telephone poles about as far apart as goalposts. Connecting their tops were two rainbow-curved bars hung with letters that spelled against the sky:

HAPPINESS FAR

Before I had half a chance to figure out what *this* was supposed to mean, a black pile-of-junk van flew up on the grass behind me, and an old woman in high-tops leaped out and ran—bluish hair streaming—between the poles and into the weedy yard. Next a sheriff's cruiser with a red splat on its windshield, siren screaming, lights whipping, cut in front of me and spit out two deputies, as close on her as smell on gym socks.

I was thinking how good she kept her lead, even though she had a net bag full of grapefruit thwacking her legs, when I saw she held in her other hand some big, ugly-looking pistol.

"Hee . . . hee . . . hee," she laughed in a way that would have sounded evil if it wasn't coming from her ropy old throat. Without stopping, she raised the pistol and took aim at a mirrored lawn ball in front of one of the cabins and fired. The ball exploded, leaving a red splatter on the birdbath where it had sat, probably blowing some chipmunk to stuffed-cheeks heaven.

"Yeehah!" she said, just as the shorter of the two deputies grabbed her and they started doing a kind of polka, the two of them whirling around and around, the bag of grapefruit bouncing off the taller, older deputy, who was looking for an opening, the wishing well getting knocked cockeyed, until finally the younger one got her shooting arm twisted up behind her, pried the gun out of her hands, and cuffed her.

"Yaaaaaaaaah! Get offa me!" she yelled, dropping the bag of grapefruit and slumping to the ground.

"Hey, leave her alone!" I heard someone shout as the door to one of the cabins banged shut and a skinny guy came running, ponytail flapping, toward the deputies and their perp.

The younger deputy struggled to get a plastic card out of his shirt pocket, which he began to read.

"Youhavetherighttoremainsilentanythingyousaycanandwill-beusedag—"

"Look, Red," said the older deputy as the skinny man got nearby. "Don't get into this."

"Jane's nearly eighty now, Darryl," he said. "Why don't you let go of her?"

"Tell them, Ronnie-boy. Tell them," she said, going stiff as the deputies struggled to haul her to her feet, finally standing her up like a tin woman.

"She was driving around taking potshots with this," said the young deputy, hanging the pistol by the trigger guard from his pinkie, Professional- TV-Forensic-Investigator style.

"It's a *paintball* gun," said Red.

The deputies said nothing.

"Did she hit anyone?" said Red.

"That's not the point," said the older man, who I could see by his arm patch was the sheriff himself. He had a mustache like the kind you draw on someone's picture as a joke, and in spite of the chase, his uniform was creased and clean. "She can't be driving around shooting up the town like some damned drunken cowboy."

"Cow*girl*," said Red.

"Cow*woman*," said the old woman. "And I don't drink."

"You shut up," said the young deputy, who you could see took his job way too seriously.

By now people started coming out of the cabins: a huge, muscular guy with a red crew cut wearing a leather jacket over a white T-shirt; a bare-chested guy with saggy boobs, wearing black tights and smoking a cigarette in a long holder; a thin woman with blond dreadlocks; another woman from the same cabin as Red, who had on sandals and a track suit and long, straight hair; and an older frail-looking Asian woman in a housedress and curlers. Maybe the place was some kind of asylum for lunatic circus performers?

"Jane's been handling firearms since she was a little girl," said Red. "If she didn't hit no one, it's because she wasn't aiming at no one."

"Freaks!" I heard someone shout. Across the road behind me a carload of kids around my age had pulled up. They got out, and a couple of them sat on the hood of the car, drinking cans of soda like they were watching a drive-in movie on a sheet stretched between the splintery green poles.

"Look," said the younger guy. "The sheriff, he warned you we were gonna stop cutting so much slack around here."

Another carful of kids pulled up next to the first, radio blaring. The deputies started taking quick glances at the two groups—one from the cabins and the other across the road.

"What do *you* say, Darryl?" said Red.

"I'm sorry," the older man said. "But it's not like I'm the sheriff of Nottingwood or something here. You people bring it on yourselves—always having to be different. We got to take her in, I'm afraid." And in spite of protests and carrying on from the inmates, they dragged her off and put her in the back seat of the cruiser, which was parked only a few feet from me.

The kids across the road started chanting: "Hip-pie scum! Hip-pie scum!" A soda can landed next to me. As the cruiser pulled away, they were whooping and hollering. A firecracker went off, a couple of people from the cabins jumped, and the guy with the red hair hit the ground. The kids laughed.

I've never known any trouble that couldn't be fixed by walking away, and I turned on my heel and started to go. But I didn't get two steps before I felt a hand on my shoulder.

"Nick?" said the blond, mighty-dreadlocked woman who had snuck up behind me.

"Wanda?" I said.

chapter 2

"NICKY, I CAN'T BELIEVE— Is that *you?*"

"Hi, Wanda," I said. Even though she's my mom's sister, she's always insisted I should "step on the 'aunt'" and just call her by her first name. "Otherwise makes me feel like some lady who crochets covers for her toaster," she explained.

"What are you *doing* here?" She held me by the shoulders. "It's been so long." She stood back a step. "I don't believe it."

She hugged me, but we don't do bodily contact in my family, so my half came out like I bumped into her and was patting her back to make her burp.

"What was that all about?" I said when she let go. I could see the inmates melting back into their cabins as the bloodthirsty posse across the street galloped off.

"Why, just your welcoming party to the Good Ship Happiness," she said. "Is everything okay at home?" she added, suddenly serious.

"Yeah, it's okay," I said.

We both looked at each other for a few seconds, neither ready to give much ground.

"You look—different," I said. Wanda had always looked like an overinflated version of Mom. But now she was thin, like all the air had been let out. And her hair—short and dark before—was now that mass of blond dreadlocks. No wonder I hadn't recognized her. Maybe she was in the witness protection program?

"Yep. Lopped off another me's worth." She turned around, her hand over her head like a dancer. "Got tired of lugging all the extra carry-ons. What do you think?"

The lightness of her hair set off her dark eyebrows, and with her warm hazel eyes, she looked—How can you say this about an older relative of yours?—good.

"You're—different," I repeated thickly.

"Yes," she said. "You said that."

Another strange, strained silence.

"Well, as long as you're here, come on in." She held onto her cheeriness by a thread. "I was just making dinner. You *are* hungry?"

Up close, her cabin was *really* beat looking. It was surrounded by waist-high weeds, and where the paint wasn't peeling, it was spotted with splats of all different colors, like some giant paint-crapping bird did a bombing run on it. A garden hose was stuck in a window.

Wanda carefully reached through a broken pane of glass on the front door and turned the doorknob from inside. "Keeps me from locking myself out," she said as she concentrated on avoiding the pointy pieces of glass that surrounded her wrist like a bracelet.

As I looked down to wipe my feet, I saw she still had her old doormat from the last place, the lettering nearly worn off. ("WELL Don't just stand there looking stupid COME ON IN.")

"Stay close so you don't get lost now," she said as she cut through the tiny, book-lined living room. I got a quick glimpse of myself in the mirror that hung in it: clothes wrinkled and ragged from sleeping outdoors, a big smudge of road dirt across my cheek. I must've looked like an arriving inmate to those kids in the cars. No wonder they chucked a can at me.

The kitchen was about the size of an elevator and had shelves that wrapped around the walls and reached to the ceiling. These were crammed with jars full of what looked like science experiments gone wrong—deformed dog brains, two-headed chicks in formaldehyde—but when I looked close, I could see they had labels on them that claimed they were peaches and pears and peas and tomatoes and stuff. Other jars were full of dried leaves and seashells and screws and paper clips and walnuts. Bunches of dried plants hung upside down in front of the windows. The place was full of moisty, foody smells, making me remember I hadn't eaten much since breakfast.

"The old woman they took away? That's Jane," my aunt was saying, "Jane Juan." She scanned a row of the jars, her head tilted back, touching the label on each. "And that's not the first time, by the way. That tall, skinny guy is Ron Branstool—Red Dog Branstool, actually—he's her grandson. She's from out West somewheres but couldn't take care of herself anymore, so Red Dog and Fawn, his wife, took her in. You like tomatoes?"

"Okay," I lied.

"I always cook for a couple, but I'll stretch this anyway." She opened the jar but stopped right as she was about to dump it in.

"Oops," she said. "Looks like the seal on this one's gone bad." She took it to the bathroom and spilled it into the john.

"Jane was getting lonesome for shooting things up, I guess," she said as she flushed, "so they got her a paintball gun for Christmas." She rolled her eyes as she brushed past me back to the kitchen. "Geniuses. She usually just shoots it off around here." She pointed to the kitchen window, which had a messy blue splat on it. "But she must've gotten an itchy trigger finger and took off downtown. They should've expected it. Give a kid a chain saw—" She shook her head. She pulled another of the jars off the shelf and opened it.

"This one's just fine," she said, pouring it in the pot on the stove, which had an overflowing ashtray next to it.

"Darryl, the sheriff—the tall one with the Oil Can Harry mustache?—he's about at the city limits of his patience, but he's okay. I think he's sweet on me. It's his sidekick, Walter, the young guy, you have to watch out for. But enough about that. Set down your pack and talk. Do your parents know you're here?" She shot me a worried look.

"I told them I was going," I said.

Which was true. The first couple hours out, I felt kind of bad and called them from a pay phone and said not to worry that I wasn't home, that I started out early. I just didn't happen to tell them *where* I started for.

And I guess it was really their answering machine I told. It's the way we do most of our talking, anyway. Some families have photo albums. We have a collection of sound bites:

Bweeeep: "Graduation went fine. Talk to you later."

Bweeeep: "I found dinner in the microwave. Don't wait up, I'll be out late."

Bweeeep: "It was just a sprain, like I told you. I gave them the med card number. I'll catch a ride. Talk to you."

"I didn't know you were coming," Wanda repeated. She was staring at the pot.

"Well—" I started to say.

"You know," she said, "I've been having trouble with this burner. I don't think it's working." She lifted the pot to another and turned it on, bouncing the palm of her hand on the burner she took it from.

"Ow," she said, licking her hand. "I guess it's hotter than I thought. So you just up and decided to give ol' Wanda a visit? That it? Well I'm glad you came. It's been about how long I've been out here and I haven't seen you?"

"A while. I don't know. A year?"

"And how *did* you find me?" she said, glancing out of the corner of her eye.

"There was a piece of paper in my father's desk with a 'W' and an address on it. I figured it had to be you."

"Your father had my address?" she said casually, watching the pot as she stirred with a long-handled wooden spoon.

"And phone number."

She adjusted the burner knob.

"Why didn't you call?"

"I thought I'd surprise you."

"Soo-prise, soo-prise," she said. "And you drive now? You have a car?"

"No. I walked."

"*Walked?*" She stopped stirring and turned and looked at me, hand on hip "From *home?*"

"Yeah," I said.

"Nicky!" she said.

"It wasn't really *that* far."

She shook her head.

"I used to walk over to your place all the time."

"Yeah," she said, "But I wasn't across the whole damn state. It must've taken you—"

"A couple of days," I said.

"A *couple?*" she said.

"Three," I said. "I don't mind. You know I like walking."

"Well, you're certainly not your mother's child," she said. "Madeline wouldn't walk across the street to pick up a fifty-dollar bill."

After a while the stuff in the pot began popping and spluttering, gobs flying off to join those of dinners of yesteryear on the walls near the stove. Wanda started adding spices from jars and other stuff she pulled from the half-size refrigerator under one of the counters.

"So that's it, huh?" she said. "That's your story. You just woke up one day and decided to walk over here."

"That's my story, and I'm sticking to it," I said—an old line we used when one of us told a tall tale. We both laughed.

"Well, you know you'll still have to pull your weight around here," she said, seeming to relax a little. "That hasn't changed."

"I know," I said.

"You can start by setting the table." She waved the spoon at a stack of plates on one of the shelves.

The dining area was the corner of the living room next to the kitchen, and it didn't take long to set everything out. Soon we were sitting down to a big bowl of some kind of brownish gumbo stuff. This was one other thing about Wanda. She wasn't such a great cook.

"Well, what do you think? Not as fancy as your mom makes, but tasty, no?"

"Great," I lied through a mouthful. "Mom doesn't cook much these days anyways, and me and Dad are hopeless."

"She still working?"

"Yeah," I said. "Still doing the real estate thing."

"Well, when you're working, you don't have the time," said Wanda.

"She's out showing houses a lot at night, and she mostly doesn't get home till late. Dad, too."

Wanda stopped eating, looked up from her plate for a few seconds, then started again.

"You want to call and tell them you got here okay?" she said.

"They're not home," I said.

"Oh, right, it's still too early," she said, looking at the half-melted plastic clock on the back of the stove.

"No, I mean they went away. On a trip. They had it planned a long time. It was like a repeat honeymoon or something."

"Where?"

"I forget. Something like Arugula. They wrote it down, but I lost it."

She put down her fork.

"Look at me, Nick," she said. "What's the story here? What's going on? I need you to tell it to me straight."

"It's nothing," I said. "Really."

She kept looking at me.

"They left me bus money to go to a meeting—an orientation. It's for a place they want me to go in the fall. This school."

"By yourself?" she said. "They wanted you to go and look at this school without them?"

"We already went there once," I said. "To look it over. Mom and Dad and me. We talked with the guy who runs it—Colonel Salter, he knows my dad—and we got the tour and everything. That's why I came here instead of going to the orientation. I figure I already saw it."

"What's the matter with the school you're going to?"

"I was kind of asked to leave," I said.

"Nick!"

"It wasn't really my fault."

"You want to tell me about it?"

"Why didn't you tell me *you* were leaving?" I said, suddenly angry. Who was she to grill me? She taught me all I knew about covering my tracks.

"No fair answering a question with a question," she said.

"Couldn't we do this after we eat?" I said.

"That's another question," she said. But then she hesitated. "Why not?" she finally said, and reached across the table and squeezed my wrist. "I'm sure whatever it was, it wasn't all that bad anyway."

"I wish you could make everybody else believe that."

We looked each other in the eye. I could hear the melted clock on the stove grinding away the seconds.

"Well, okay," she said, releasing her grip and patting my wrist. "So what do you think of all this?" she waved her fork at the room around us.

"It's nice," I said. "It's so—"

"Neat, right? Go ahead, say it. This is the new, improved Wanda you're looking at here. The weight, the hair"—she plumped it with her hand—"all those jars in the kitchen? Fawn taught me all about canning, and we have a big communal garden here. Grow all my own stuff. I painted all the rooms, and this was old furniture I fixed up." She lifted a corner of the plastic tablecloth to show me the scarred plywood underneath. "It was like starting a fire from wet wood, but I was determined this time."

I faked my most sincere smile, trying to show I was happy for her, but a new Wanda was nothing new.

"I've really turned things around this time; not just a new leaf—a whole new tree," she said, like she was trying to convince herself. "I've even got my own business now. No more workin' for the Man."

"You own a business?" I said. Maybe she really *had* reformed.

"Yes," she said, sounding hurt that I acted so surprised. "Well, I'm *half* owner—with a friend of mine. It's a doughnut shop."

"Doughnuts?" I said, surprise on top of surprise. Given her lack of talent in the cooking department, serving up any kind of substance for human consumption was the last thing I ever thought Wanda would do.

"I had to jump at it when it came up. That's why I had to leave so quick. I was going to write you or give you a call, but I didn't want your mom and dad— As soon as we get it going, it's really going to be *the* thing." She stopped and grabbed my wrist again. "I know you've heard that from me before, but this is something I'm really, really good at this time."

"This shop," I said, an idea bubbling up in my brain like gas in a swamp, "maybe you could use some help?"

"I don't know," she said. She thought for a few seconds, like she was carefully picking her words. "Nick, I would *love* to put you to work for me." She let go of my wrist. No pat this time.

"But, like I said, we haven't turned it around yet. We're still kind of short on cash. And we have a girl there already. She's pregnant, and I can't put her out on the street."

"But I could work for free," I said. "Just to help out. To earn my keep."

"I don't know if the insurance would let us. I'll have to check it out." She flashed a quick toothy one.

"How long you planning on staying, anyway?" she said.

"I don't know. For a while, I guess. Is that okay?"

Flick-of-an-eyelid pause. "Sure," she said. "Hey, you want some dessert? I have ice cream." She went to get it out of the refrigerator. "It doesn't keep so good in here anyway, we've got to finish it up."

As she was getting down the bowls, I scooped up the last mouthful of the gumbo stuff and popped it in my mouth. I'd been pushing this particular gob around my plate, thinking it was a stringbean, but when I couldn't chew it, I spit it out in my spoon. Even though it was all mangled, and had sauce and stuff on it, I could clearly make out what it was: The filter from a cigarette.

I stashed it in my napkin and stuffed it in my pocket.

"You like chocolate syrup?" said Wanda over her shoulder.

"Who doesn't?" I said.

chapter 3

*I'M TRYING TO FIND MY WAY OUT of some big house. It's familiar, like I've been here before, but a long time ago, and I've forgotten my way. I'm walking through a long hall, then through one of the doors that line its sides, into a big room, then out another door into another room and a door and a hall again, around and around, realizing I'm getting nowhere, finally hearing a pounding, pounding on one of the doors from the other side, but as I go to open it, I fall, all caught up in something, groping across the floor in—*I was in Wanda's living room, lying next to her couch, tangled in a bedspread she must've thrown over me the night before.

"Who is it?" I said, as a hairy gorilla paw appeared through the broken pane and turned the inside knob, swinging the door wide so it barely missed me sprawled on the floor.

Standing there was the built guy with the red crew cut who hit the dirt when the firecracker went off the night before.

Up close I could see that his nose had been rearranged by something hard, moving fast. The corners of his mouth were creased with smile lines, and his eyes were wide-set and blue. He wore the same leather jacket over a white T-shirt and ripped jeans, which looked like maybe he slept in them.

"You're probably looking for Wanda?" I said, finally getting free of the bedspread and getting to my feet.

"As a matter of fact," he started to say, but then asked, "Who're you?"

"Her nephew," I said, smoothing my clothes.

"Oh, yeah," he said, "she told me about you. Sister's kid, Nicky, right?"

"Nick," I said.

"Deke," he said, sticking out a big hand that wrapped around mine like a tortilla. "Deke Henehan." One of his eyes was bloodshot, giving him an unbalanced look.

"Nick Doran." He pumped my hand so hard my teeth rattled.

"Is she here?" he said, looking around.

"Yeah, I guess. I don't know, I just woke up."

He blew past me into the cabin.

"Wanda?" he called. Then he saw a note on the table.

"Oh, right," he said. "Today's a late day at the shop. She says for you to have breakfast, that there's stuff in the refrigerator. Eggs okay?"

"Uh, yeah," I said, still not sure I wasn't dreaming.

"Mind if I join you?" he said, pulling a frying pan off a hook and putting it on a burner—the good one, I noticed.

"Yeah, sure, I mean, okay, I guess. You know Wanda?" I added.

"Yup," he said. "We're bueno buds." He soon had coffee boiling in an old percolator pot on the stove and was frying up a half-dozen eggs, humming a tone-deaf tune.

"Saw you come in last night," he said, as I was folding up the bedspread. "Where you runnin' from?"

"Why does everybody ask me that?"

"No wheels, the backpack, sleeping on the floor in your clothes." He talked offhandedly while he worked.

"I wasn't sleeping on the floor, I *fell* there," I said, "and I'm not running away. I really just needed a break from home, is all."

"I've heard people say that," he said, shaking his head as if it was some strange custom from a faraway land. He expertly flipped the eggs and caught them back in the pan.

"Egg sangwidges, okay?" he said in a jokey country twang. He dug into them with the spatula, tearing them in two and plopping each half on a piece of bread that he topped with another, fried egg hanging out the sides.

"Sure," I said.

He poured the coffee into a couple of Styrofoam cups from the stack next to the sink. "Too nice to eat in here. Let's go outside."

"So how long you know Wanda?" I said in between bites as we sat at a picnic table between Wanda's cabin and the next.

"About a year now," he said, looking off past me as he chewed. "Ever since she moved in. That's my place." He glanced at the cabin next door. "She's a fine lady," he added.

Looking around as I ate, I saw that someone had straightened the wishing well after the beating the old woman and her pursuers gave it the night before. In the harsher light of early morning, the cabins looked even rougher. Where they didn't have big polka dots of paintball splats, most needed paint. Some of the roofs had bald spots, and others were patched with shingles of all different colors. A few, like Wanda's, were wild with weeds and woolly shrubs, and others, like Deke's, were surrounded by packed brown dirt with not so much as a blade of grass. The one had all the junk surrounding it. I saw no sign of activity from any of them.

"What *is* this place, anyway?" I asked Deke.

"The Far?" he said. "Come on, I'll show you."

We finished our "sangwidges"—Deke swallowing his in three or four gulps—and I followed him to a fat oak in back of his cabin. As we got close, I noticed gray slats of wood nailed to the trunk that led up into its branches.

Deke scrambled up these slats like a squirrel, never spilling a drop from the coffee cup he still held in his hand. Even after I set my coffee on a rock and climbed with both hands, it took me much longer, especially since I didn't trust the warped boards and tested each before I put my weight on it.

When I finally got up to the first big branch, I saw what looked like a pile of old lumber wedged in much higher up.

"Up here," said Deke from somewhere up in the pile. As I

picked my way up branch by branch, I saw it was a tree house—maybe more like a tree shack. When I got close enough, Deke reached down and grabbed my arm in his massive mitt and hauled me up the rest of the way.

"You sure this thing is solid?" I said. It looked like it was nailed together from pieces of old packing crate, some of which had faded red Chinese symbols painted on them.

"Look," said Deke, jumping up and down and making me wish I hadn't asked. "It's been here *years*," he said. "It's part of the tree." He pointed to where the trunk had grown around the boards. "But take a good look around," he said, spreading his arms and slopping some of his coffee. "It's another country up here."

He was right. You could see miles in every direction. On one side was a woods of smaller trees. Beyond them the banks of a brownish stream curved around the jut-out of land that was the parking lot for the cabins. In the other direction was one of those brand-new, bare-looking developments, with houses that had broad roofs of an all-the-same grayish color.

Down on the ground, the cabins had looked like they were laid out in a circle, but from up here you could see they actually formed a giant Valentine heart, with the wishing well dead arrow in the center. Paths led out from it like arteries to each of the cabins.

"All this here, was set up—oh, I don't know exactly—maybe fifty, sixty years ago by some Chinese guy," Deke said. "Was all part of a farm he owned, and when the road out front there was improved, he built these cabins—'housekeeping cottages,' they called them back then—mostly trying to pull in honeymoon couples from the city who wanted a hideout. But the deal went bust."

"Why?" I said.

"Well, the bypass came through and turned the road into a cow path. And even back then not many people would drive all the way upstate to ride cows on their honeymoon. So the guy sold off the cabins one by one. Story goes that this treehouse was built by his brother they sent over from the old country who had problems." Deke tapped his finger to the side of his head.

"What's with the 'Far' thing?" I said.

"Well, like I said, it was a farm to begin with, and he—the Chinese guy—used the name of it—Happiness Farm—when he built the cabins. But some time or other, the 'M' fell off, or got knocked down or stolen and, like they say around here, the rest is histor."

"Histor?"

"That's a joke," he said.

"Oh," I said. I wish I'd had my coffee with me. Another half cup, and I would've got it.

We sat looking around quietly for a few minutes.

"You come up here much?" I said.

"Whenever I need adjusting," said Deke. "Makes everything look so tiny, you wonder how it could trouble you."

"You know a lot of the others who live here?"

"Oh, yeah," said Deke. He must've heard the worry in my voice. "Forget about last night. Most of these people couldn't hurt themselves. Nicest bunch you ever want to meet." He started pointing out cabins. "The Branstools—Red Dog and Fawn? That's their place. Jane—the old lady with the paintball gun? She's Red's grandmother. And the one with all the iron junk in front of it, that's Rode Kool's, who's from Iceland or somewhere, he says. He's a welder. Then next one over belongs to Roger—I don't even know his last name—we call him 'Jolly Roger.' He's . . . well, he's just Jolly Roger. And then O. K. Sunbeam, nicest little old Japanese woman—runs one of those 900 numbers out of her house. She can make her voice sound like—you wouldn't believe. And Loosie Starshine—she's—no one knows where she's from. Just showed up one day—works for a vet in town. Her place is always full of owls with busted wings and snakes in casts and things. And next over is a black guy, goes by Clatoo Burada—we call him Clat. And around the bend there is Mysterious Willie—claims he's an old boxer—nobody ever really understands what he's talking about. Plays a mean bagpipe, though."

"Where did they get those names?" I said.

"The names?" said Deke.

"Yeah, I mean they all have these weird names."

"You think so?"

"Jolly Roger?" I said.

"Oh, well, those aren't their *real* names, anyway."

"How come?"

"Let's just say most of them have a past they'd be happier about if it belonged to someone else. But, like I said, they're harmless. Don't worry, Wanda will introduce you around. We have big dinners outside in the middle there on the Green. Wanda started that. She's really pulled things together since she's been here. We're all just one big slap-happy family."

Suddenly there was a screeching of tires from the road and the whine of an engine revving much too high and coming in our direction. There were trees in the way, and I couldn't see at first, but then a pickup truck with a lightning bolt logo painted on its side roared into view going backward at high speed, throwing chunks of turf and lawn statues and wire garden fences every which way. The truck was blaring its horn, and the people inside were screaming and laughing and hanging out both sides of the cab. Two young guys in gray sweats with the hoods up and bandannas over their faces sat in the truck bed. It looked like they were going to ram the wishing well, but they skidded to a stop at the absolute last second.

The two guys in back and two others from the cab, also in bandannas, jumped out and grabbed the wishing well, each by an upright. They started to move it, but could only raise it a couple of feet.

"Come on," said one. "Lift! Dammit!"

"I am. I am," said another. "It's stuck."

"It's chained or something," one of the four said, trying to hold it up while looking inside.

Meanwhile Deke was halfway down the tree trunk. "Hey, you!" he was shouting. "Leave that alone."

The guys dropped the well, and three of them quickly jumped back in the pickup, but the fourth glanced up, trying to see where all the noise was coming from, I guess. He saw me, and we stared at each other a long second. But then I could see from the eyes— dark violet colored, long-lashed, and all made up—that it wasn't a guy at all, but a girl.

"Come on. Get in!" the others were shouting, and she broke off as if from a dream, jumping in the back the second the pickup peeled off, horn blaring, something—a loose fan belt?—squealing from inside its engine compartment. "Wake up hip-pies!" they shouted, the second syllable as in "apple."

Meanwhile Deke had jumped the last four slats to the ground, and by the time I picked my way down, he was halfway across the Green. But the truck had a good lead and was already roaring out under the entrance. Deke trotted to a stop and watched it take off down the road.

"Damn!" he said when he got back, breathing heavy. "Never saw *that* truck before. Damn kids come up with new stuff alla time. You get a good look at any of 'em?"

"Nope," I said.

chapter 4

"SO YOU MET DEKE," said Wanda late that afternoon when she got back from work, smelling of cinnamon, her jeans dusty with flour.

"How did you know?" I said.

"Didn't think you could make this much mess on your own." She slapped my hand as I grabbed for the bag of day-olds she brought home.

"Not until you clean this up," she said, pointing to the dirty frying pan and dishes that were the remains of breakfast. She tossed me a wet dishrag before she went into her bedroom to change.

"Remember the rules?" said Wanda through the bedroom door. "They're on the refrigerator."

She was talking about the same wrinkled yellow newspaper column she had posted on the refrigerator in the old place: HOW TO MAKE A HOUSE A HOME was the headline, and under it were a dozen things like:

If you take it out, put it away.
If you make a mess, clean it up.
If you borrow it, bring it back.
If you value it, take care of it.
If you blah, blah, then blah, blah, blah.

I'd already read the list so many times that it looked more like a piece of wallpaper pattern instead of words that made any sense. I did take a second, though, to reread the last one:

"If you want to live with others, get your own house in order."

Tacked on the end of all those practical putting aways and fixings and cleaning ups, it had always seemed so meaningful. Trouble was, I wasn't exactly sure what it meant.

"Did you hear what happened?" I said, raising my voice as I began scraping the plates.

"Hear what?" she said through the door.

I turned on the faucets, but only a thin stream of water dribbled out, then immediately stopped.

"Use the hose," said Wanda as she came out of the bedroom.

This was the garden hose sticking in the window over the sink. I squeezed the pistol grip on the nozzle and hosed off the rest of the crud on the plates.

"Some kids—Deke said they were locals—tried to steal the wishing well," I said.

"Again?" said Wanda."You think that would be old by now."

"They tried before?" I soaped the dishes up and blasted them with the hose, stacking them on the drain board.

"Yeah. Last time they put it on the courthouse lawn downtown." She sat at the table and tapped a cigarette out of the pack setting there. "So what happened?"

"Nothing," I said. "They didn't get away with it. Deke showed me how he chained it down."

"Chained?" Wanda shook her head. "Sometimes I think he takes this all too personal."

"We could see the whole thing from up in the treehouse."

"He took you up in that rickety thing?" She lit up with a wooden match from a red, white, and blue box. "Could you see who it was?" she said, blowing out a lungful.

"Nope," I said, thinking about the eyes of the girl in the pickup. "Not really." I didn't know why I wasn't telling my aunt about her. The girl had looked right up at me. Dead *into* me. I could have picked her out of a crowd in a football stadium. "Can't the cops do something?"

"Sheriff Darryl?" said Wanda, settling back into the chair. "Well, first of all, he was ticked at *us* last time the well wound up downtown. He called me; asked if I had anything to do with it."

"He blamed *you*?" I said.

"He was just looking for attention. You know, like when you pull on a girl's pigtail?"

"When you're nine years old," I said.

"Like I said, he's sweet on me." When she smiled, her eyes got into it too. I suddenly found myself looking at her as a person, separate from being my aunt. I could see why she might attract attention. "'Sure, Darryl,' I told him, 'lugged it on down there myself. Carried it on my back in the dead of night on my break from the doughnut shop. You gonna put your big ol' handcuffs on li'l ol' me now?' . . . Besides, folks in these parts get kind of itchy when you talk about getting 'the Authorities' involved. Not like they have anything to hide, mind you." She raised her eyebrows and pursed her lips.

"But why doesn't he do *something*?" I said.

"There's another piece of it," said Wanda. "You see, after stunts like with the Branstools' granny? Darryl has made it *very* clear that under *no* circumstances does he want us bothering his head with anything short of murder. Though if those kids keep it up, I might be able to arrange something."

"What's their problem, anyway?" I said.

As I finished washing and stacking the other kitchen stuff, Wanda explained that from the time Stone Coach Woods—the fancy houses with the slate-colored roofs I'd seen from the tree-house—opened a couple of years ago, the residents of the Far had been the butt of ever-increasing sabotage. When she moved in, Deke told her it used to be only the wishing well they messed with. But then the Green had been turfed and garbage dumped on it, the door latches on all the cabins were glued shut one night, and lately people awoke to find their cars rolled into the shallows of the Molasses River behind the parking lot.

"Stoners," she said shaking her head. "Won't leave us in peace."

"You're sure it's them?" I said.

"It's them all right," she said, grabbing a towel off the back of a chair and starting to dry.

"What's their problem?"

"Who knows? Testosterone poisoning, carbonated hormones, MTV, bad nutrition, too much time on their hands. I expect basically they just don't like our kind."

"So your hands are tied?"

"Behind our backs," said Wanda. "Darryl doesn't want to hear anything about what he calls 'mischief.' Besides, he told me once in a moment of weakness—after I'd stuffed him full of free doughnuts—that these kids are from all the big-garbanzo families in town, and it's impossible to make pranks like that stick in court."

"It's kind of beat, anyway," I said. "The wishing well."

"Deke wants to rebuild it," said Wanda. "But he's got this old house of his he works on that occupies nearly all his time when he's not working his regular job."

I wiped my hands on my pants and fished a squashed creme-filled doughnut from the bag on the table.

"Just one," said Wanda, bunching the top of the bag down and clipping it with one of the all-purpose wooden spring clothespins she kept in a basket on a counter. "Don't want you to ruin dinner."

I knew Wanda could do that without my help.

"Deke seems like a good guy," I said.

"He's the best," she said.

"Are you and him—" I started to say, when a big gob of filling squished out of the doughnut and ran down my chin.

"Why, Nicky"—she threw me the damp dish towel—"no wonder your parents want to send you away to school. Didn't you learn any manners? Prying into peoples' lives. The answer is no, anyway. Deke's very independent; he's been on his own since he's your age."

She rinsed the sticky dish towel under the hose. "And anyway," she added, "I'm afraid that Deke's first love is Old Vic—his big old house. He's like a kid with a toy. His cabin is full of old lumber and pipe and furniture and stuff he plans to use. He's always collecting things for it and dreaming about it and talking about it. Everything else is second."

As she spoke, she wrung the dish towel out like she was strangling it. I got the idea that she had strong feelings on the subject, and I let it die.

chapter 5

foot notes

People like to throw stuff at you when you're walking alongside the road.

I've been hit by half-eaten hamburgers, lit and dead cigarettes, full, half full, and empty beer, juice, and soda cans and bottles, shoes, maps, ice scrapers, dirty baby diapers, candy wrappers, and just about every fruit, vegetable, and other food you could name except maybe soup.

I have a theory about why people do this: First off, if you're walking, you're weird. Who was it that said some people walk out of step because they hear a different drummer? Well these days anybody *walking* is hearing a different drummer.

I mean, you see kids giving you the slit-eye out their minivan windows as they fly on by like their daddy just pointed you out as the latest brand of Strange and No Good. ("Now you keep away from people like that. Ya heah?")

And let's face it: You *are* weird. There's no noise or smoke coming out of you. (Unless maybe you had burritos for lunch.) You aren't using any special as-seen-on-TV equipment. There's no evidence you even *bought* anything lately. You're just not hauling your weight. You represent Everything That's No Good in the World Today.

And there *they* are, up in their SUVs or pickups or station wagons, wallowing in their plush seats in piles of their *stuff*, their music and onboard movie and game consoles, Moon Pies stuck in their faces. And it's like you're giving them the finger.

"Looka that guy, willya? Over there. He's *walkin'*, fer crissake. Right in fronna the kids!"

It's disrespectful. What, are you trying to make *them* look bad?

So what do they do? They throw stuff at you—usually something near at hand, which explains the assortment.

Throw stuff at the weird person.

You'd think with all this I might get mad—carry a pocket full of rocks and a slingshot. But no; I'm at a place where it actually gives me some kind of satisfaction when I get whacked with a gnawed-on Twinkie.

I'm making a point, don't you see?

I'm actually *connecting* with somebody.

chapter 6

AS IF TO PROVE WANDA WAS RIGHT about his obsession with Old Vic, Deke volunteered me the next afternoon to help him pick up a piece of street furniture that he planned to use for the big old place. Wanda was still sleeping, and I left her a note.

"Heyup, here we are," he said as we drove up to it in his tiny rusted pickup. "Perfectly good. Perrrfectly good. Shame to see it go to waste." It was a giant old dresser someone had painted white and left at the curb. After wrestling it onto the truck and off again at his cabin, I thought it would be a perrrfectly good idea if it *had* gone to waste, or at least to someone's firewood pile.

There was no more room in the cabin, so he stood it on end and covered it with a tarp on a deck under a shed roof he'd built in back.

"Thanks," he said. "Should have a whole houseful by the time I'm through."

"How come you don't keep it there—at the old house?" I asked.

"Not such a great neighborhood," he said. "And with nobody home, someone would just walk off with it."

Another good idea, I thought.

By now it was getting to be dinnertime. Deke worked second shift at a shingle factory and had to take off. I figured Wanda would be up by now, but the cabin was empty, her bedroom door wide open.

I found her sitting at her picnic table on the side of the cabin opposite Deke's, a canning jar full of iced tea in front of her, smoking a cigarette and watching inmates of the Far who were frolicking about.

She waved to a girl who was trying to do cartwheels, collapsing halfway through, but trying over and over. The girl wore a floppy hat that fell off and a long denim skirt that fell down over her head each time she went over. This might have been educational, except that under the skirt she wore a pair of men's boxer shorts with big red hearts on them.

"You're getting closer," she shouted, and the girl waved back, smiling. "Maybe if you take off your hat?"

While I'd been helping Deke, the Green had become thick with Frisbee-throwing, dog-hugging, guitar-strumming, flute-playing GVMs, for "Groovy vibes, man!"—what we used to call them in school—who looked like extras in some fruity Summer of Love made-for-TV movie.

"Hasn't anybody here ever heard of TV?" I said.

"Sit down here for a minute," she said, her smile fading as she looked from the Green to me.

I climbed over the bench and sat opposite her.

She looked down at the tea that she sloshed in the jar.

"I'm deciding what to do," she said.

"What to do about what?"

"You."

I said nothing, having learned that it's best not to confess to anything, at least until you hear the charges.

"While you were gone with Deke," she said, "I got a phone call."

This couldn't be good.

"From Madeline—your mother—of all people."

"And?" I said.

"I thought you said you told them you were leaving?"

"I did."

"Your mother said she found out when they checked the answering machine."

"They checked the answering machine from Arugula?" I said.

"Aruba," said Wanda.

"They were already gone, like I said, and that's how we usually leave messages anyhow."

"Why don't you tell me more about it . . . this deal with the school."

"Well, first of all, it's an awful place. It's supposed to be military—the Millstone Military Academy—but it's more like the Confederate military. They make you wear uniforms, but they're kind of casual about it, so everybody's is slightly different. And they don't even *have* TV. It's supposed to make you more disciplined, they said. But I talked to somebody in the bathroom last time when I escaped from their dancing armadillo show for a minute, and he said that the guys had these tiny sets, and after lights-out they'd get together in the supplies room and watch it."

"Forbidden fruit," said Wanda.

"Yeah, well you should see this crappy place. Makes this look like paradise."

"Which it is, of course," said Wanda as a golden retriever with a bandanna around his neck dragged a tree branch on by.

"I mean," I said, "they make you wear these shirts with military patches on the sleeves and *shorts* in warm weather."

"Alcatraz," said Wanda. "So what would all this punishment be for?"

"Well, like I told you, they asked me to leave the school where I was going, and Mom and Dad thought I would be better off in a place where they had more of what they call 'structure.'"

"Nick," she said, looking me in the eye. "Come on, don't make me pry it out of you. Tell me why they made you leave. This is me, remember?"

And it *was* Wanda. The same Wanda who always took me in, no questions asked. For a couple of years there, I found myself sleeping on her sofa a couple of nights a week. If I had a bad day at school, I would just leave a message on the machine and tell my parents not to worry, I was okay, I would get my homework done, I was staying overnight at Wanda's. She was always there when I needed someone guaranteed to take my side.

Like once when I got into this scrape where they wanted us to do a project for the Junior Board of Commerce and I taped this infomercial on a company I called "Useless and Dangerous Products, Ltd." If they let me get past the first five minutes or so, they would have seen that I really had some good insights about marketing and it wasn't really that negative at all.

"It's great to have ideas," the assistant principal, Mrs. McKee, said at the meeting she called for me and my parents, "but there have to be limits."

Which, of course, my parents agreed to right away, being comfortable with great, limited ideas.

But when I showed it to Wanda, she thought it was hilarious, especially the part with my table at Junior Commerce Day at the mall. I'm wearing this white coat and plastic nose and glasses and pocket protector full of pens and trying to sell people this product I came up with called Belly Button in a Tub: basically this pink foam I shoved into a margarine container with a pink button glued in the middle and a Q-Tip and a booklet that told you how to take care of it and clean out the lint and had a coupon with which you could send away for a ring.

"But what are you supposed to *do* with it?" this woman on the tape keeps asking.

"That's the beauty," I say. "It's just something to consume."

"You eat it?" she says.

"No. You don't really do anything with it."

"Oh," she says.

And through all of this, Wanda and I had this unspoken pact

of no secrets and no lies. That was one of the main underpinnings of our relationship, and now I knew I would have to deliver. But suddenly I remembered something.

"What if I told you a story about something that happened to someone?"

This was the opening of a bit we used when we wanted to confess something we weren't so sure about. The great part was that you got to make up stuff along with what really happened. Then later you could back off from the *really* bad parts you made up.

"Go ahead," she said. "I'm all elephant ears."

Good! She remembered. Saying something corny like this was part of the thing.

"Well, it's about this guy who gets in trouble—but for stuff he did that he didn't really mean to be so bad."

"It *wasn't* so bad?" she said.

"Well, no. He just didn't *mean* it to be bad."

"Oh! Of course," she said. "Like what?"

"Well, like he was late for school," I said, "or he had this gym teacher who didn't like him and was always giving him detentions, or he caught a house on fire, or he had to take band class and be in this stupid pep band and he would cut and wouldn't go to games, or when he answered questions in class in an original way, they said he was just being smart."

"A capital crime in my book." Wanda took a sip of her iced tea. "Go back to the thing with the house and the fire for a second, though," she said. "Whose?"

"Yours."

"*My* house? That old place I used to rent? It *burned* down?" she said nearly choking on her tea.

"No," I said, shifting on the hard bench. "Just got damaged. Kind of bad, though."

"How would something like that *happen*, Nick?" she said.

"Well, one day when this guy hadn't seen his aunt in a couple of weeks, he gave her a call but got a recording that said her number 'was no longer in service.' He thought that maybe she blew the phone money again—"

"Easy there," said Wanda.

"—so he took the long walk over and knocked on her door. It was getting dark, about the time she was usually home, but there was no answer. Even stranger, her doormat with the funny saying was missing, along with the piece of paper with her name on it in the mailbox. He tried the key she gave him, and it didn't work. When he looked in the window, the furniture was still there, but he saw all her books were gone, and he knew something was up.

"When he got home, he asked his mom if she knew anything.

"'About as much as you,' said his mother. 'Maybe less.' She was looking at her computer screen, where she was closing some big-ass real estate deal. 'She missed payments on the loan we cosigned,' she said, 'and the phone is disconnected, so we guess she's skipped again.'

"'But you never told me,' the guy said to his mother.

"'We didn't know for sure,' she said, not looking up. 'We didn't want to think it, I guess. But there it is.'

"The guy always expected his parents were jealous anyway. You see he shared so much with his aunt and not with them, and they probably were not all too sad she was gone—except for the money."

"Not enough to get a *decent* car," said Wanda.

"After that, when he went walking, he always seemed to wind up in his aunt's old neighborhood, going by her old house. After a while, there was a For Sale sign in front, but it stayed empty, being kind of small and run-down and all."

"That's how his aunt got it to begin with," said Wanda. "Her sister, the real estate lady, convinced the owner to rent it when she couldn't sell the dump for him."

"Anyway," I continued, "one time, when this guy found himself across the street, tired and thirsty and having to go to the bathroom after the long walk over there, he said, 'Screw it,' and went up and knocked on the door. The sign was still up, but he wanted to make sure. Nobody answered, and he walked around back and knocked on the back door, all the time looking for one of those key boxes that real estate agents lock the house key in. But there wasn't one. Then I remembered about that door."

"*He* remembered," said Wanda.

I didn't feel like playing around anymore.

"Well, *I* really had to take a pee," I said, "and there was that little bathroom right off the basement stairs? And I pulled up hard on the doorknob and pushed, and sure enough, it popped."

"I must've asked the landlord to fix that a hundred times," said Wanda.

"So I walked in and called, 'Hello, anybody home?' which, of course, anybody wasn't, so I went to the bathroom, and then I thought I'd stay and just take a look. It was amazing," I told Wanda. "Except for all your books being gone, it was like you never left. They didn't change *anything*."

"None of that stuff was mine," said Wanda. "It all came with the place."

"There was that fake sheepskin rug—with the head on it—in front of the fireplace and the table that was made out of the old telephone-company wire spool and the two ratty armchairs. And I was tired from all the walking, and I sat in one of the chairs, and I must've fallen asleep and—"

"Wait, don't tell me," said Wanda. "The three bears came home, and the Papa Bear said in his great big voice, 'WHO'S BEEN SITTING IN *MY* CHAIR?'"

"Wanda," I said.

"Okay," she said, "but hurry up and get to the good part."

This was working better than I thought.

"I must have fallen asleep, and when I woke up, it was dark and I left," I said.

"You *left?*" she said. "So how did the house burn?"

"It didn't that time."

"Nick!" said Wanda.

"I'm getting there," I said.

I told her how every time I came back, the house was still empty. And one time—it was nearly fall by then—it was chilly and I happened to be sitting in the living room. I had cut out of school early, but it got dark early and I pulled the drapes and was doing some homework. I had some camp food I brought with me—you know, like the beans and franks in the little cup? So I microwaved it and ate. But I was cold, and I didn't want to turn up the heat. It was on, but way low, and I figured the bill would tip somebody off, so I started a fire in the fireplace, using that wood from the pile out back."

"That was the same pile from when I moved in," said Wanda. "I never trusted that fireplace."

"Well, that was probably a good idea," I said. "'Cause I get a good, roaring fire going, and a half hour later there's this pounding on the door. 'Hey, anybody in there?' someone is shouting—scared the hell out of me. 'The house is on fire.' BAM! BAM! BAM! I think maybe they see the smoke coming out of the chimney and they're thinking the place is burning? And I don't know what to do, but I have one of these collapsible cups in my pack, so I run in the kitchen and I fill it with water and throw it on the flames in the fireplace.

"I do this, I don't know, maybe five or six times, and the pounding doesn't quit, and by now I'm hearing sirens, too. But the flames are pretty much out, so I go running out the back door, and I'm halfway through the yard just as I hear the front door get knocked open and I hear some guy calling, 'Hey, anybody here?' and as I look back I see the *chimney's* on fire—there's smoke pouring out the top and sides—all over—but I keep running. After a couple of blocks, I figure I'll attract less attention if I walk, and I'm walking when the first fire truck goes by."

"So you didn't get caught?" said Wanda.

"Nope," I said. "Not until they found my name in my backpack that was sitting in the living room and arrested me at school."

"Oh, Nick," she said. "It was an accident."

"That's exactly how Dad's lawyer played it. He's like: 'Since when is starting a fire in a fireplace an act of arson?' and they gave me a suspended sentence for breaking and entering and put me in Mom and Dad's custody. I think the owner was just happy to collect the insurance money, anyway."

"And the school kicked you out for that?"

"Like I said, there were other things, too. That just happened to be the shove that sent me over the edge."

"And after all that your parents left you home alone?"

"That was months ago, and it was some big trip they went on; like I said, they had it planned for a long time, and by the time they left I was a model prisoner anyway. I had a girlfriend, and I was supposed to start this job washing cars for this dealer after I came back from the orientation. I even like mowed the grass around the house and everything." I thought of how long it must be getting already since I left.

"Your mother was really worried," Wanda said.

"She's just worried that I'll be in some kind of trouble and it will be trouble for them."

"It sounded genuine to me," she said. "But leaving her the news on their machine? What were you thinking?"

"I swear, that's the main way we talk these days. They were probably checking to see if I left one. Which I did, of course."

"And so did this Salter guy, from the academy."

"Colonel Saltine. . . . So how did they guess to check here?" I said.

"They called a couple of other places, but your mom had this hunch, and she just happened to have my number written down in her address book."

"Which, being Mom, she took along for postcards," I said.

"How do you suppose they got it to begin with?"

"Your number?" I said. "You're asking me?" The tone in her voice—it was like she was blaming me. I tried to shift the topic. "They want me home?"

"No," said Wanda. "She really burned my ears, though. Like I was to blame. But I finally calmed her down. I told her you were okay here and that you could stay if you wanted and this was the best place for you, anyway, for the time being. The call must've cost a fortune. I convinced her they shouldn't cut their trip short. She made me promise I would have you call when they got back home."

Wanda was a good talker.

It was full dark by now, and the residents of the Far had retreated inside or to their own picnic tables, except for one diehard guy sitting out there playing guitar and singing a tune through his nose—same tune my parents had on one of those big records they'd get out and play on the ol' stereo after a few drinks.

She was quiet for a while, swirling the last couple of pieces of ice around in the jar, her cigarette stubbed out with a dozen of its brothers.

"I always hated that house," said Wanda. "I don't think I ever realized—" She didn't finish.

"What?" I said.

"How much better it is finally having my own place."

"For me it was like home," I said.

"Speaking of which," she said, "how long *are* you planning on staying?"

"I don't know," I said. "A while."

She gave me a sideways glance. "You know you *can* stay as long as you—"

"I know it's maybe a little tight," I said quickly, "but I don't mind sleeping on the couch, and I was thinking maybe, since you don't need anyone at the shop, I could find a job somewhere else in town and throw in a few dollars."

"There's not much work around here," she said. She hesitated for a few seconds before going on. "Do you think maybe you *should* go back?"

"For what?" I said. "The orientation will be over, and Mom and Dad hardly know I'm *there*. Like I said, they're working all the time. And remember, they wanted to send me *away*."

"We'll talk about it," she said, "but it's getting late."

As we went back in the cabin for the night, I had the feeling, for the first time ever with Wanda, that maybe, just maybe, I was less than one hundred percent welcome.

chapter 7

"HOLD TIGHT NOW."

Deke pulled the starter cord on the power auger, and the thing roared like some movie monster that had eaten a couple of automobiles a few days before and was having one nasty bowel movement. I held one handle of the vibrating beast, Deke the other.

"Ready?" he said.

I nodded.

He put it in gear, and it began bucking and kicking, trying to rip itself free from our hands as it dug into the packed ground like a giant, motorized corkscrew.

"I'm planning to fix it so's this thing don't go nowhere," Deke had said, patting the wishing well on its roof after he roused me out of bed that morning.

"How?" I said.

"Come along, and I'll show you," he said.

We took a short ride in his pickup to a rental place where a friend of his passed the auger out the back gate.

"It's got to be back by twelve," said the guy, who wore a tiny beard under his lower lip and looked around like he was holding.

"They don't get much call for this on weekdays," Deke explained, "so I get a deep discount."

We stopped at a building supplies yard and picked up a couple of six-foot four-by-fours, bags of cement, and a handful of long bolts and then drove through a fast-food place for some breakfast.

"Why is it such a big deal anyway?" I said, finishing the last bite of an English muffin as we tooled through the puny downtown past rows of cars parked diagonal to the curb.

"The wishing well? Why, it's only the very soul and solid center of existence of the whole Far," said Deke sipping the coffee he held in one hand as he steered and shifted with the other.

"Come on," I said.

"It's true," he said. "It's kind of like I imagine there's these cables connecting it to all the cabins. Kind of holds them in place, like they would go flying off without it. I mean, that time when it got kidnapped? It was like 'the center cannot hold.' Who wrote that? It's like there was *nothing*."

I looked at him to see if he was serious. He seemed to be at least half. But all this cosmic stuff about missing the well really didn't fool me. The more I found out about him, the more I believed Wanda was right. It *was* a personal thing with him. It was like his reputation was at stake. He took pride in having things in order, whether it was the big old Victorian house he was working on or the little fake wishing well.

Wanda thought it had something to do with his crazy background. She explained how his mother named him Deacon, hoping he would take after the name and not his no-good father. After Deke was born, the old man miraculously got clean and sober, and Deke's mother started to relax. Then one day the guy broke the zipper on his pants and couldn't go on his next call—he was a salesman for cleaning stuff, laundry soap and floor wax and things—and stopped in a tailor's to get them fixed.

Next he was waiting in borrowed pants on a barstool next door, and next he was there all day and half the night. His mother knew there was trouble when he came home loaded, wearing big, strange pants hoisted up to his armpits. A couple months off the wagon, and he was fired. And one day not long after this, Deke's mom, who had been holding it together all these years, finally let it all go. She left Deke with a friend to go for groceries and never came back. Deke was six.

"Heave now," said Deke. The worst part was hauling the auger up once it had screwed itself down in the ground. "I'd of done it myself if it wasn't for this," said Deke as we lifted, "but my back just ain't what it was." When we got it out, there was a neat, round hole that went down a full three feet.

After we'd repeated this three more times and set the machine aside, Deke had me take out the gold coffee can that hung by a lamp chain in the wishing well.

"Somebody using this for an ashtray?" I said, dumping it out.

"Nope," said Deke. "People write wishes on pieces of paper and put 'em in there and burn 'em."

"Wishes?" I said. "Like what?"

"It's secret, but I suppose it's things like trying to win the lottery, or get a woman—or a man—or have a kid, or not have one."

"Does it work?" I asked.

"Sure," he said.

Deke disconnected the wishing well from where he had chained it to an eyelet buried in the ground, and I helped him lay it down on its side.

"I mean, I don't get it. We had our fun when we were pups," he spoke while he worked, "but it was like sticking a For Sale sign in the minister's yard or putting a couple eggs in the principal's umbrella outside his office. We never picked on anybody wasn't asking for it."

He started cracking up laughing, so the pencil mark he drew on the four-by-four was wiggly.

"You ever notice how when someone opens an umbrella, they always look up in it?" He wiped the back of his eyes with the hand that held the pencil. "Whooo," he said.

He cut the two four-by-fours in half and drilled holes through one end of each of the four pieces. He then drilled holes in the legs of the wishing well and connected them to the pieces of four-by-four using the long bolts he'd bought. When we stood the well back up, it was like it was on stilts.

Then we poured a quarter bag of cement in each of the four holes we'd dug and, adding water from a pail, stirred the mixture in each with a stick. We picked up the well and lowered its long legs down in the holes into the wet cement so it was about the height it had been before. We kicked some dirt in the top of each hole, and when the job was done, if you didn't know better, it looked exactly as if we hadn't done anything.

"That ought to do it," said Deke. "Give her a day to set up, and then I'd love to see 'em even *try*."

As we drove back from dropping off the auger, I happened to see a doughnut shop: the Donut Works, it was called.

"Hey," I said to Deke, "Is that Wanda's place?"

"Where she works?" he said. "Yeah."

"Let's stop," I said.

Inside the shop, Wanda was busy cleaning out the bottom shelf of a display case.

"Hey, lady," Deke said. "You got any asparagus ones left?"

She looked up, surprised and, I thought for a second, panicked, before she broke into a smile.

"Nick! Deke!" she said, coming out from behind the counter to give us each a floury hug. She had on an apron with "Donut Works" on it and underneath, "Building Better Donuts for America" with a big wrench levering on the O in "Works."

A big woman in a similar apron came out from the back room of the place, took a quick frowning look at Deke and me, and went back.

"How's that cheery old bag of moldy muffins?" said Deke.

Wanda put her finger to her lips and shook her head. This must be her partner. Wanda had said how this woman and Deke didn't get along. "What trouble are you guys up to today?" she said.

"A bit of work at the Far," said Deke.

"We just cemented in the wishing well," I said.

Wanda looked at Deke.

"They figured it out," said Deke, like he was apologizing. "With the chain. It was a matter of time, so I just planted it a little more firm."

"Deke," said Wanda. "Really."

He shrugged.

"Nice place," I said to Wanda, looking around the shop. There was a mural covering the long wall that showed cartoon doughnuts sliding down a chute out of a factory with a tall, puffing smokestack with the shop name on it. The doughnuts were floating down a river like tire tubes, swinging on doughnut swings, rolling along in dune buggies with fat doughnut tires, riding on a Ferris wheel made from a big doughnut, and having all kinds of other doughnutty fun.

"Glad you like it," she said. "Well, what can I do for you?" It was like she was trying to rush us along.

"Got a couple of factory rejects?" said Deke.

"Besides you two?" she said

"Hey, they broke the stud-muffin tin after they made us," he said.

"Looks like it was dented already," she said, poking him in his belly.

The bell on the door tinkled, and a man in a suit came in. He smiled and nodded at us and started looking at the doughnuts in the case.

"You've got to see it," I said. "The way we socked it in, you couldn't move it with a bulldozer."

"Can't hardly wait," she said.

"Wanda," said the other woman, poking her head out from

behind the swinging door that separated the counter area from the kitchen. She nodded at the man in the suit.

"Seriously," Wanda said. "I have got to get back to work." She picked up a tray of doughnuts. "You want something?"

"Nah, that's okay," said Deke. "We're gonna get some lunch. Nick here just wanted to see the place."

"See you guys later," she said, but when she turned with the tray of doughnuts, she bumped into the register and half of them slid to the floor.

"Wanda!" The big woman suddenly appeared and started bawling her out in this tiny, high-pitched voice as Wanda picked the doughnuts off the floor. "Take care of that customer, will you? I'll get these."

Wanda shrugged and gave us a sheepish smile as Deke, making like he was tiptoeing, slipped out the door, and I followed.

"Whew-ee!" he said. "She's a witch with a capital B, that lady."

"Why does Wanda let her boss her around like that?" I said as we walked to a diner a couple of stores down.

"Alberta?" Deke said. "'Cause she *is* her boss."

"Her *boss*?" I said, "I thought they were *partners*."

Deke stopped in front of the door to the diner. "Who told you that?" he said.

"Wanda," I said.

"Wanda?" he said. "Partners in a *business*? Where would she get that kind of money?" He laughed as he pushed open the door. "Wanda doesn't own a pot to cook a run-over cat."

chapter 8

IT FEELS WEIRDLY like—was it only a week ago?—when I walked out of my parents' house. Here I am again, my backpack loaded, its frown of a bedroll slung over the top, ransacking the cupboards for road food.

Some people have special talents. Maybe they can touch their nose with their tongue, do long division in their heads, or take off their undershirt without first taking off their shirt.

My special talent is the ability to be already gone. I don't need a lot of incentive. Don't waste your money giving me a few bucks and telling me to get lost. I'm halfway there. Not only can I tell when I'm not wanted, I can tell *before* I'm not wanted. Anticipating when people don't like me is what I do best.

Like Wanda, for instance. Whatever her reasons might be, and whether she knew it yet or not, it was clear to me that our old relationship had already left the building, and unlike Elvis, there were no sightings.

I had to be quiet because Wanda was asleep in the bedroom. She had stumbled in after her shift early that morning, waved to me, and crashed in her room. But otherwise it was nearly the same as when I left my parents: No schedules, no good-byes, and this time, as an extra added attraction, no particular place to go.

The weather forgot to check the calendar and had showed up overcast and cool that morning, which made me shiver all the more as I headed across the Green, stopping only to give the wishing well a test shove.

Solid.

The downside of walking is that it forces you to think, and as I plodded along out toward the entrance to the Far, I couldn't stop trying to figure why Wanda had been so chilly to me.

Maybe she was just stressed about "her" business. Beyond the fact that she only worked there, maybe some kind of trouble was brewing that she didn't want me to know about. Or maybe she had some master scheme to hook up with Deke, and I was in the way. Or maybe it was that she didn't like being tracked down in the first place. After all, she did take off without telling me and never made any effort to get in touch. Added to this was the fact of the money she owed to my parents: Just when it looked like they were going to forget about it, to write her off, I got them back on her case.

Or maybe it was that Wanda simply just had enough of me and my troubles: whining about school and my parents, sleeping on the sofa, my stuff exploded out around me, the prize pig in the parlor. She had a lifetime supply of her own, after all.

I mean, her name alone should be a tip-off that she'd be mad, bad, and dangerous to know. Aunts should be along the lines of Millie or Clara or Abigail. But *Wanda?* Where would Dorothy have been?

"Oh, Aunty Wanda, there's no place like home!"

That's for sure.

Knowing it was an alias hardly helped. As Mom tells it, her sister Alice ran off one long weekend and, when she came back, wouldn't answer to anything but "Wanda." And although she eventually stopped writing it with hearts where the *a*'s should be, it stuck to her as permanently as the tattoo of the flying dove that had landed on her shoulder that same weekend.

Even as long as I had known her, Wanda had jumped from job to job—waitress to manicurist to store clerk, from place to place—apartment to duplex to house, and from lover to lover—

Tom to Dick to "Zookie" (don't ask), like she was crossing a boiling stream on slippery rocks.

"At least she had the good sense," said my mom once, "to never *marry* any of the idiots or punish any children by bringing them into the world." Which, it turns out, was no fault of her own, since as Wanda told me once, she wasn't able to have any.

One time she even did a hitch in the Peace Corps. Went to Brazil and helped poor people down there dig wells and stuff. "After that," my mother told me, "Wanda always said that everything here in the States seemed so wasteful. That she couldn't stand it when people threw out newspapers or watered their lawns. Being down there really seemed to do her in. At least she stopped going with such losers after that." So said my mom.

Out on the main road, I started walking away from town. The unknown had always held more promise for me, and I hadn't explored in this direction. A rain so fine it was almost like powder started to fall. I put up the hood on my sweatshirt and walked into the round piece of gray countryside it made in front of my face.

Wanda had lied to me. I couldn't believe it. And after I had gone and spilled my guts to her. Told her the whole story of my downfall.

She no more owned that doughnut place than I did. Who knows what else she made up. Maybe the cabin wasn't even hers. Maybe she had even bigger secrets she was keeping from me, some *real* reason she left without telling anyone. But I should have expected as much. I had the feeling from the beginning that the whole thing with Wanda and me just wasn't the same.

Like I said before, we'd had this kind of pact, this bond; not spoken or written down, but as strong and real as if we'd slit our palms and mashed them together. No matter what we'd done, no matter how much we'd screwed up, we'd always be *honest* with each other. I told her when I lost my first girlfriend, and she told me when she lost her tenth boyfriend; I confessed to her when I'd cheated on a test, and she told me how she cheated her tightwad boss at the restaurant where she was waiting tables.

For the couple of years she'd settled in that old house—the one I'd caught on fire—there had been no secrets between us. At least I thought so. And although leaving without telling me may have been forgivable, it was *unthinkable* that she would lie.

All I knew is that right now I was ticked off enough *at* her that I didn't feel like talking *with* her. I was tired of long, gloomy stories with unhappy endings—sadly twanging banjos swelling up on the sound track—my own or anybody else's. It was time to walk again.

I was no more than a quarter mile from the Far when I saw one of those low-to-the-ground signs for something called "Stone Coach Woods—A Planned Community" and the winding street lined with puny trees that led into it.

This must be the cushy new development that Wanda had talked about where the hoodlum locals lived and that I saw from Deke's treehouse. As Deke said, "Having us butt up next to them is like sitting next to a fat smelly guy on a bus. Maybe he was there first but it don't make it any nicer."

Deke. Now, *there* was someone I liked. I think Wanda liked him too, despite what she said about his obsession with his house. Although, given her history with guys, the fact that he was reasonable, reliable, and hardworking might count as three strikes against him as far as she was concerned. I'd miss him, anyway.

After a few more miles, I came to a small roadside grocery—a couple of gas pumps out front, weeds growing around them. I thought I'd buy a soda and get the rain off me for a few minutes.

Blocking the entrance was a dirty, dented silver sports car, its engine running, nobody in it. I squeezed around it through the ad-pasted door of the store. The rain was falling heavier by now.

Inside it was all creaky wooden floors and loaded fly strips—a bait shop and guy grocery, with fishing tackle on the walls over plastic tubs whose handwritten signs read "Sandwerms" and "Grubs," and dusty cans of green beans and corn, the real food action being in the snack aisles, where bags of chips as big as bed pillows overflowed wire racks next to drums of peanuts and barrels of jerky. But all this was only a buildup for the main attraction—the coolers where all the beer was kept, or more like temporarily stored.

Behind the counter was a clerk in a hunting hat in a tasteful checkerboard pattern, with earflaps that stuck out—probably because his ears did the same—and a three-day growth under a pair of red-rimmed eyes.

I had to wait to get into the cooler, since a girl in tight-fitting jeans and a loose nylon jacket had the other sliding door pushed over and was looking over the brands of beer. She was bent over and had her head inside, and I couldn't get a good look at her, although I liked what I could see. She finally picked a six-pack and let the door slide shut. Our eyes bumped for a second, then she turned with almost a snap.

I'd seen those eyes before. Violet, long-lashed.

I figured she was about my age, and I wondered how she thought she was going to get away with it.

She picked up a bag of chips and, while she was still behind the rack, loosened one of the cans of beer in its plastic cuff as if she was going to take it out and drink it right there.

The guy at the register was just about to say something as she slammed the beer down on the counter and the loose can popped out and went flying across the slick surface and off the other side. As the clerk bent to pick it up, she grabbed a fistful of candy bars from the rack in front of the counter and stuffed them in the gaping side pocket of her jacket.

"Some ID," said the guy as he put the can of beer back on the counter.

"Don't have it on me," she said, not even making the show of patting her pockets, looking him level in the eyes. "I'm twenty-one."

"No I-D, no drink-ee," he said, like he just graduated stand-up comedy school and this was his valedictory.

"Just this then," she said, paid for the chips, and was gone.

As I left with my soda, there was the girl sitting in the car. I had to squeeze past again, and on impulse, I rapped on the window.

She rolled it down, showing not even the least bit of curiosity. "And?" she said.

"Slick," I said, looking at the candy bars she'd tossed on the passenger seat.

"How would you know?" she said, her eyes narrow.

I was speechless. For a brief second her features softened like in that mime trick where they pass their hand in front of their face and their expression changes. "You're the new guy at the Happy Hippie Home," she said.

"The Far?" I said. "I guess."

"Well, here," she said, "save you some food stamps," and she tossed me a candy bar before rolling up the window. I had to flatten myself against the wall as she drove off.

I walked on down the road for a while. There was no doubt it was her—the same one with the crew who had tried to steal the wishing well. How else would she know me? I thought about that for a while. I thought about her. The rest of her face was in keeping with the eyes: the curves on each side of her nose sliding beside high cheekbones, her cheeks fuller and fleshier than the druggy-looking, need-a-meal models in the magazines, opening in lips that, although she wore no lipstick, were red and full. Her short, spiky hair highlighted three or four small, gold circle earrings that ran up the outside edge of one of her ears.

After a while the wind shifted, and the rain started getting in my face. I walked a little farther. Then I turned back.

chapter 9

NICKY, how did you get your clothes so soaked?"

Wanda fingered my sweats and jeans, hanging from the shower rod in the bathroom.

"Walking," I said, not looking up from the screen of Wanda's old black-and-white TV, which I'd rolled out of the closet on its cheesy little cart.

"Of course," she said. "What are you watching?"

"I don't know," I said. In fact it was that old TV show where a group of people are supposed to be on a boat tour and get stuck on this island and drive each other nuts.

"That ancient thing?" said Wanda, taking a glance at the screen and shaking her head. She went in the kitchen and began slinging pots and pans.

"You been here long? I guess Deke hasn't been around?" Wanda said.

"Nope," I said. The goofy guy who's always causing trouble has convinced the others they can escape by building a helicopter, and he's busily at it, using palm fronds for the blades and an old bicycle for the power. (Where did he get the bicycle? From some fish?)

"He gets busy at work," Wanda was saying. "They get big orders in, and he has to work overtime for weeks on end."

I didn't say anything. The guy finally gets the thing together, has some palm moonshine at the big, bon voyage banquet, and sneaks out to try it, just as a storm comes up.

"It's a real hole he works in," Wanda said, "the shingle factory?"

The guy is pedaling and pedaling, and sure enough, his helicopter contraption begins to lift off the ground.

"He's been there too long," said Wanda. "They're hiring new people in at almost as much as he gets."

Right when he gets it high up above the huts, a stormy blast hits and a frond breaks off, and although he's pumping away, the thing falls with the sound of a shot-down plane, dead on top of the hut where everybody's sitting around toasting each other, landing right in the middle of the banquet table and bringing the hut down around everyone.

Suddenly my aunt was standing in front of the screen. She gently took the remote out of my hands and switched off the set.

I looked straight ahead at the wrench on the Donut Works apron she was wearing. "At least you weren't laughing at it," she said.

She sat on the arm of the sofa next to me. "What on earth is the matter, Nicky? You're not homesick, are you?"

"No," I said.

"Well, what is it then? Look at me." She put her hand on my chin and gently tilted up my head so I couldn't avoid meeting her eyes.

"Nothing," I said.

"Nothing? Nothing would make you pack up all your stuff and walk around out in the rain?" she said, nodding toward my backpack, leaning against the wall.

"You lied to me," I blurted out.

"Nick . . . !" she said, dropping her hold on my chin.

"Deke told me," I said, glaring at her. "The other day when we were in the store." I nodded at her apron. "You just work there."

"Deke talks too much," she said, standing up and smoothing the front of her apron.

"You aren't, are you? Partners."

"Let me turn down the pot on the stove," she said.

When she came back, she sat across from me, slumped in a stuffing-sprung chair. She lit a cigarette from the pack she had in the apron pocket.

"Things don't always work out how you plan," she said, breathing out smoke as she talked. "I had some money in my pocket—the most I ever had in one big piece in years—the money your parents lent me. It was supposed to pay off my card and leave me enough for a decent car."

"Why didn't you let me know you were going, or where you were?"

"Wait," she said. "Let me finish." She puffed out a long, sighing, stream of smoke, blowing one of her Rasta curls off her forehead.

"I had all this money in my pocket, and then, out of the blue, who should call but Alberta. I knew her back when we rode together, and I hadn't talked to her in years, since . . . Well, that's another whole story. Anyway, she says she's starting a business, and we talk for a few minutes and we make some plans to meet."

"That woman in the store?" I said. "She didn't look so friendly."

"If people want to stay friends, they should never work together," said Wanda. "Well, we meet, and it's a beautiful day and we talk about old times—'Big Bert' we used to call her back when she rode her Harley with this Christian motorcycle club— the Holy Muthers—and she looks so happy with this big dream opening up in front of her, but she says it's tough going it alone and on a whim, for a joke, I ask, Could she use a partner?"

"You were always saying you wanted to work for yourself someday," I said.

"Yeah. Well, I should have been suspicious when she took me

up on it so quick. To make it all happen, though"—she looked down at the rug—"I had to split town. I couldn't very well ask your parents for more money, or tell them what I planned to do with what they lent me. Besides I had just broken up with—you probably remember him. Johnny Lee?"

This would have been the prophylactic-vending-machine tycoon.

"—and I needed a change of scenery."

"Why didn't you tell *me*, though?" I said. "I wouldn't have said anything."

"Well, like I said, I couldn't tell *them,* and if I told you, I thought it would put *you* in a bad spot having to keep a secret like that. I had to clear out quick, and besides, I figured, based on what Bert said about the business, that I'd be able to pay them back right away. I figured it would only take a month or so, and then I'd tell you; I'd call. But one month led into the next, and—"

Wanda started to snuffle, and pulled a wad of tissues out of her apron pocket. "Anyways, when I moved up here, as it turned out, I learned a lesson in business talk. Turns out that 'Needs a partner' means 'Is running out of cash.'"

"It's not making money?" I said. "The doughnut place? It looked like it was going good. You were pretty well cleaned out when Deke and I were there."

"Oh, it's doing great, but you've got to pour so much in at the beginning—to start it up anyway—and I ran out. Meantime, Bert came into some money, and when I couldn't put in any more—I was scraping by as it was—she bought me out."

"So you only *work* there?"

"Hourly pay; no benefits. Pays the mortgage, puts gas in the car, and I eat on whatever's left. Plus all the day-olds I want." She pointed to the big, greasy bag sitting on the counter.

"You should have *told* me," I repeated.

"Once things straightened out I was going to, but they never did." Her eyes were leaking badly now. The cigarette, forgotten, was burning down to a long ash. "I also had the feeling that you *believed* in me, and this was another screwup. I was hoping you'd forget about me and write me off. Nicky, you know I've told you before, I think of you like my own kid, and I didn't want to set a bad example for you, I guess."

She was quiet for a while. I didn't know what to do.

"The very idea," she said, snuffling, "your aunt Wanda setting a bad example." At this she burst out giggling, the cigarette ash falling down the front of her apron, causing her to laugh all the more. I got caught up in it, both of us hooting so hard after a while we were crying.

"Come here," she said, when she caught her breath. She stubbed out the cigarette in the ashtray by her feet and brushed her palms together. I went over and wedged myself in the chair with her, and she hugged me, both of us still sniffling.

"I'm sorry," she said, kissing me a loud, wet one on the forehead. "You're gonna think this is really crazy, but I was so paranoid when I first saw you standing out on the road there with your backpack last week, I was sure your parents sent you out to *spy* on me."

"Speak into my lapel, please," I said, pulling on my collar.

"Oh, Nick," she said, hugging me close. There was a crinkly sound from my shirt pocket, and she said, "What have you got there?"

It was the candy bar the girl had tossed at me.

"Where did you get this?" she said. "Don't you get enough sweet stuff around here already?"

"Down at that little store, just past the development," I said.

"That fleabag place?" she said. "How did you get all the way down there? Wait, don't tell me; you walked."

I smiled and moved to grab back the candy bar. But she was too quick.

"Not till after supper," she said, slipping it into her apron pocket.

chapter 10

foot notes

Sometimes I find myself on some old footpath that I swear has been there a thousand years.

It's like I'm on a perfectly ordinary roadside path when all of a sudden, instead of crossing a bridge up ahead, it jogs and drops to the river below. And following it down, I find a land that time has skipped, like a flat stone over still water. Maybe there's a ring of blackened stones and a brush lean-to looking like some Neanderthal left it that morning to go hunt mastodon.

The whoosh of cars grows fainter and fainter as I continue on this path—this trail—which spools out on the same track it's been as long as people walked this river, which is to say forever—a way as natural as the way veins snake through a leaf or through your hand.

You can find lots of trails like this if you just look. Little kids know them, but like the games you play at school, you forget when you get older. And most people don't take the time to explore.

You see, if you think about it for a minute, at one time everywhere in the world was in walking distance. It *had* to be. And there *had* to be trails to take you to hunt, flee, go to market, haul water, march, migrate, and visit Grandma.

Even when people finally learned to ride horses or camels or llamas, they mostly followed paths already there. And it wasn't until civilization showed up that serious roads got built, usually right over these paths of least resistance. I read where even Broadway in New York City was once an Indian trail.

I like to imagine there's still a whole world of these ancient trails underneath the tons of tar and brick, cobblestone and cement, that's been laid down on them over all the centuries. And when it all crumbles and blows away, people will walk on them once again.

But like I started to say, every once in a while, I find myself on one of these unpaved originals; one that's the easiest line to a spring or around some big outcrop of rock; one that has the stored-up wisdom of centuries telling you, "This is where your feet go." Sometimes, on a trail like this, I'll even pass through a cool pocket of air I'm sure is the ghost of some earlier traveler who's sneaked back just to swing his legs one last time.

But from the deep dust, I see no mortal has been on it for years.

My footprints are like those the astronauts left on the moon.

chapter 11

"IT'S MAAAAMBO TIME!"

The hysterical voice blasted from the speakers wired to the record player. And I do mean "record"—this black ancient thing as big as a pizza, called *Dance, Latino! In Ten Easy Lessons!* with this schmoozy woman on the cover in a tight green dress and big puffy do, sucker-puckering the camera. And next everybody was jerking around like they were on skates on a runaway flatcar. In fact one of them *was* on skates—Jolly Roger had on a pair of these gold spray-painted roller rink numbers, which he was leaping around in.

"Get those party parts shakin'," he shouted over the scratchy blare of the record as the needle gouged its painful path.

I would count it from about here that the party at the Far actually got started.

It had been literally minutes in the making.

After dinner, a couple of voices echoed "Party time!" across the Green, Wanda ran out the door, and I grabbed my pack, thinking maybe it was code for a raid.

But no, people were dragging picnic tables and setting them up in a horseshoe shape around the wishing well. Rode Kool—resident welder, electrician, and plumber (and former bomb maker, according to Deke)—ran wires to the well, propped the record player on it, and hung speakers from its roof.

O. K. Sunbeam rolled out an old bathtub filled with ice, and a couple of others dumped in cans of beer and soda. Clatoo Burada rolled out a huge grill made of a fifty-five-gallon drum cut in half and laid over with oven racks and got it fired up.

Loosie struggled around the paths with an armload of bamboo poles, stopping in front of each cabin to slide one inside a piece of pipe sunk in the ground, and everybody ran a string of Christmas lights from their cabins out to the tops of them.

Within a half hour, with the blinking lights, clouds of charcoal smoke from the grill, and scratchy dance tunes blasting from the speakers, the place looked, smelled, and sounded like the midway of a one-drunken-clown traveling carnival.

Then came the food. Deke hauled out a laundry basket full of potatoes and corn on the cob wrapped in foil, which he threw into one of the grills. Little by little, others brought out what Wanda said were their specialties: big salads and pasta dishes and cakes and pies and mounds of fruit piled up in scrubbed garbage-can lids. I wouldn't have been surprised to see someone hauling out an ox on a spit, except that Wanda told me most residents of the Far were vegetarians.

Mysterious Willie wove through the group, playing his bag-pipes, the gold wishing-well can hanging on a string around his neck.

"For Jane's lawyer," said Wanda as she dropped a few bucks in the can, Jane being due in court in a few days to defend her shoot-ing spree.

After dark, things got really interesting. Deke slapped an As-troturf doormat on a table, jumped up on it, and karaoked with one of the records—some old musical about dreaming an impos-sible dream. Then a fast tune came on, and others formed a conga line. Some of them just sat looking dazed, having their own pri-vate good time.

I don't dance, so I stayed near the tables, watching Wanda and Deke and listening to Mysterious Willie in his straw hat with the burn marks all around the top.

"You know," he was telling anybody who would listen, "when

you're living your life, it feels like a train where you ride down the tracks in one straight direction, but if you look at it from above, you see all these other tracks goin' off whichever way or another that your *other* selves are always taking off on. So say, like I leave the house, but forget a shoe and I come back to get it, well there's another *possible* me out there who didn't forget his shoe, who's still—"

"Willie, shut up, will you?" said O. K. Sunbeam. "I'm trying to enjoy the party."

"—walking down to the river. And that's happening all the time." He ignored her and went on. "So like your leg doesn't hurt you, and you sleep an hour past when you did yesterday, or skip taking your onions—"

"Willie," said Rode, "don't tell us no more, we'll wait for the movie."

Deke and Wanda were dancing slow now, forehead to forehead and talking and laughing.

Another rousing rumba came on, and next I knew, Loosie had hooked me over the head with a scarf and pulled me out to dance. It was dark and she didn't move so fast and no one was looking anyway, so I did just fine.

While I was out there hoofing around, Jolly Roger came up behind and stuck something on my head. I took it off and saw it was a paper crown—a giveaway from some hamburger place.

"Put it on! Put it on! Wear it! Wear it!" The others, chanting and clapping hands, formed a circle around me and Loosie. Old Jane Juan danced up and took it out of my hands and stuck it back on my head. I felt dumb and embarrassed, but it wasn't like in high school where everyone was posing, watching to see if you would make a goof out of yourself. Here everybody was *already* a goof, and nobody cared. Rode, for example, was wearing a hat made out of blackened aluminum foil from the roasted corn, which he'd molded around two corncobs so they looked like horns, and Mysterious Willie had stuck lit candles around the brim of his beat old straw number, which explained the burn marks.

So after a while, I started to relax and dance away with the others.

Throughout the night, I'd seen cars pulling up outside the entrance to the Far, and kids gathering by the entryway. A couple of times I thought I heard someone calling out things, like when I'd first got here.

When I looked later, though, the cars were gone.

The music was getting that echoey kind of way it gets when it's late, and a couple of people had even started to drift back to their cabins, when I heard the first *splat!* and got splashed with something. At first I thought nothing of it, since the air was full of beer and soda and other flying fluids anyway. Maybe someone had sprayed a drink while doing some wild dance stunt? But a minute or two later there was another.

Then somebody yelled, "Incoming!" and three or four people jumped off their benches as some giant flying thing smacked into one of the tables. I could see from the pieces that it was a rotten cantaloupe. I looked around for a clue as to what was going on, but most people were behaving as if nothing particularly strange had happened. Was this part of the fiesta? Then a minute or two later, Jane was knocked flat.

"Hey!" I shouted, running over to help drag her, drenched, to her feet. A piece of bright green rubber was stuck in her hair. Somebody had hit her with a water balloon.

"You okay?" I said, looking around at the others, trying to figure out who would do such a thing.

"I'll live," she said, "but it cleaned my flipping clock. Help me home."

As I began to walk with her toward her cabin, something scored a direct hit on the wishing well and knocked the record player off with a squawk that sounded like a stuck bird.

Over the next few minutes, more rotten fruit, water balloons, a road-killed squirrel, and a couple of bags of garbage rained down on us like meteors.

Loosie and O. K. hid under picnic tables, laughing. Jolly Roger was dodging the stuff, leaping about, pretending he was in a ballet; Willie sat at a table, melted wax dripping off his hat brim, as if nothing was happening

Deke was pouring sweat, running in circles and looking anxiously up in the surrounding trees.

"Stoners—must be catapulting the stuff in," I could hear him saying to no one in particular when I got close. He took off for the fence bordering on Stone Coach Woods.

"Deke," Wanda shouted after him. "Give it up. Let's call it quits," but he gave no sign of hearing her. "Damn!" Wanda dodged a bouncing laundry detergent bottle. "Always somebody who wants to ruin a perfectly good time."

It was getting dangerous to be outside, and with the music knocked out, more and more residents slipped away. Wanda and I called it a night ourselves, and after a while, most of the lights outside had been turned out and the bombing had pretty much stopped. Much later we heard Deke come back cursing and swearing and the door to his cabin open and slam.

"Well, Nick." Wanda ran her finger along the jags of my crown, which was sitting on the table between us. "How does it feel to be an officially initiated member of the Happy Far Family?"

"Is that what this was all about?" I said.

"Mostly," she said.

"I don't know," I said. "Pretty good, I guess."

chapter 12

NOW THAT the deal with Wanda and the doughnut place was out in the open, she had nothing to hide and promised she'd ask Bert if they could put me to work.

Meantime, I had time on my hands.

Wanda had asked me to cut down the weeds around her house, but all she had to cut them was a sickle—this dull, curved knife thing with a handle that you used by stooping down and whacking. So, needless to say, I didn't get all that far. Maybe Deke had an old mower somewhere in the mountain of junk in his house. I'd have to ask. Instead I cleaned up around inside the place, which took all of fifteen minutes, it was so small. Got to earn my keep somehow.

I rolled the TV out for a while, but daytime shows reminded me too much of when I was in the hospital for my appendix.

> *"Allen, you have to know by now*
> *it's only you I've wanted all these—"*
>> *-click-*
> *"So you're telling me that you and your son hired yourself*
> *out to other people in the trailer court as male—"*
>> *-click-*
> *"Lucy, 'splain to me how you get*
> *your toe caught in—"*
>> *-click-*
> *"Sorry, the correct answer is 'phlegm.'*
> *Dan, what do we have for—"*
>> *-click-*

It felt like my life was leaking out.

So I walked.

I don't know if I've said, but I'm built pretty well for getting around this way. Sit me down, and I'm your average height, but stand me up and I'm all of a sudden a head taller, thanks to these way-long legs I've got. This makes being up there on skates or skis kind of scary, but for walking it's great. And out the front door I went on them, swinging one foot in front of the other in long sweeping arcs, trying not to think about anything in particular.

When I looked up, I saw my legs had led me to the entrance to Stone Coach Woods, and this time I went in, pulling myself up to my full height and trying to look my best for the surveillance cameras.

The houses were all big and fancy and painted white. Many of them had flags out front that said "Welcome" or "Summertime" with flowers on them or had the name of the people who lived there. It looked like the set for an old movie where someone comes home from the war.

Not me.

There were a couple of trucks—rug cleaners, plumbers, and like that—parked in driveways, but there wasn't a living person to be seen, or squirrel, bird, chipmunk, or ant for that matter. Windows and doors were sealed tight, and air conditioners were humming, although the day wasn't really that hot. I imagined the people inside sitting in some huge, cool basement bar with a built-in bowling alley, or lounging in the back by the side of some giant pool, the only sweat in the whole place on a glass with a tiny umbrella in it.

I'd only walked a block or so when a Jeep all painted up with gold shields and topped with a revolving yellow light rolled slowly past. A private cop. He must've picked me up as an alien invader on one of the spy satellites. As he went by, snapping a piece of gum, his elbow cocked casually out the window, he gave me a hard look through his wraparounds like, What is scum like you doing in here?

I smiled and waved.

He frowned and drove.

Jeesh! Just tryin' ta be friendly-like.

I rounded a curve in the long street and could see three guys shooting free throws in a driveway up ahead on my side. I thought of crossing over, but it would have been too obvious, like I was scared of them or something, so I kept going, looking like I knew where I was headed.

They were heavy into it and didn't seem to notice as I walked past. I'd only walked a few houses down, though, when I heard a shout:

"Hey, freak!"

I kept walking.

I thought maybe that would be it, but then, as I got farther on, I could hear the sound of a basketball being dribbled on the sidewalk behind me.

I didn't need to turn around to see they were following.

"Faggot."

The odds weren't so good. I walked faster.

"Hey, you. Don't walk away when I'm talking to you, freak-o."

The street lead to one of those dead ends you get in fancy developments, with a circle with plants in the middle and houses all around. I kept walking, buying time till I figured what to do.

The dribbling got closer and closer and the footsteps with it faster and faster, and then *thump*, something—the basketball—hit me in the back. I stopped and turned. They surrounded me.

"Nice catch," said the lead guy. I remembered seeing him leaning on a car the first night I got to the Far. He was a runty dude with a stubbly attitude haircut and a scraggly goatee. He wore a black T-shirt with some kind of weird symbol on it, black jeans, and boots. The other guys—one with a baseball cap on backward, another with a big, oversize shirt—were anybody you might see loping around in a pack at a mall, sniffing at people and lifting their legs on trash cans. They were grinning, but only along for the ride, and backup muscle if needed.

"What are you *doing* in here?" the runty guy said, dribbling the ball as he talked. He had perfect white teeth that took away from his bad-boy image.

"Is there a problem?" I said.

"You," he said.

I said nothing.

"Freaks belong in the freak show." He nodded in the direction of the high fence that ran along back of the houses on the block. Behind it off in the distance I saw the big tree with the treehouse inside the Far.

I still said nothing. I've learned that shutting up forces guys like this to use their imagination, which doesn't get them very far and gets the situation over with quicker, one way or the other.

"You know any freaks live around here?" he said to the droogs.

"Nope," one snortled.

"I wonder where he could be going?"

He was watching the ball as he dribbled and talked. Mr. Yarber, my gym teacher, would have fined him a dollar for every bounce he watched. On an up bounce, he flicked it at my chest, thinking maybe if he could hit me in the back, he could hit me in the chest. But I grabbed it.

He tried to swat it out of my hands, but I was too fast for him. I faked left, went right, and drove through the droogs, dribbling down the street, heading back toward the entrance.

"Hey!" the runty guy said, and I could hear him flapping after me in his stylish clunky boots.

I got down a couple of houses, ran up to the front door of one, and shot a long looping hook with a nice spin on it up on the roof. I guess they thought they would snag the rebound and take after me, but it bounced around on all the gables and railings and crap up there as they watched it, heads bobbing for a second or two in sync with its bounces, giving me enough time to cut down the driveway of the next house, heading for the back fence and the Far.

I was halfway down when I heard the single *broop* of a police siren and an amplified voice. "Sir," it said.

I kept going.

If I could just get to the fence . . .

"Sir," said the amplified voice, more insistently. "I'll have to ask you to stop."

I hit it—eight feet high and solid wood—foot first and jumped to grab one of the pointed slats, missed, and fell back a step or two when I staggered around to see the guy jogging up the drive—the cop in the sunglasses, cuffs dangling from his belt. I flashed on how cold the ones felt they'd clicked on my wrists at school when they caught up with me for the house fire.

"Are you looking for someone in particular?" He was being all Mr. Very Helpful, although I saw he had the holster unsnapped on his pepper spray.

"Well, no," I said. "I was just taking a walk."

"Up this driveway?" he said.

"Seemed as good a place as any," I said, puffing lightly from the run. Somebody stop me.

"This is private property, you know," he said, getting less polite now.

"Really?" I said looking around bewildered-like.

"Let's see some ID," he said, dropping the helpful act and showing teeth as he chewed his gum.

I sighed, pulled out my wallet, and gave him my photo ID from my old high school. I looked past him to the street. The Stoners were gone; probably got scarce as soon as they saw the cruiser.

"How did you wind up so far away from home?" he said, looking at my address.

"Walked," I said.

"Oh, a smartmouth, huh?" he said. "Well, I wonder if you'd be interested in walking on over to have a little talk with the sheriff? Maybe you can shed some light on the break-ins around here lately."

I was probably about to say something *very* stupid at this point—something that would cause me to spend my first three months in the military school's stockyard or stockade or whatever they call it. In fact, the words had begun to form—something like "If you weren't sleeping it off all day in your cruiser, maybe you'd be a little more clueful about your local criminal activity." I was about to push out the chestful of air that was to carry them when I heard someone shout "Josh!" and heard the slapping of a pair of slides on the pavement.

The cop turned, and I saw coming down the street right at us a girl wearing a light beach robe.

"Josh," she said as she came up the driveway, her flimsy wrap flying open to give us a healthy flash of tanned breasts barely held in place by the top of her skimpy two-piece. The cop still had his feet planted facing me, but somehow had turned the rest of his body nearly all the way around to take her in.

It was the girl with the eyes. The one who tried to heist the wishing well and tossed me the candy bar.

The cop turned back, eyeing me suspiciously. I looked at her blankly over his shoulder.

She gritted her teeth and made a fist like, Pick *up* on this, you dope.

I smiled and raised my hand. "Oh, hiya," I said.

"Josh," she said brushing past the cop and right up next to me. "You got the address wrong. I'm a couple more down."

"Oh, yeah," I said. "Right."

"I thought you'd *never* get here," she said, breathing heavily, the sweet smell of bubblegum and coconut tanning lotion filling the air around her.

With all this distraction, the cop forgot that my ID showed I was from the other side of the state, that it read "Nicholas," not "Josh," and probably also what year it was and who was president.

"Thanks, Smitty," she said to the cop, taking my arm and leading me away.

"No problem, miss," he said, tipping his cap like he was in the movie where the friendly cop walks the sexy woman across the street, not realizing he was actually in the cartoon where he's Elmer Fudd, and Bugs Bunny in drag has stolen his watch.

The girl talked to my frozen smile about the weather or something. I could hear her words, but with my arm clamped up against the side of her breast, I didn't exactly understand them.

As soon as the cop drove off around the curve, however, she let go and gave me a shove. "You *are* slow." Her face went through another of its monumental changes, this time from smile to scowl as she jerked the wrap tightly around her.

"Thanks," I said. "I mean for the help," I added, just so she didn't think I was agreeing with her about my lack of swiftness.

"Come *on*," she said, her shoes slapping faster on the sidewalk. "You got to watch out for Smitty; he's over-Dudleyed." She kept looking down the block like she was afraid someone else would see me with her.

Around back of her house was an amazingly blue pool, much like I was imagining was behind these very houses, overhung with a tree and set with a couple of tables and lounge chairs. I'd seen smaller pools in public parks. A couple of girls—maybe about ten and twelve years old—were playing in the water.

"What do you think you were *doing* out there?" she said. The question was getting monotonous.

"Just walking," I said.

"Nobody 'just walks' around here," she said, "unless you're . . ." But she let it trail off. "Where are you from, anyway?" she said.

I told her.

"So you're just visiting Happy Hippietown, is that it?"

"I guess," I said. "I don't know." Dumb answer. "Why do you call it that?" I was getting annoyed.

"'Cause that's what it is, or didn't you notice that, either?"

She glanced over at the two girls in the pool, who were whooping and splashing in the shallow end paying no mind to us, then sat down at a table in front of a half glass of soda.

"You want something to drink?" she said. The first friendly words I'd heard.

But I'd absorbed all the hospitality I could take for one day from the people around here.

"Thanks," I said, "But I need to be going. Do you mind?" I pointed to the back fence, same as the one I'd tried to climb a few houses down.

"Be my guest," she said. "Here, use this." She pointed to a plastic milk crate that had some big bottles of fancy soda in it. As I took out the sodas, she said, "What is your name, anyway?

I told her. "And yours?"

"Diana," she said. I walked around the pool and placed the empty crate next to the fence.

I was just about to step up on it and climb over when I looked back to see her standing there looking at me.

"Can I ask you something?" I said, raising my voice to reach her over the distance between us.

"Ask," she said.

"What made you rescue me like that?"

"I think you're cute," she said, hand on her hip propping her wrap open for the full frontal show.

From all the way across the pool her smile stuck crosswise in my chest.

I nodded at this piece of information, turned, and climbed back into the Far.

chapter 13

"WAKE UP! WAKE UP!"

One thing about living at the Far was that it was far from predictable—like in expecting to sleep in on any given day, for instance. It felt like I had just slipped under the waves and here was Wanda already dragging me up, dripping, with "Time to go to work."

"Wurrrk?" I said, realizing I was lying in an empty bathtub fully dressed—something Wanda said nothing about. Instead she said, "Yes. Come on, hurry up." She explained there was some kind of complication with my pregnancy and I wasn't feeling so good and had to go home and stay with my mother. Or maybe that was the girl who was working for them in the doughnut shop. I was sure I could figure it all out later.

"Let's go, we're late," Wanda said.

I suppose there wasn't any good reason I should be hostile to Wanda for not telling me before about this, except maybe I wouldn't have sat up so late watching her old ghosty black-and-white TV, which I had rolled out of the closet into the living room. That is, until Wanda said it was keeping her from her pre-work nap, so I took it in the bathroom and set it on top of the toilet seat and closed the door. There was nowhere to sit, so I put a couple of couch cushions in the tub, and I guess I fell asleep.

And now instead of happy dreams of the movie I was watching where the sailors mutiny against the evil Captain Bligh and get to live on a tropical island among the lusty breadfruit trees, here I was facing the cold reality of Wanda's bathroom. The small bare bulb she snapped on over the medicine cabinet burned straight down in my eyes. No matter what my watch said, the black square of bathroom window told me it was still night out there.

I could barely eat anything so early, so I sipped on a half cup of coffee from a foam cup Wanda had stuck in my hand as I stumbled out the door.

The parking lot for the Far was full of what looked like the losers of a demolition derby—leaking, rusted, and dented cars, vans, and trucks of all makes and models. There was even an old truck up on blocks ("Bledsoe's Bread: Good, Anyway You Slice It!"); no surprise to find out it was Deke's.

Wanda had inherited her giant old road beater—the one my parents had lent her the money to get rid of—from her last boyfriend, who had the sense to leave without it. "Meanest thing he ever did to me," she said. We had climbed up in it and she was about to turn the key when she said, "Damn!" got out, and whacked the hood.

"You need to do *that* to start it?" I said.

"You need to do *that* to get Yasgur out from under the hood," she said. "Mysterious Willie's cat," she explained when I gave her a dumb look. "Climbs up in there to get warm at night."

She turned the key.

Ruh-RUH-rer-ra-ruh-RAH-rur-ra-ruh (cough, cough).

Ruh-ruh-RER-ra-ruh-rah-RUR-ra-ruh (Aaaack!).

She said a bad word and waited a few seconds.

"Always when I'm in a rush," she said.

But then she tried again and it cranked right up, sounding like a cheap suit of armor tumbling in a clothes dryer.

The moon, shining in the bathroom window when I fell asleep, must've gotten tired and gone to bed. Even the streetlights were dark as we clattered down the empty streets. In a few minutes we were driving toward a weird, flickering bluish light in the downtown, which turned out to be the neon sign in the window of the Donut Works. As it flashed, a blue wrench turned the white doughnut O in the otherwise red lettering of the store's name, lighting up the street and sky above like a beacon for the doughnut demented. The cost of the sign alone must've eaten up Wanda's pitiful life savings.

Wanda introduced me to Alberta, her former partner. "Bert," as she was known, looked like she ate up a lot of the profits. Sticking out from under the short white sleeve of her uniform, was the image of a bearded chin, its mouth open in a laugh. Wanda told me later this was a tattoo—and I am not making this up—of a laughing Jesus, a leftover from her Holy Muther days. The face on the tattoo was in stark contrast to Bert herself, who didn't wear so much as a grin at this time of day, or any other, for that matter. It was Wanda who showed me the routine I would learn to know and love.

Basically, my job would be to keep a couple of big, churning mixers full of ingredients that would end up as doughnut dough. There was no science to this—little measuring or timing or anything much else that involved common sense or good judgment—which is probably why they zeroed in on me for the job.

You started by pouring a large bag of the basic mix into one of the huge metal bowls, added water from a special plastic container with a line on it that showed just how far to fill it up, and turned on the mixer. Once it got working, you followed a wipe-off checklist of flavors that Bert had already filled out for that night— chocolate, sour cream, blueberry, whatever—and for each separate batch, you poured in a little bag of stuff. Depending on the bag, the doughnuts became chocolate, sour cream, blueberry, whatever. The bags even had helpful pictures on them in case you were out sick the day they taught reading. The mixers buzzed when the dough was ready.

Wanda next got to do the fun part, which was to take big

scoops of the mixed-up stuff and dump them into the hopper on the doughnut maker. This machine grunted out perfectly round, raw dough circles, which then moved slowly down a long conveyor belt, giving them time to plump up as the yeast began to work. The belt, which was made of mesh—like a stiff fishnet—then gently eased the puffy circles of dough into a pool of hot grease, where they floated along like happy munchkin innertubes as they fried on one side and then—this was the cool part—ran right into a revolving metal paddlewheel that scooped them up and flipped them over so they fried on the other side.

When they were done, they slid down a metal chute, where Bert and Wanda scooped them up with long-handled wooden paddles and put them on a table where they added frosting or sprinkles or powdered sugar, or whatever.

Even though I watched it all happen for thousands of doughnuts, hours on end, it was still magic to me how the big gloppy tubs of powder and water turned into the tasty, round, crispy O's.

The work kept you busy, and soon I noticed everything was brighter. At first I thought they turned on the store lights, but then I saw it was the sun.

It got to be opening time, and the bell over the door was constantly ringing. By then all the doughnuts were long cooked, and I was scrubbing up the huge beaters and washing out the bowls, throwing out the trash and mopping down the kitchen floor.

When I was done, I peeked out the door to see people lined up, Wanda and Bert busily filling bags, the cash register beeping and chattering away. It felt good seeing people waving cash, elbowing each other, and bellying up to the counter to get something you helped make. And if, like they say, you are what you eat, then a good percentage of the people in town that morning were part doughnut.

By noon, Wanda dropped me at the Far and ran off to do a few errands. It felt strange to be home with a whole day's work behind me and most of the day left. I was tired, though, which also felt strange at noon, and I thought I'd lie down, but before I could get settled on the couch, the phone rang.

"Nicholas."

I snapped wide awake.

"Dad," I said.

"Why haven't you called?"

"There's a lot going on here. I was going to—"

"'Wuz gonna'?" he said.

"I have a job and all," I said, getting angry already.

"You had a job here," he said. "One I got you, I might add."

I took in a breath. It wouldn't be good to get in a fight with my father right when things were starting to show some promise.

"Dad, look. I'm sorry. I know I should've called. I apologize. You did get my message."

"We got it all right; just after Colonel Salter's. Mom was worried and called all over the place. But I knew right away that Wanda had something to do with this," he said.

"Wanda?" I said. "I didn't even *see* her for a whole year. I came out here completely on my own. She didn't even—"

"And so much for her promise to get you to call."

"Dad," I said. "You can't blame *her* for that."

"I'd ask how you found her," he said, "but I saw the paper with her address and phone was gone from my desk. . . . Why didn't you go to Millstone?"

"I *was* there already," I said, "with you guys."

"Colonel Salter was worried," he said.

"I don't even know if I want to go," I said.

"Nicholas, we've gone over this. I know these things aren't easy, but remember we told the judge we'd keep you out of trouble."

"But, Dad," I said, "a *military* school?"

"Nicholas—" He sounded exasperated. "It's insurance, and anyway, what are we supposed to think about your taking off like this? We trusted you—"

"Look, Dad, I *was* going to call," I said. "And it's not like I'm *not* going. I just skipped the orientation. I'm doing fine out here. Like I said, Wanda found work for me. She's helping me."

"—and the first chance you get you run out on us. The grass was up to my knees." Dad always finished his sentences. If he was conked on the head and woke up ten hours later, he'd pick up right after his last semicolon.

"But I'm not in any trouble," I said. "I just need some time."

"Wanda found you work?" he said. Actually listening. This was a start.

"Wanda is trying to do something," I said. "She's a partner in a place. I want to help her." I thought it wouldn't hurt to keep Wanda's story going a little longer, given the circumstances.

"I wonder where she got the money," he said.

"No, really," I said, ignoring the swipe.

"Your mom said it was a business. Some store?"

"A doughnut shop. She bought it and she's all organized and cooks and everything. And she gave me a job there. It pays better than the dealership."

"You're working in a *doughnut* shop," he said, as if I'd told him I was a rodeo clown.

"Yeah," I said. "I told you she was different. She's got this place with a friend. When they start to break even, she'll pay you back."

"And pigs will start their own airline," he said. "Wanda's lucky your mom stopped me from calling the police back when she left town."

"How did your trip go?" I jabbed with my left.

"It was fine," he said. "The ship was huge. We ate too much. We hit some bad weather. Your mom and I missed you."

"Like I said, it was really more for you two. It would have been dumb for me to go," I said. "I don't know what I'd do on a cruise for ten days. Tell Mom I'm fine. I'll talk to her."

"I'll call Colonel Salter," he said, "and explain. You can go to the late orientation. And Nicholas," he said patiently, "if you're looking for a role model—"

"She's not a role model," I said. "She's a person. I'm okay here. Wanda said it was okay to stay."

"Your mother was worried sick."

"Tell her I'm okay. Everything is fine, really."

"I'll talk to Colonel Salter," he said. "They have a short program if you can't make the regular orientation. But you have to go a day or two early. Before the term starts."

I couldn't believe it. Was this truly my dad? It sounded like he wasn't going to insist I come back. Maybe it was finally getting through to him that I needed to have my own life.

"How is Mom?" I said. "Let me talk to her."

"She's out showing a house. She was supposed to be back by now, but I didn't want her to be disappointed if you weren't there, so I called."

"Thanks, Dad," I said. In the long silence afterward, I could hear the crackling and sputtering of Wanda's old telephone line. Suddenly, so far away, he struck me as being—I don't know—a different person.

"I'll tell Mom, and we'll talk," he finally said. "Love you, son."

"Love you, too, Dad," I said.

I kept the phone up to my ear after he hung up. I don't know what I was listening for.

chapter 14

SUMMER SATURDAYS were slow days for doughnuts, so Wanda told me to stay home. The Pony Express didn't stop at Deke's with the news, I guess, since he showed up banging around the cabin before dawn anyway.

"I wish my parents would just leave me alone," I found myself telling him as we sipped coffee twenty minutes later up in the treehouse. My dad's phone call had been kicking my brain around like a flat soccer ball the last couple of days. "I don't want to live in their house. I don't want to go to their school. I don't want anything to do with them."

Deke seemed to be thinking about what I'd said, or else he was staring at a black bird with red-edged wings that had landed on a nearby branch.

"And I feel kind of bad about getting my parents onto Wanda. It's like she tunnels out of there with a spoon and *eats* all the dirt, and when she finally sticks her head up outside the fence, I set off Roman candles."

"You said your dad already *had* her address. Right?" said Deke, still staring off into the leaves.

"Yeah," I said. "But he wasn't *doing* anything with it, and now that I'm here, maybe it'll start to annoy them more that she skipped with their cash. And I'm sure they're already blaming her for the fact that I didn't go to the orientation at their stupid military school."

I drained the rest of my coffee and wished I was skilled enough at climbing up here to have a whole cup. "What was the sheriff here for yesterday, anyway?" I said.

"Darryl?" said Deke, finally looking at me. "I heard it was bad smells from Jolly Roger's place—somebody in Stone Coach complained—his cabin is right over the fence from them. Why?"

"Whenever I see him pull up, I half expect he's there to haul me away or maybe Wanda for kidnapping or harboring a fugitive or something. Maybe I should move on and cause trouble for someone I don't care for as much."

"All the more reason to stay," said Deke.

"Huh?" I said.

"It's hard to find someone you care about so much you don't want to cause trouble for them," he said.

"Or I expect my father will show up one day."

"Worse things happen," said Deke.

"Such as?"

"Such as he might *never* show up."

"I should be so lucky," I said.

He shot me a puzzled look.

Wanda told me that after his dad left, Deke used to stop and look at the man's picture in the front window of a photo studio he passed going to school every day. I saw a yellowed copy of this, creased like it had been folded, that Deke tacked up in his cabin. The guy was handsome in an ancient-movie-poster way—slicked-back hair and a cigarette in his hand with smoke drifting artistically up.

Over the years, that picture was the most that Deke, who had no brothers or sisters, would see of his dad. Then his mom left, and he was passed like a sandbag from relative to relative, till the last in line dropped him and walked off. He was fourteen.

"I mean, you got out on your own so early," I tried to argue.

"The down side being I was dead broke and living on the street."

"How did *you* make it?"

"Snuck around apartment buildings—this was out in Chicago—stealing newspapers. You could get big bundles right from the lobby if you went real early in the morning. Sold 'em for meals. Until I got caught, anyway."

"The cops got you?" I was looking for a partner in crime.

"Nope—the guys who delivered the papers. Knocked me around a little, but then they felt sorry for me, I guess. Wound up letting me stay with them in some beat place—a room—in one of the guys' apartments. He didn't let us use the tub, but it was okay for a couple of years anyway, until I enlisted."

"What was that like?" I said.

"I'll tell you sometime," he said, tracking a squirrel as it hopped from a lower neighboring tree and then up the branches of the one we sat in. "Why are you so interested in leaving home, anyway?"

"It's a long story," I said.

"I'm not going anywhere." He pulled up a crate and motioned me to sit on another.

"You see, I had this brother," I said, leaning back against the main trunk of the tree and spinning out the whole sad tale.

Mom and Dad and Donnie and me used to do a lot of fun things together—weekends at the beach, fireworks shows, miniature golf, car trips to Disneyland and the Grand Canyon, Christmas trees with trains running around them—the typical TV family stuff.

Right up until Donnie died.

Donnie and me were in the back seat of the car. I had this new game, and he wanted it. We fought, and my father got off the next exit, stopping to put Donnie in the front seat with him while I got stuck in the back with Mom—doubly unfair. As we started to go back on the highway, Dad was fuming mad and he made a left turn at the intersection and there was a flash and a boom and suddenly I didn't have the game in my hands and we were parked in the grass facing the other way. I remember Dad looking over his shoulder—"Madeline, Madeline, are you all right?" Mom was pretty beat up and bleeding, being right where the other car hit. I could see between the seats up to where Donnie sat in his seat belt, untouched and asleep. For good, as it turned out. He was ten.

After a few years, I didn't remember much of him, since I was only five and barely house broken when it happened. He had a bike, hung around with some other big kids, played ball, sometimes played games with me and my friends when he was bored or had nothing else to to. I remembered him looking like he was peaceful, asleep in the front seat of the car. But mostly he was something that had been *there,* like rain or TV—enough to notice that when he wasn't anymore, all of a sudden there was this *space.*

My parents, I guess for my sake, tried to make believe that everything was just fine so this space, this hole he left, wouldn't seem so big and empty. But the more they tried to squeeze it down and make it less and less noticeable, the denser it got, until finally it was so dense it was like one of those *black* holes that suck all the light out of everything.

It got to where my mom couldn't take being around the house—everything reminded her so much of Donnie. There was only me to take care of anyway, so she went back to work. She had been selling houses before she met my dad—in fact that's how she met him, at some open house—and she went back to it, putting me in day care with a neighbor lady who took in kids, taking me to open houses. On top of all that my dad got transferred to a job out of town a year or so later, and I didn't see him for weeks on end.

For years I wore Donnie's too-big hand-me-downs. I could see the pencil marks on the door frame in the basement where

Dad had measured him on his birthdays and where he now measured me. Finally one time my mark was above the last of his—I remember my dad looking at it, surprised—and they just stopped. Stopped measuring me. Stopped a lot of things.

"It was like it was my fault for growing up," I said.

"What made you think that?" said Deke.

"Oh, they never *said* anything," I said. "It's just how, you know, you *feel* something." And I told him about one time when I was twelve and we went on this car trip out west. It was supposed to be like old times, except just the three of us. And one time, we must've been driving all night and I was sick and I finally fell asleep in the back seat and when I woke up, I could see my dad in the gas station paying and my mom looking at a magazine and I had to take a pee, so I went around the side of the place to where the bathrooms were, and when I came out, my parents were gone. I kept looking at the space where the car was, thinking maybe it would just appear again. Then I went back in the gas station. It was one of these places like a store with bright lights and bags of charcoal and gallons of milk and stuff, and I looked all around. I asked the guy behind the counter—he was only a few years older than me—and he said they left. I got this panicky feeling and threw up, right in the store, and the guy was all pissed and threw me out, and I was standing out front looking around for a good long time, trying to figure out what to do, when they pulled up. My mother *leaped* out of the car and ran and hugged me and said they thought I was under the blankets in back and they drove over the grass in the middle of the highway to come back as soon as they realized I wasn't there, and they were laughing like they thought it was a big joke."

"And that's it?" said Deke.

"That was just one thing," I said, "an example. There was a lot of other stuff, too."

As I got older and did things Donnie never could do—skiing or driving—I got to feel like I was throwing it in their face, comparing myself somehow with Donnie, with what he couldn't do because he was . . . dead. I got to feel that by just living my life, I was doing something wrong. Like I was violating his sacred memory or something.

"Do you see?" I asked.

"I don't know," said Deke with a smile. "They did come back."

"But it was always like I was to blame, somehow. It was like they lost it when Donnie died."

"They're just people," he said. "It must've been hard for them."

When it looked like Deke didn't get it—how my parents were—I said "Yeah, I guess," and that I'd try to remember what he said and let it drop.

I COULDN'T ALWAYS SLEEP SO WELL; it was hard during the day, and while I was lying there, all I could think about was Diana—how great she looked standing there with her hand on her hip, and what she'd said about liking how I looked. I tried phoning her a couple of times, but they always left their answering machine on except for once when I got someone—probably her father—and hung up. Between Smitty the Boy in Blue and the local thugs, I didn't feel like risking a stroll through Stone Coach Woods again.

Besides, she was one of *them*—with the group that had tried to steal the wishing well, and maybe a player in the bombing of the party as well. Seeing her would be like consorting with the enemy, going over to the Dark Side, betraying Deke and Wanda and all the rest of my newfound friends.

One afternoon after work I gave up; sleep just wouldn't come. Wanda was deep out of it in her bedroom, and I thought I'd get out and walk around a little. I had that unreal feeling you get when you've been up all night. Like you're always just thinking of something but you always just forget what it was.

The day was so bright it hurt my sinuses. But I slogged along anyway, this time back toward town.

I'd gotten about halfway when a familiar silver sports car sailed past me, off the edge of the road so close that it popped gravel in my face—something else I was used to while walking. What was different this time was that the car stopped a hundred feet ahead and backed up, wobbling wildly so I thought the driver was trying to run me down and I jumped in the ditch, landing up to my ankles in muddy water. The car slid to a stop as the window rolled down.

"What are you doing?" came a voice out of whoever was folded up in the car's dark insides.

I couldn't put words to everything going through my tired head except for "What?"

"I almost ran you over!" Like it was my fault. A head appeared in the window to go with this charge.

It was Diana's.

"Yeah," I said. "Twice."

She looked up and down the road. "You run out of gas or something?"

"I'm just walking," I said.

"Again?" she said, as if this was some nasty habit she kept catching me at. "What do you think this is?"

I didn't know how to answer. A road? America? The twenty-first century? One o'clock?

"I'm just walking," I repeated duh-ly.

"Well, get in, and I'll drive you," she said.

This is another thing: I get offered rides all the time. Actually it's more like people *demand* that I ride with them. They can't imagine why I might be hiking it alone. I usually have to insist that I don't want a ride; that I'm walking by choice. This time, though, I said yes. Or really I didn't say anything. I just stumbled up the side of the ditch, my shoes squishing, and got in.

She looked me over. I looked back. It wasn't hard.

Her denim shorts bunched up past the tan line on her thighs, and she had on a blue halter top that showed off—among other things—her bare midriff, which had a fingernail-size white scar to one side of her navel. Her black, short hair—cut above her ears— was gelled so it looked spiky-wet, like she'd just gotten out of the pool. There were the rows of earrings. I noticed that her nose and cheeks were speckled with a few freckles. And her deeply tinted, liquid eyes, even at this early hour, were carefully made up. She stared at me, her lips pursed as if she'd been sucking on a lemon, her tanned bare foot nervously tapping the accelerator. I stared back slack-jawed.

"Well?" she said, after a few seconds. "Where to?"

"I'm not going anywhere," I said.

"Fine," she said, and we lurched back on the road with a screech and a rooster tail of gravel.

The interior was covered in so much cushiony leather, I felt like I'd been swallowed by a cow. "What is this, anyway?" I said.

She gave the name of some high-end sports car I'd only ever read about, glancing at me like I was some kind of goon who had never seen a wristwatch.

We were quiet for a quarter mile.

"Where you from, anyway?" she said. Driving seemed to calm her, and her voice softened.

I told her—some small town she'd never heard of, of course, and I had to explain where it was, way over in the center of the state.

"You from here?" I said.

"Lately," she said, as the car sickeningly hugged the hills and curves of the two-lane, past rail fences strung with a thin strand of electric wire and borders of bright blue chicory. "Before that, just about everywhere. My father works for this big company, troubleshooting. They have offices and factories all over, so they ship him all over the place every couple of years. My mom says a family isn't an amusement park; you can't just do it on weekends. So we go, too."

"Must be hard to get used to," I said.

"You get used to it," she said.

There was a plastic orange barrel up ahead, sitting slanted in a pothole. She headed right for it, and I automatically put my arm up as the car hit it, sending it spinning. The car bounced through the hole with a spine-stubbing BAM.

"What're you *doing*?" I said.

"Damn!" she said. "I thought they only put those in the big holes."

"You did that on purpose?" I reached for the door handle—something I learned before I'd learned not to hitchhike.

"This thing is tougher than I thought," she said, throwing a grin at me. "He still hasn't figured out how the suspension blows so fast, though."

As we drove along, she aimed at and hit everything on the road: chunks of blown tire, bolts, a muffler, road kill, tree branches, sunken sewer grates, pieces of lumber. You name it, she hit it.

"What are you doing?" I said, feeling the doughnuts I'd eaten a few hours ago start to crawl up my throat.

"Just trying to piss him off," she said. "My dad. He thinks this car is so hot. He got it for me, like I'm supposed to be eternally grateful. So how long you been here?"

"Couple of weeks," I said.

"You moved here?"

"No," I said. "I don't know. Just for the summer, I guess."

"What's it like over there in Happy Hippietown?"

"Better than where I was," I said, suddenly feeling like the doughnuts were ready to leave. "Let me out here, would you?" I meant just for a minute, until I could get everything back together.

"Sure." She instantly jerked the wheel and dug the car to a stop.

"Thanks," I said, getting out and closing the door, putting my hand on the roof for balance.

She powered down the window. "You walk around like that a lot?" she said, lying across the passenger seat to look up at me. I could see into her top.

"Yeah," I said.

"Maybe I'll see you again," she said.

"Yeah, sure," I said, still dizzy. Before I could say anything else, she took off, so I nearly fell from where I was leaning on the car.

chapter 15

foot notes

We're built for walking. And I don't mean it's just the way our legs are attached; it's the way our heads are screwed on, too.

Have you ever flown somewhere warm in the winter and heard someone say, "I can't believe it; only a couple of hours ago I was shoveling snow out of my driveway"?

Sure they can't.

Flying makes no sense at all to our earthy heads.

I remember seeing a show on TV once about some ancient people who believed that wherever you went, your spirit always followed on foot—sort of like your shadow, right on your heels. This was okay as long as people walked, but when they started riding horses, trains, cars, *airplanes*, it took longer and longer and longer still for that plodding, footsore shadow-spirit to catch up.

So I have this theory. I think the real reason people feel so groggy getting off a plane—jet-lagged, or whatever—is that their spirit hasn't caught up with them yet.

You see, when you walk, everything is *connected* to everything else. You go from one thing to the next to the next with things blending into each other—no quick cuts like in commercials.

I heard about this guy once—this old rock star—who walked across the United States in pieces, a little at a time. He started from his front door and walked as far as he could in one day, then had his limo pick him up and bring him home.

The next time he felt like it, he had his limo driver take him to the exact place he left off, and he'd start again and finish for that day and go home again and like that until he crossed the whole country, piece by piece, staying in motels overnight or flying back and forth when the distances got too much for his limo to come get him.

While he walked, he listened to books and studied foreign languages from flash cards he taped to the tops of his shoes, I guess to help pass the time.

I'm not criticizing him. I think it was a cool idea, and in all my walking I've never gone half that far. But for me, as far as I'm concerned, walking is for doing uninterrupted. For *not* doing something else in the meantime. For keeping at it all in one continuous piece. For *not* skipping the boring parts.

If you keep your eyes open while you walk, you see how there *are* no boring parts, anyway. Everything is just one *big* part. It gets so big it fills you up.

And if you keep your ears open as well, you'll hear your spirit walking along beside you, whispering in your ear. It's that little voice in your head? The one you ignore most of the time?

Some people say it's the one that's telling you right from wrong.

I think *they've* got it wrong.

I think it's simply telling you what *is*.

Listen closely.

chapter 16

THE WAY I LOVED WALKING?

Diana loved driving.

"It makes me feel like I'm free and in control," she told me. "Both at once."

I think I understand the "free" part—you could get in your car and drive to Peru if you wanted. It's part of what walking does for me.

But when I tried to ask what it could possibly be that would make *her* feel like she wasn't in control, all she did was shake her head like she was shaking the water off her hair when she'd come up from diving in a pool. "Don't worry about it," she said. "It's not like I'm helpless." But I couldn't get her to say more.

I knew all this, by the way, because we had started to meet regularly and talk. Not like it was planned, but more like this: As I wandered the roads around town, she would roar up behind me and stop—so close I could feel the heat from her car's engine—and I would get in and we would drive around.

It would have been nice to go somewhere, especially with the way she drove, but her place and mine were off-limits, and parking was no good, since her fellow Stoners knew all the spots and were bound to bump into us.

"So tell me," she said, next time she picked me up, "what brings you here to Loserville?"

And I played her the whole sad tune—the troubles in school and with the police and all the rest of it, minus the stuff about my brother. That could wait.

"You actually *burned* the place down?" she said, her face lighting up when I got to the part about catching my aunt's old house on fire.

"Not really," I said. "It was an accident; just a chimney fire."

"Oh," she said, disappointed.

"But they dragged me out of school in handcuffs."

"Cool," she said, interested again. "So then you ran away from home?"

"Walked, but not right away."

I told her how my parents wanted me to go to the military boarding school, and my aunt's was the only place I could think of.

"So you *did* run away."

"Not exactly."

"Oh," she said.

Seemed like I would be an endless disappointment.

"I'm sort of just *staying* here for a while. My parents know I'm here."

"You just show up, and your aunt takes you in, no questions asked?" Her voice rose as she got to the end of the sentence.

"Well, yeah," I said. "I never thought about it like that. She did ask me a few questions, but I knew she'd do it. My aunt and me have a good relationship." I described how I always felt welcome at her place when everywhere else seemed closed to me.

"Sweet," she said swerving sharply to run over a tire iron lying beside the road. I suddenly felt dizzy again.

Remember how I said I nearly lost my doughnuts the last time I rode with her? Well, I may have mentioned it already, but there's another big reason I walk: I get carsick.

I know, I know. It sounds like such a kid thing, and it's never going to make Disease of the Month:

BARF FLOODS NATION'S HIGHWAYS
AS CARSICKNESS SWEEPS NATION

But what can I tell you? My parents took me to some doctor after they got the car steam-cleaned one too many times, and he said there was something wrong with my inner ear and that it was tricky to fix and gave me some medicine that mostly made me sleep.

And yes, I tried *everything:* leaving the car windows open—snow and rain and all kinds of crap blowing in; wearing these goofy elastic bands on my wrists with a button on the inside that's supposed to press on some acupuncture place; breathing in and out of a paper bag; wearing these wacky sunglasses my father sent away for with a level in the lenses; and every other crazy thing that anybody ever said to try.

Finally, when I was old enough, I'd make up some excuse about having to do homework or something, and my parents seemed only too happy to drive off without someone in the back seat who was always tossing up his lunch for their approval.

Of course, this would have made it tough to ride with Diana to begin with, but she didn't help by swerving all over the damn road, hitting every pothole and piece of junk she could find.

"Would you mind?" I said, putting my hand to my head after she ran over a bag that must've had a cinder block in it.

"What?" she said.

"Could you pull over for a minute?" I said.

"Again?" she said.

"Now!" I said loud enough that she hit the brakes, diving the car onto the gravel.

I quickly jumped out, retched in the ditch, and wiped my mouth with a wadded-up tissue I'd grabbed off the floor of the car.

"Pleasant," she said, when I got back in the car. "Get rid of that, will you?" she said, meaning the tissue, which by now looked and smelled like some internal organ I'd ripped dripping from a fresh corpse. I hung it out the window until we got to a sewer and dropped it in.

"This happen much?" she said.

I explained the carsickness thing.

"You tried—" she started to say.

"Everything," I said. "If you took it a little easier—"

"Okay," she said. She cut down to ten miles over the limit.

"Go over again why you need to hit everything in the road," I said, pissed off at myself for getting sick and at her for bringing it on so fast.

"Active aggression," she said, giving me a sidelong smirk.

"I give up," I said. "I don't get it."

"Let me explain it like this," she said, downshifting on a long curve. "One day we get this new social studies teacher at school, and she's cutting on us. Like if you don't have a pen, she makes a big deal of giving you a Snoopy pencil and stuff—so we decide to bust her. We just keep screwing up when she says to do something. We're like: 'Oh, you want us to fill out *both* sides of the form?' and 'Mr. Kornblum said that we were supposed to have the test *next* week,' and stuff like that. And she says—she was a psych major in college—that what we're doing is called 'passive aggression,' where you don't tell the person that they've done something to piss you off, but you try to punish them anyway—usually by *not* doing something. Do you follow?"

"So how does beating up on your car fit with this?" I said.

"Well, nobody ever said I was passive about anything. So instead of *not* doing something, I *am*. My dad gets me the car, and I'm like, 'Thanks, Dad,' but I pound it into a pile of bolts. You see?"

"I guess," I said. "But why are you so pissed at your dad?"

"Let's just say I am," she said, looking straight ahead. "He's only worried about how things look, anyway."

I let this last comment drop. I didn't know if I wanted to get this deep into it, and besides, right now something else was bothering me more.

"So when you guys bomb the Far, is it passive or active?" I heard myself say.

"You mean slinging in all that crap?"

So Deke was right, it *was* them.

"Slinging?" I said.

"Yeah, they use this big slingshot thing. Like two people hold it—each one has a handle and someone pulls it back in the middle and lets it fly. Must shoot stuff like half a mile."

"Well, what about it?" I said.

"That's just goofing," she said.

"Well, you know, some people get ticked off when they get hit with a water balloon that's been shot a half mile."

"Wow!" she said. "We actually *hit* somebody?"

"Yeah," I said. "An old lady. And what's the thing with stealing the wishing well and all?"

"*Stealing?*" she said, flashing those eyes at me. "We never 'stole' a thing. It's just a prank. You're new there yet, you'll see. They like to think they're oppressed and everybody's out to get them and crap, so we help them out a little. I think they have as much fun trying to stop us as we have doing stuff."

"Well, I don't know, but there's at least one guy who lives there—Deke—he's got a red crew cut?"

"Yeah, I know who you mean," she said.

"He doesn't seem too happy about it." I explained how he and I had dug the holes and cemented the well into the ground.

"So that's the end of that, I guess," she said, smiling, like it was some private joke.

"I guess," I said as we bounced over a piece of a wooden pallet that had fallen off a truck. "But with your father, why not just tell him?"

"My father?" she said. "He *knows*. He got the car to get rid of me, to get me out of the house, and I want to show him—"

"Get rid of you why?"

"It's too complicated. Get down!" she said, suddenly pulling on my sleeve.

"Huh?" I said.

"Get *down*," she repeated, looking panicky.

"Where?" I said. The car was so small.

But she kept pulling down on my shoulder, and I finally got scrunched down in front of my seat, my head resting on her thigh. Out of the corner of my eye I could see the underneath of trees streaming by faster and faster overhead as she accelerated, and then I heard her shout "Hi!" as she kept rolling.

"Damn," she said. "They're turning around. I've got to lose them. Stay there."

I was happy to: my head resting on her warm thigh, getting a close-up view of her leg as I was and a noseful of her smell—mostly coconut oil and chlorine from the pool.

"They're still behind us." She seemed to be on a straightaway and set her hand gently on the side of my face and left it there.

"It's okay now," she said after a while. "They turned off."

"Who was it?" I said, sitting up.

"A couple of my friends," she said. "We shouldn't do this," she said, suddenly nervous. "Can I let you out here?"

"Okay," I said, and she pulled the car over.

"Bye," she said, flicking her hand at me as I closed the door, the car instantly taking off in its usual spray of gravel.

Where her hand had rested, my ear and jaw were hot.

chapter 17

"THAT'S IT, WANDA, DAMMIT! That's the last straw; I've had it with you."

We were getting close to quitting time at the Works, the early stream of customers out at the counter now trickling to a late-morning dribble, when I heard Bert's high-pitched squeak back in the office.

Next I heard Wanda shout something, kicking off some heated back-and-forth yelling. I was scrubbing the big beaters from the mixer and couldn't make out much of it over the water running in the sink, so I turned it off to hear better, but just as I did, Wanda came stalking through the kitchen, ripping off her apron and firing it into the murky mess in front of me.

"I'll come back for you later," she said. I could see her eyes were all red and teary.

"What happened?" I said, fishing out the soggy apron. "What *is* it?"

But she was already out the back door, and I heard her big jalopy hock, spit, haul itself up on its tires, and rattle off.

Bert went out front and started slamming trays and kicking the rubber trash can around.

"What's up with Wanda?" I said when the big woman finally came back to the kitchen.

"What's up?" she squawked, sounding like when you let the air out of a balloon while pinching its neck. "Look at this." She reached in the trash she was carrying and pulled out a white paper bag.

It seemed ordinary enough—slick with grease, rumpled, coffee grounds stuck to it.

"Open it," she said, shoving it at me.

Inside were three doughnuts—chocolate iced. The top one was half eaten. Out of its remaining half stuck a cigarette butt with lipstick on the filter.

"Guy who brought it back said he was driving when he bit into it and thought it was a nut or something and when he looked, he saw *that*. He heaved on his suit and put his car into someone's front yard. Lucky nobody was hurt."

"Oh," I said.

"I'm sorry," said Bert, looking kind of teary-eyed herself, "but I can't do business like this. She's no good with the register; she cracked one of the showcases cleaning up last week. . . . It's hard enough. Here, get rid of this," she said, handing me the trash.

When I came back in, she was wiping her eyes with the bottom of her apron.

"I tried to give him a free dozen, but he didn't even want them," she said. "Can you blame him? This is a small town. And it's not the first time."

"Should I stay?" I said.

"Yes, you should stay," she squeaked. "I didn't fire *you*." The bell tinkled on the front door. "It's probably the health inspector," she said.

An hour or so later at quitting time, I heard Wanda's car clatter up to the back door, then heard her beeping the horn.

I got out as quick as I could, but not before she started leaning on it.

"All right, all right," I said.

"I hate her!" she shouted, thumping the steering wheel with the palms of her hands. "I mean, what am I supposed to *do?*" she said, as the car staggered into gear. Riding in Wanda's car, by the way, was more like sledding down a rocky hill in a cardboard box, so I usually didn't get sick. "How am I supposed to pay the bills?"

"I'm still working," I reminded her. "I can kick in something."

"I don't want to take your money," she said. "I'm a grown person, and I can't even make it as a doughnut lady. This *should not* happen."

She was driving pretty wild, cigarette in one hand, wiping her eyes with the back of the other, not really paying attention, when I noticed a silver sports car coming from the opposite direction, veering toward us.

"Damn," said my aunt, but the other car hit a pothole in the center of the road and swerved back into its lane before she could do much of anything.

As it went by, I could see Diana at the wheel. I don't think she saw me, though, intent as she was on looking for other stuff to hit.

When we got back, Wanda immediately went to her room to try to sleep it off, but before I could even begin to doze, she was back in the kitchen, talking to herself and slamming things around. I decided I wasn't going to get any sleep with her like this, so I shook off the covers and sat with her and ate some cereal. She was reading the paper, snapping pages and blasting cigarette smoke out her nose.

"Nick." She suddenly put down the paper and grabbed my wrist. "How can I be the New, Improved Me when all the same old stuff keeps happening?"

"You're asking *me?*" I said.

"I mean, if I just had half a chance," she added, letting go, her grip leaving white finger marks on my skin.

"I shouldn't have asked you to take over for me," I said. I'd had to take a leak, and she must have dropped the butt in the mixer when I called her in from her smoke break out back by the Dumpster.

"Don't blame yourself. It's totally my fault." She looked at the cigarette she was smoking: "Damn cancer sticks. . . . You know, that's the irony of it. The one bad habit I keep? It's the one that gets me." She crumpled the cigarette pack along with the remaining one or two smokes inside into a tight wad and flung it over her shoulder. It bounced off the cupboard and, like a miracle, landed in one of the mugs sitting next to the sink.

"Let's see you do that again," I almost said, but I could tell she wasn't in the mood for joking around.

"You can get another job," I told her.

"But I really *liked* that one," she said. "It was my dream."

"Everybody in town knows you."

"That's another problem," she said.

"I'm sure something will come up." I clinked my spoon in the bowl and carried it to the sink. "It's not like you aren't a good worker or something."

She looked at me as if I *was* trying to joke around.

"Coffee?" I said.

"Okay," she said.

I wasn't looking and filled a couple of mugs before I realized the first had the crumpled pack of cigarettes floating in it. Fortunately Wanda was facing the other way and didn't see me as I fished it out and dropped it in the trash. Nothing could hurt *that* coffee much, anyway.

In spite of drinking it, however, Wanda started yawning and soon went back to bed.

But I was wide awake by then, of course, and thought I'd go out for a walk.

I hadn't gotten a half mile when Diana pulled up like she'd been cruising around, looking for me.

"I saw you before," I said as I climbed in. "Earlier. I didn't think you got up that early."

She looked burned out—her eye makeup blurry, her blouse wrinkled like she dug it out of the hamper.

"Yeah, well—" she said, and then she was quiet, looking ahead as she drove.

"Is everything all right?" I said, although I didn't want to know. Didn't think I could take two basket cases in one morning.

"The usual."

We drove in silence through town, catching all the lights except for a few that we sailed through anyway, and soon we were on a winding road in the countryside. As we bounced along, I started getting that old queasy feeling again, but even stronger from all the tension back at Wanda's along with too little sleep and too much coffee.

"Look," I said. "I think I'm going to heave if we keep driving around. Would you do me a favor?" She shot me an annoyed look, but when I asked, did a one-eighty in a wide spot in the road. In a quarter mile, we passed a faded For Sale sign with an arrow pointing down a no-name gravel road. I'd caught a glimpse of it as we tore on by the first time.

"Here," I said. "Turn here."

Having the bottom of her car scrape on the high spots and gravel nick its sides seemed to improve her mood. She was smiling by the time the road curved and limped by a lonely-looking one-story house with an attached garage. The long grass nearly hid the For Sale sign in the yard. There were no other houses in sight.

"Stop."

She glanced at me sharply, worried, like I was going to blow here and now.

"Pull in the driveway," I said hoarsely.

"What is this?" she said.

"Wait here a second," I said, popping the door before the car was entirely stopped and grabbing a quick look around as I sprinted up and opened the storm door.

Sure enough.

In a few seconds I had the key, unlocked the front door, and slipped on in. In another few I opened the garage door and motioned to Diana to drive into the big, bare space, which she did, a mystified smile on her face.

"Whose place is this, anyway?" she said, still sitting in her car as the door clunked behind us.

"Hell if I know," I said.

At this she smiled broadly.

chapter 18

I'D BEEN AT WANDA'S for almost a whole month now, running through my stash of summer, and I didn't feel any closer to figuring out what I would do once it was all gone.

It was a shaky plan for starts that I'd ever convince my parents to let me stay the next couple of years with Wanda, go to the local high school, and—what?—ride around with Diana, make doughnuts, sleep on the sofa and in my spare time watch TV in the bathtub?

It was even shakier now that Wanda didn't have a job. I knew this wouldn't go down at all. Once my parents found out she was fired from a business that wasn't hers, on which she had squandered all their (stolen) loan money, they would conk me on the head with this solid new Louisville Slugger evidence that Wanda was mad, bad, etc., and drag me off to Millstone. I didn't have the nerve to bring it up yet, but it might be possible that even Wanda—whipped as she was—wouldn't support my brilliant self-serving plan to live in her cabin as a permanent guest.

And there was no way I could bring it up anytime soon. You see, after she got canned, Wanda got all caught up in this sticky gloom. She would sit up in bed all day, reading magazines, smoking cigarettes, watching her fuzzy old TV, not budging from the cabin. She even told Deke when he came knocking that she didn't want to see him.

"Hasn't *ever* been this bad," he said, shaking his head. "She usually bounces back after a couple days."

In spite of being turned away, he came around anyway, always bringing something—a pound of coffee, a bag of apples, a couple of rolls of toilet paper, all industrial-grade, generic army-surplus stuff in plain brown wrappers.

Likewise there were knocks on the door at all times of the day and night, and when I staggered to open it in my socks and underwear, I'd usually find something really weird—like a dozen eggs superglued on top of one another and leaning against the cabin, or a gallon of milk in a beach ball or a pig piñata full of flour. One morning after some strange scratchings I opened the door to see O. K. Sunbeam walking away, waving her hand. Hanging on the doorknocker was a ropy wreath of Cheerios.

There was also all the stuff from the communal garden they grew out along the river, whose rich earth even this early in the summer was beginning to pump out green beans, peas, summer squash, sweet onions, radishes, and carrots.

I managed to slip in a thing or two myself. Like when I saw Wanda was low on shampoo, I bought some and filled up her bottle—burying my empty in the trash. I would casually bring home milk and bread and other basics from the old supermarket downtown. It felt good being able to pay back some small piece of all that Wanda had done for me over the years.

Also the outdoor dinners were more regular, and even though they couldn't get Wanda to come out, there always seemed to be extras—salads and casseroles and pies—that made it to her refrigerator. One evening Garcia, the old, lame golden retriever, showed up on the doorstep, a fat envelope full of small bills in his mouth—exactly enough to take care of Wanda's next mortgage payment. Wanda tried to chase him away, but he wouldn't budge until she took it. She told me to give it back, but what could I do? I knew nobody would take it. So I stuffed it in the tin valentine box full of newspaper recipes that Wanda kept in the kitchen.

With Wanda zonked and time on my hands, I wound up spending a lot of it on my feet—walking. In the few days since we had opened the old house by the gravel road, I hadn't run into Diana. It was just as well. I needed time to think.

For me opening houses was ordinary. I'd done it hundreds of Sundays since I was a kid with my mom. While she showed off the wonders of plaster ceilings and country kitchens, I'd find whole rooms full of other kids' stuff. People were forever being startled when they found me off in a basement rec room playing with a truck I'd borrowed from some kid's toy box.

Later when I was older, I'd get into houses on my own, like I did at Wanda's old place, to rest or get a drink of water or use the bathroom midway through some long walk.

But ordinary as it was for me, Diana had been all excited.

"Wow!" she kept on saying as she walked through the rooms. "This is *great!*"

Although the place was stripped of knickknacks and electric mixers and other junk, a lot of the main furniture was still in it. This wasn't so strange, since when people moved they got new stuff, or went into a smaller space, or their old stuff just didn't fit. Even if they did take it with them, the agent might have them rent furniture so the place would look lived-in.

"How did you know there was no one here?" Diana said.

"It's kind of a sixth sense," I said. I had told her how my mom was in real estate and how you could tell if the grass wasn't cut and there were old newspapers in the driveway and no lights at night and the drapes and blinds were all always closed and things.

"But once I see it's got one of those key boxes, I know for sure," I said "You know, it's like a little safe hanging on the door-knob, and it has the keys locked inside?"

"How did you know how to open it?"

I got the one off the front door and showed her. The thing had a combination lock on it with letters instead of numbers, and I twirled it back and forth and popped it.

"One agency will pretty much use the same combinations for all their houses in town."

I explained how the combination almost always spelled something *real* imaginative like D-O-O-R (as in "front") or R-E-A-L (as in "estate") or H-U-N-T (as in "for houses.") The one my mother's agency used—if you can believe it—was K-E-Y-S (as in "stupid.")

"I thought over the years they would have thought up less dumb ones," I said, twirling the dial, "but you know what this one was?"

"Not a clue," she said.

"Watch." I turned the dial to the letters H-O-M-E, and it popped.

"Cute," she said.

"That's another one."

She rolled her eyes. "But what if somebody comes while we're here?"

"Unlikely with this place," I said. "Also you hold onto the keys, which gives you time to get out while they're figuring how to get in. Just got to remember to put them back before you leave."

Diana started poking through the kitchen cabinets. She found a bottle opener in one of the drawers.

"Now if we only had a bottle of something," she said.

She went on to do the whole tour, looking in closets, the drawers of night tables, even under the beds.

"This is just *great!*" she kept saying. The tired, worn look she'd had that morning had been permanently changed to the grin she'd given me when she first drove her car into the garage. She looked gorgeous in her sandals and cutoffs, although that day she wore a sweatshirt instead of her usual narrow tube top.

I suddenly realized it was a lot different having her in a house with me than my mother, or just being alone after a long walk.

The possibilities of the situation suddenly washed over me in a wave. I remembered Diana's hand, hot on the side of my face.

After a while we sat on a sofa in the basement family room. My mom would have pointed out the wet bar with a refrigerator underneath and the full downstairs bathroom and even the stove burners built into one of the counters. I had been wondering why there was a bolt *inside* the door at the top of the stairs, but when I saw all this, I knew it was set up as what my mom would call a "granny flat" so a grandmother or mother-in-law or an older kid could live down here.

Back in an old coal cellar there was even a separate entrance—a flight of cement stairs running up to a couple of big doors you had to swing back off the ground—but the room was full of rusty tools and window screens and cobwebs, and it looked like no one used it. I made a mental note that it would be a good emergency exit.

Diana absently picked up the remote and pointed it at the scarred console TV and pushed the power button. It came on. "Hey, it works," she said.

I explained how it also wasn't so strange to leave the electricity on in a house and the gas and water, too. You needed lights to show the place at night and gas for the heat so the pipes wouldn't freeze. And as for the water . . . "It's not so good," my mother would explain to sellers, "if someone sits down for a test drive on one of your toilets and when they go to flush nothing happens. They're usually afraid to come back."

Diana sat there next to me, cross-legged, but you could see by the way she was staring at the screen, the sound low, she wasn't paying it any attention.

"It's so peaceful," she said. "With no one in it."

"Yeah, I guess," I said. I put my arm around her over the back of the sofa. She leaned on it.

I told her I was pretty much used to that.

"You don't have any brothers or sisters?" she said.

"No," I said, "but I did."

She gave me a questioning look with those dark, up-close violet eyes.

I took a deep breath and dove into them, pretty much telling her the same sad, gloomy old stuff I'd told Deke about Donnie dying, his ghost and me haunting the empty house—my mother out selling houses to other people, my father off in the city doing whatever he did, and so forth and so on.

"But that's why I left all that," I said. "So why keep dragging it up? I guess I envy you having sisters and all." I tried to change the subject.

"Don't," she said.

She told me how her father, with his troubleshooting job, hauled them all over the country—Seattle, Fort Worth, Pittsburgh, Pasadena—and although they moved with him, he was never home much anyway. Her mother put most of her efforts in these places into meeting other women, who were usually in the same situation she was in. So she was mostly off somewhere playing cards, going to fashion shows or garden club meetings, being charitable anywhere but home. Diana and her sisters were left with sitters or alone when Diana was old enough.

Sometimes her mother and the other women would come to Diana's house and sit talking out by the pool, reminding her of a tree full of birds chattering before they flew off for the winter.

Diana rested her hand—narrow and pale despite how tanned she was—on my thigh like it was the most casual thing in the world.

"My sisters and me, we were always the new kids in school."

"I saw your sisters at your house that time. You never talk much about them," I said pulling her closer so her hair—smelling of chorine and gel—brushed my cheek. "I don't even know their names."

"Caitlin and Katherine? Kit and Kat we call them. What's to say? They're kids. There's about four or five years between us. They're only a couple of years apart." I could feel her voice vibrating through her body as she spoke. "So there's this gap. They always seemed to have each other, but it wasn't so good for me."

"Why was that?" I said, finding it difficult to imagine how guys wouldn't always have hung around her.

"I was stuck in that whole tired braces and pimples and glasses thing. Seemed to go on forever, but funny thing was, I never believed . . . I knew if I could just get through it—"

She moved away slightly, but then pulled my head down on her shoulder, stroking my hair. Why didn't I think of this before? All those wasted hours driving around in her cramped car.

"You know all that stuff about *listening* to what people tell you?" She shifted, getting more comfortable. "Well, my whole life, since I was old enough to know, was about ignoring what I was told."

"Like what?" I said, casually putting my face in her neck and lightly kissing it. It felt like I'd stuck my face in some warm tropical flower.

"Like I was a dumpy little kid who wasn't going to be anything and might as well face up to it."

I could feel her shiver slightly, although it wasn't cold.

"How far from the truth could that be?" I said, working my way up from her neck to behind her ear, her tiny earrings brushing my nose. "Who would tell you that?"

She didn't say anything but drew back slightly and looked at me with those powerful eyes. Then she closed them, and I kissed her on the lips. She was willing and yielding and put her hand behind my head. But after a few seconds she broke off.

"I realize now," she said.

"What?" I said, dreamily.

"What he was doing," she said.

"Who?"

"My father."

I started to kiss her again, thinking maybe if I could get her to stop talking she would get into it, but she broke off after only a few seconds.

"He was trying to cut the legs out from under me so I wouldn't go anywhere, so I would be around the house and convenient."

"Convenient?" I said. "For what?" But as soon as I asked, I knew. It shot through me like when you start the first drop on a roller coaster.

She put her hands over her face like she was going to push her hair back, but then she kept them there. I felt her stiffen under my arm.

"It's hard for me to talk about it," she said.

I waited. Gradually the words began to leak out from behind her hands.

"Nights when I was little," she began, "he came into my bedroom. Everyone was asleep, or my mother was off at one of her things. The room was always so dark. He insisted."

She sniffed and wiped her face with the palms of her hands, drying them on her sweatshirt.

"He never said anything. I couldn't even be sure it *was* him; this dark, shape—tickling me all over, laughing this low, creepy laugh. More a big weight on top of me, holding me down. I couldn't do anything. When I saw the man sitting at the table next morning drinking his coffee, it didn't seem it *could* be him. It was something else that happened, or like a dream. It took me so long to realize—"

I kissed her wet cheeks, but she wouldn't let me kiss her on the mouth, which was all thick with saliva and tears. She took a tissue out of her pocket and blew her nose.

"And I thought *you* were the disgusting one," she said, holding up the soggy tissue. She laughed a little, but that seemed to bring on the tears again. I waited for her to say more, but she just sat there, the crumpled tissue in her hand, blotting her eyes.

The light from the high basement window gradually dimmed, and soon all I could see of her face was from the bursts of light that came off the TV.

Suddenly the floor lamp in the corner snapped on, and both of us jumped.

"Must be on a timer," I said. "But we probably shouldn't stay here too much longer."

She nodded, and after a while we went upstairs. I went out the back door, walked around the side of the house, and scouted out the road to make sure no one was coming. It was easier when it got dark, since you could see headlights long before you could hear anything. But there was nothing to see, and all I could hear were the crickets chirping and an occasional car whooshing by on the paved road before the turnoff.

I knocked on the garage door, and like we had worked it out, it started to roll up, and she backed out into the driveway. Before the door was even entirely up, I ducked into the garage and hit the button to lower it again, jumping out over the cutoff beam and dropping into the low, silver car.

Once we were on the main road again, she seemed to pull herself together.

"Sorry," she said. I glanced down to see her pale hand, gleaming in the dim light from the dashboard, resting on my thigh.

chapter 19

DEKE'S PICKUP wasn't half as bad as the Wandamobile, since it wasn't half as big. Otherwise the rust and ride were about the same. Deke himself was so large, it was more like he *wore* it than drove it, and I think he invited me along sometimes just to balance it off.

The reason he *said* he needed me that morning—after I had only a few hours sleep again, of course—was to give him a hand with what he called his "lifelong project and soul task" of fixing up his old derelict house.

"This is yours?" I said, as we pulled up the driveway through the high black iron fence, which came to rusted points at the top.

"Yep," he said. "Every rotten bit of it."

Wanda had told me, but I never imagined. . . . It looked like a set from a comedy horror movie. It was dingy gray, with arched windows—some of them covered in plywood—and had a tower that rose up over its third story. A wide porch, a few of its supports missing, ran around most of the first floor. As Deke explained, the garage on the side was actually made for a horse and carriage. It used to be open in the back so you could drive through to the carriage house—now a pile of bricks behind the house.

Seems like Deke was the last of a long line of drunks—dried out himself, thanks—who had owned the place. The last two—his father and grandfather—had lived there on and off and attempted different repairs.

And I do mean "attempted" and "different." "Sins of the fathers," Deke called them, since even I could see they were done by people who maybe could tell a handsaw from a cheese grater but were shy about letting on.

The place reminded you of someone who had fallen face first off a moving train and then dropped in for plastic surgery at a local kindergarten. Outside were the plywood windows and falling-down porch; inside, these fake, cafeteria-type ceilings hiding where the real ceiling above had collapsed. Candle wax and duct tape covered the drainpipes under sinks; pipes in the basement took off every crazy way. Painted two-by-fours were sledge-hammered in at angles in the living room to shore up sagging floors above.

Sealed up in an unfinished area of the attic, Deke found an old water heater tank, a couple of unconnected bathtubs, dusty bottles, and boxes of bottle caps—all leftovers from a brewery. And strangest of all, someone who squatted in the house during the years it sat empty had painted murals that took up whole walls of the place: one of strange big-footed characters, their legs stretched out in a long step and "Keep On Truckin'" painted underneath, another of a large caped devil, looming up behind a black mountain.

"Dunno what they mean," Deke said, hands on his hips and shaking his head as he looked at a third one, this of a big, yellow, happy-face sun, "but I couldn't bring myself to paint over 'em."

The place even had a ballroom that took up half the third floor, with a bandstand on one end. Its dusty floorboards hadn't been walked on for so long they made cracking sounds that took off from under our feet in all directions, like ice creaking on a frozen lake. Paint peeled from its walls like loose scabs.

Painting was the least of Deke's worries about the place, however, which didn't even have running water. In fact the very reason he needed me that day—aside from balancing off the pickup—was to help him with some plumbing he was doing, replacing the jungle gym of old steel pipes in the basement with shiny new copper ones.

"So you inherited all this?" I said, wiping the back of a sooty hand across my forehead after hacksawing and pulling down old pipe in the basement for a while.

"Yup. When my dad died, they shipped me a box of his stuff, and here was this deed. He'd never talked about a house. I was sure by then it must have been sold for back taxes and bulldozed for a strip mall. But I drove down to take a look, anyway."

Amazing to tell, it was still standing, and even more amazing, when Deke checked at the county courthouse, the taxes had been paid right up until the month before the old man died.

"Had some idea about coming back, no doubt," said Deke.

"So you moved down here to work on it?" I said, holding a piece of replacement pipe while he blowtorched the joint.

"Living over this way actually cut off some drive time to my job," said Deke, his white teeth shining against his otherwise blackened face.

"Why didn't you move in?" I said.

"The place was a *real* wreck then. Full of broken beer bottles, old mattresses, hamburger wrappers, chicken bones, mice, bees' nests—you name it. Took me a month to get the old junk out, a couple of years to get it even in this shape. And besides, I found the cabin at the Far, and it right away felt like home to me. And there's Wanda." The silver solder melted and flowed into the pipe joint, binding the pieces together.

"You thought about selling it?"

"You know how I don't like to waste stuff? Guess I was afraid somebody would just knock it down for the land. Hand me that coupling, willya?"

I should have figured. Even the longer runs of pipe we were using came from a demolished house. "Once you cut off the elbows and couplings, it's fine," he explained. "Never rusts out, shame to toss it."

"What are you going to do with the place when you're done?" I asked.

"I heard that 'if' in there," he said, grinning through the swipes of soot on his face. "I dunno—sell it. Maybe live here." He glanced at me.

"You'd really think about that—living here alone in this big old place?" I said, worried that he was serious.

"Yeah, well—" He kept the blowtorch flame steady on the fitting he was heating. "Once I move my furniture and stuff in, that would start to fill it up. I could close it off some, like maybe just live downstairs."

"And leave the Far?" I couldn't imagine it without him.

"My place there? It's pretty beat, you know. Next piece."

I handed him up a length of pipe.

"The Far's a good place for a while," he said when I got quiet, "for getting yourself together. You probably don't have long there yourself, you know."

"Did Wanda say something?" This is what I was afraid of.

"No, no," he said. "I just mean in general. Hold it still. Don't worry, I won't burn you." I was holding the pipe with my hands as far away from the torch flame as I could.

"It's like a halfway house," Deke added. "People don't usually stay too long."

"I think I'd like to stay there for a while, anyway," I said.

"What's her name?" said Deke, not even looking at me.

I hesitated for a second. How did he guess?

"Oh, it's nothing like that," I lied. "It's just I'm not ready to go back. Besides, they still want to send me to that school—my parents. I was hoping maybe they would let me go here instead, in the fall."

"Can't say as I blame you," Deke said. "That seem likely?"

"How could I talk them into it?" I asked.

"You're asking me?" But he seemed to think about it for a while. "Maybe the ol' self-reliant approach," he said.

"Meaning?"

"Meaning you tell them you've got a job here and somewhere to stay and you're out of where you were getting in trouble, and—"

"And isn't that what you wanted to accomplish by sending me away in the first place?" I finished.

"Right," said Deke.

"I told my dad some of that already, except about wanting to stay here for good and the school part. They still want to send me away to Millstone, I guess."

"Hold that now, till I get the next fitting." He worked cleaning the end of it up for a few seconds. "You really think that's why they want you to go there? To send you away?" he said.

"Partly," I said.

"What makes you think that?"

"It's just like . . . It seems like I'm in their way or something. They got in the habit of driving places without me." I'd told Deke how riding in cars generally made me sick. "And lots of nights. It always seemed they had something to do. Something dumb. Like dancing lessons or something. It was like they just wanted to get out of the house, and . . . I don't really feel like going into it."

I mean, Deke should know what it was like without me having to explain.

"You joined the army," I said, remembering what he told me of his life.

"Yeah," he said. "But I wasn't running away." He put the fitting on and started to solder it.

"And I'm not either." I felt myself getting pissed. Why did I have to keep explaining myself?

He stopped what he was doing and looked at me. "I know," he said. "I guess I was talking about me."

We were both quiet for a few seconds. "The short piece," he said, and when I handed it to him, he started scrubbing the ends of it with steel wool. He explained how it was important that the surfaces you soldered were super clean, or the stuff wouldn't stick and the joints would leak.

"So what was that like?" I said. "You said you'd tell me."

"What, the army? For me it was like finding a home," he said. "It was the best I was ever treated, if you can believe it. I went from sleeping jammed in some tiny cold apartment with four other guys and raggedy clothes—sticking newspapers in my shoes to cover the holes—to a nice warm barracks and nice shiny boots. Lots of friends. I had a decent job and my name on my pocket. Even basic training . . . I mean, it was like they cared for me and taught me all that stuff so I wouldn't get my ass blown off. It was great. Until Vietnam, anyway."

"You went there?" We'd studied it in history—Mr. Parkman's class—guys slogging through the mud and listening to Jimi Hendrix and taking dope and fighting the Vietcong and coming home in body bags.

"Yeah, yeah, tail end of it."

"You ever have to shoot anybody?"

"I don't know if I *had* to, exactly," he said.

"But you did?" I said.

"Hold that up there, now," he said. He started working on soldering the next piece again while I held it in place with long-handled pliers. It was very short, and I didn't want to risk it. As he worked, he talked, the blue flame from the torch flashing on his sweaty face.

"I had typing in high school, so I got assigned to a communications unit. They had me in a trailer most of the time—sitting there on flat tires—punching out messages with a couple of other guys on old teletype machines. The technology was way beyond that even then, but the idea was that if the bird—the satellite—died, we'd be the fail-safe backup for the base. A little higher," he said, motioning me to slant the end of the pipe up more. "Well, I had about a month to go before I was supposed to get my papers and get rotated back to the States, and the base gets attacked and a whole bunch of guys get shot up."

"Did you get shot at?"

"They didn't get as far as this trailer, but I was like, Hey, these are my guys you shot. It was like they were my brothers; it was like my *family* they had attacked. So I vowed someone would pay. That they wouldn't catch us sleeping again, and every time I'd hear a chicken fart, I'd whip out my pistol."

I laughed, but Deke kept working, not cracking a smile.

"One night I'm on duty, banging out messages. It's maybe two in the morning, and I hear something. I go out, and there *is* something in the bushes on the other side of the perimeter fence and—remember, I'm also a short-timer, and I know my number is up—so I don't call out or anything, I just start shooting. Okay, give me another ninety-degree."

"And?" I said, holding the fitting hostage.

"And it turns out it's some kid. They find him the next day. Some V.C. kid. Dead in the bushes. Let's have it." He held his hand out until I gave the fitting to him.

"A kid?"

"He was about fourteen or so. You couldn't always tell with them, even the adults, they were small. But he was younger than you."

He said nothing for a while, as he worked at cleaning the fitting.

"What happened?"

"Nothing. That was it. Turns out that he was packing some

homemade grenades, though. Probably would've blown me to bits if he saw me first."

He was quiet again, and we both worked for a while in silence. Then he breathed out—"Hmmph"—as if he thought of something funny.

"What?" I said.

"Met this guy once years later," he said, "who was chief honcho for communications in-country at the time. Told him my assignment, and he laughed. Turns out the backup system I was working on? The satellites already *had* a backup system, he said. There were already other birds up there, so if one went down, they would come on line."

"So what were you guys doing, then?"

"With the teletypes? That's what I asked him. Turns out we were kind of a decoy."

"I don't get it," I said.

"The real backup birds they would actually use? They were *spy* satellites. Only they didn't want anybody to know about it— that they had them—so they had us typing away like we were it. Like we were all they had."

He finished the final joint in the run we'd been working on, wiping it clean with a rag.

"It gets better," said Deke. "There we were, morning, noon, and night, hours and months typing out messages, and—this is the kicker; guy I met swore this was true—the teletypes weren't even *connected* to anything." He shook his head as he polished the pipe overhead, holding both ends of the rag like he was shining a shoe.

"Come on, let's go eat," he said, snapping the rag.

chapter 20

Diana and I had a routine by now.

Before we broke for the day, we'd set some time and place to meet. Most times it would be at some new house we'd opened. I explained that going back to the same one was against the code—we'd get lazy, and we'd get caught.

Once we opened one right in town, but I was so nervous I jumped for the back door every time a car slowed, and we wound up staying less than an hour. So we specialized in houses that were farther and farther out. I'd check the newspaper ads and have a place in mind when we met. Diana liked surprises, and I wouldn't tell her where we were going, but just to take a left here and a right there.

She didn't always like what I came up with, though, so I told her a secret my mom told me: You *never* get the house you want. The ideal home with the white picket fence and the nice old neighbor who baked you pies is a myth made up by real estate companies to keep people unhappy with what they have so they'll keep selling and buying. The secret of being happy, she always said, is to find something you know is good and hold onto it—in spite of whatever grass happens to look greener.

When all else failed or we didn't have time to check out a new house, we went back to our old standby: the first place out in the country we had opened together. It was set up perfectly for getting in and out of with nobody seeing us and had been sitting empty so long I think even the agent forgot about it. After a while I had spare keys made so we could get in quicker.

Diana had been gradually warming up to me after she'd pulled away the first time, but even though there were plenty of beds and couches and comfortable carpeted floors in the houses we got into, we never got too far—something that really wasn't my idea, you understand.

I mean, let's face it, Diana was capable of running her own life and deciding what she did or didn't want from it and from me. And the funny thing is, she *did* seem to want something from me. I know I wanted her. She was the most beautiful thing I'd ever seen up this close, and we connected on a level I'd never experienced before. My head spun every time I thought of closing the door behind us in some house we'd opened. Just the two of us alone in all those rooms.

It was so different just being with her. It made me feel like with other girls I'd been with, I'd only been practicing. And honestly? Most of the time, after that first rush was over, there wasn't a lot there.

Before I met Diana, I even wondered why I didn't get that feeling you always see people get in the movies, where it's like they're *insane* for someone. Oh, yes, I had some fun, and I learned a lot, and there were times . . . but mostly it was going through the motions.

Take Samantha, for example. . . . Toward the end there, she went out with this other guy I knew and told me she'd done it just to see my reaction. I guess she didn't like it when I didn't have much of one.

"You don't get it, do you?" she said. "How do you think it made me feel when you didn't say anything or do anything? You were supposed to be jealous. You're a good-looking guy, but that just isn't enough."

The secret was that by that point I had stopped caring so much about her. Like I said, in those days I was doing a lot of practicing. It was pretty obvious that she was, too.

That's why I think it's unfair that guys get run down for stuff like this. How else are you supposed to know if you *like* a girl unless you know what she's really like, and how are you supposed to find out what she's really like unless you really get close to her? And how are you supposed to really get close to her if you don't try stuff? And what are you supposed to do *then* if, let's say, you find out she wheezes out her nose while you're kissing, or she thinks that tasting stuff off her plate is disgusting, or she hates your parents (even if you don't like them so much), or you just plain don't like her? You don't find out stuff like this at some polite distance.

I mean people get down on guys for playing with girls, for using them when they're not really interested, but I think both guys and girls are only trying to understand what other *people* are like—especially people they may spend their whole lives with. And sex is part of it.

Fool around when you're sixteen, and they call you irresponsible. Get to twenty-six without fooling around, and they call you strange. Where's the sense in it? *Something's* got to happen. And I know for sure it never will if you don't try out some moves some time with someone—someone you may discover is not the love of your life, or even your week.

Figuring it all out had to be even harder and more confusing for Diana. Maybe what she was going through was like after the time I went on this trip with my parents.

It was after Donnie died and was one of Dad's efforts, I suppose, to make us all jolly and happy. We went to some place by a lake and stayed in this cabin. Boring as hell: no phone, no TV, and the nearest pizza twenty miles away across a couple of bridges. And, I don't know what it was, I ate something rotten or got bit by a poisonous spider or a tsetse fly, but I got sick. I sweated so bad I took a towel to bed and soaked it through. The room was spinning.

Of course we had to stop and buy T-shirts before we left. They didn't have one that said, "I puked my brains out and all I got was this lousy T-shirt," so I settled for one with just the name of the place. But here's my point: For years, every time I took that shirt out of the drawer, I couldn't put it on. I'd get sick looking at it. I finally gave it to the Salvation Army.

For Diana, sex was a trip that brought up bad memories. Things that had happened to her in the past brought her up cold or worse. Every time we'd get comfortable and friendly, we'd get just so far, and then she'd want to stop; have to stop.

I was trying to be patient, but finally, one day I couldn't take it any more. We were in our old house, it was getting dark, we'd been down on the sofa in the basement, and things were starting to get interesting. I ran my hand under her top and then low down her back under the waistband of her shorts, and she jumped.

"What is it?" I panicked, thinking she'd heard a car in the driveway.

But she was teary again.

"It's all a mess," she said.

"What did I do?"

"It's not you," she said. She'd seemed more and more moody the last couple of times we were together.

"What is it then, dammit?"

"It's my father," she said.

Over all the times we'd met, Diana hadn't told me much more of the sad, sick story of what had happened. What more was there to tell? But she did say that as she got older, she started feeling there wasn't something right about it—about what he was doing to her and making her do to him—and she started to resist—tried to tell her mother. But her mother wouldn't hear about it. You know how parents can be when they don't want to know. And finally she would scream and cry when he was at it, and finally, as she got older, he seemed to lose interest anyway and stopped.

Listening to all this made me mad and made me feel guilty somehow because . . . because I really don't know why: Because I hadn't been there to protect her? Because her father was a guy and so was I? Because people can do such bad things? I don't know.

"I thought you told me he'd quit—" I started to say.

"I think he's planning a move on my sisters."

I felt sick now on top of the anger and guilt.

"Can't you get your mother to do *anything*?" I said.

"She's like, Don't ask, don't tell," Diana said. "She gives me this funny look when I try to talk to her about it, and besides—"

"Or the cops?" I said.

"I can't."

"Why not?"

"I just can't," she repeated.

"You know, I saw it on the news, cops these days get special training, and they have women cops who—"

"There's something else," she said.

Talking in the dimming room like she was talking to herself, tears leaking down her cheeks, she told me the rest of the story: When she started going out with guys, she realized something wasn't right. All that unwanted experience with her father left her confused about how to act with guys her own age. She just had no sense for what normal people wanted or did, where the lines were, or even *what* they were.

It's like this guy in our class who visited Paris? He goes in the men's room in this expensive restaurant to pee, and there's this big fancy thing spouting water in the middle, so he unzips and has at it. Like, this is *France*—of course they have urinals with fish spitting water. He's right in midstream when this woman—the attendant—

comes out screaming French stuff at him while he's standing there holding himself and throws him out before he can even zip up—everybody in the place laughing at him. Finally someone tells him it was a *fountain* he was peeing in—the urinals were inside the next door. Who would know?

For Diana sex was a foreign country where she didn't know the rules. So when she started dating, she went from guy to guy to guy. At first she thought it was just the way her father had run her down that had wrecked her confidence so she couldn't stay with any one guy for very long. Then she overheard some girls in the bathroom at school laughing about how everyone thought she was a tramp.

This was right when all the stuff about date rape started coming out, and she saw this show on TV, and it hit her all at once. She was suddenly mad as hell: at her father, at the guys who'd passed her around, at the world in general. The father and the world she couldn't do anything about, but the guys . . . All crying and hysterical, she barged into the guidance counselor's office and told him she was date-raped. He had to follow up on it—the school had policies and all. And next these guys are being dragged in for questioning and it's in the paper—no names, but everybody knows who it is.

But when it came down to it and the cops talked with her about how she would have to testify, she couldn't go through with it, and she withdrew all the charges. She transferred schools, and it took some tricky footwork by her dad's lawyers to keep *her* from being charged, but that was the end of it. Meantime her dad got scared by all this, that she would even go to the cops, and bought her the car, the unspoken meaning of which was that he was trying to make it up to her and shut her up.

"So you see how screwed this all is," she said. "I can't go to the cops; my mother didn't want to hear about it to begin with, so she *really* doesn't want to hear about it now; my father knows it and thinks he's bought me off; and my friends—I mean, it's a different school, but word gets around and guys are nervous around me—and it's all a mess."

I had to agree, and I had to learn to be content with just holding and kissing her in the dark. Funny, even though I'd never met her father and never wanted to, it was like he was always somehow *there,* sitting between us on the sofa.

Things had gone on like this for a couple of weeks since the first open house—driving around, opening other houses, making out in the limited way we did—until this one time when she was supposed to pick me up at this abandoned gas station right outside town, and it got way past the hour. There were times when she couldn't get away, and I thought maybe this was one of them and started walking back to town. I hadn't gotten a half mile when I saw her coming the other way, then driving across to my side of the road and pulling up next to me.

"Let's go," she said, nervously checking the rearview mirror. "Come on. Get in."

"Okay, okay," I said, and when I opened the door, I saw she had her sisters crammed in the tiny back seat.

"Hi," I said.

They melted to a pool of giggles.

"Are you Di's boyfriend?" said Kit, the younger of the two, when we got going.

"Don't pay any attention to them," said Diana.

Diana drove straight to the old house, saying nothing the whole time.

"Let us in, Nick," she said as we pulled in the driveway.

"Diana," I said, "do you really think—"

"Nick," she said, looking at me.

I quickly got into the place and opened the garage and she drove in, the girls chattering and looking all around.

"Di brought you over one day by the pool," said Kat. "Whose house is this, anyway?"

"Quiet now," said Diana. "You can't be making a lot of noise. Right down the basement."

Diana lingered at the top of the stairs for a moment. "He's coming home early from work," she told me, her voice pitched low. "I know he's up to no good, but I hate even being around him, so I can't stay, but if I'm not going to be there, I don't want them to be there alone with him."

And soon we were all down in the family room: the girls watching a movie that Diana brought, Diana and I on the couch behind them, my arm around her shoulder, slightly frustrated, but feeling good just to be there. But it wasn't long before the movie ended and the girls started fighting about whose turn it was to take it out of the player.

"Got to go," I said.

"Already?" she said sleepily.

"I don't want Wanda to be worried about me on top of everything else." I had explained to Diana about my aunt losing her job and all. "And I've got to stay on her good side," I added.

"You really like that place, don't you?" said Diana, meaning the Far.

"It's home," I said, "for now, anyway. People there have been good."

"Must be nice," she said.

"It is," I said, and she walked me to the top of the stairs, where I leaned her against the kitchen wall and gave her a long, lingering kiss and body-length hug. She didn't pull away this time.

Next morning I awoke to the screech of tires and a crashing, crunching sound and someone shouting, "Wake up, Hip-pies!" and when I pulled myself together and went out on the Green, the mists still rising in the morning sun, I saw Rode Kool and

Jolly Roger and a group of the others gathered around the wishing well.

When I got close, I could see one of the uprights was broken like a matchstick.

"What happened?" I said.

"Don't know," said Rode. "Heard a noise, and when we went out, the well was all busted up like this. Looks like someone hooked a chain around it and tried to drag it off." He pointed to a couple of fresh ruts in the grass.

"'Course they couldn't get anywhere with it, but they sure messed it up good," said Jolly Roger.

"Let me help," I said as we pushed it so the two broken parts of the four-by-four fit back together and it stood up straight. Rode nailed a couple of plywood splints on the piece to keep it together.

"Deke won't like this none when he gets back," said Red Branstool. Lately Deke had been working mornings at his big old house. It was like all of a sudden he was in a big rush to get it done.

For some reason, right at that second, I remembered Diana's mysterious smile when I told her about how Deke and I had sunk the well in cement so it couldn't be stolen.

"So that's the end of that, I guess," she'd said.

chapter 21

"DEAR NICKY, HOW ARE YOU?"

I knew the letter was from my mom before I even opened it.
If I hadn't recognized her handwriting from the address, the envelope from the real estate company would have been a dead giveaway. I found it propped against the sugar bowl one afternoon
when I woke up.

> *I hope you're doing well. Dad says he talked with you. I told him
> Wanda promised you would call. He said it had been a week, and
> . . . Well, I just wish he'd waited until I came home. I was out
> showing a house, and the people were late. He's just too impatient
> sometimes. In fact, I'm at an open house right now; only one
> snooper so far. I would have written you before, but we've been so
> busy. Things are finally slowing down, anyway. But he said
> everything was okay with you and Wanda?*
>
> *We miss you. I think you've disrupted your poor father's
> routine.* [The horror! The horror!] *I've seen him look up from
> the paper when we're at breakfast as if he's waiting for the upstairs
> bathroom where he likes the shower better, and I even forget and
> put out three settings sometimes.*
>
> *That girl you went with for a while, Samantha? She called
> once, but I didn't know what to tell her except you were gone and
> I didn't know when you'd be back.*
>
> *Nicky, I know you think I don't, but I do completely
> understand why the way Wanda lives seems attractive to you. I
> know she seems so wild and free as a bird—she always was
> rebellious—and that must be more fun than your dull old mom*

and dad. But what I have found out as I get older is that the things that all seem so solid and all are . . . Well, they're not just there; you have to keep working at them.

What I'm trying to say is that we never talked about it with you but when Donnie was gone your father and I had problems. On top of everything else he heard of an opportunity for another job farther upstate that he thought might work out better. We didn't want to sell the house or anything right away until we saw how it did work out, so I stayed here with you and he commuted back on weekends. Well, it was just plain disastrous, so he quit and he couldn't even get his old job back but he wanted so bad to come home and be with us, to be there for you, especially with you just starting school and all. He isn't so good at showing it, but he really does care.

But I guess I should be happy with you for wanting to get out of a rut and do something different.

Everything else is fine here. We're having the porch painted, and the man redoing the downstairs bathroom is supposed to start tomorrow. I have learned with selling houses that people do a lot of things to a house just to sell it, but we want to enjoy it while we're here. So when you come back I wanted to warn you everything's a mess. Maybe it's good you're not here, anyway, I mean with all the noise and dirt and everything.

Sorry, but I have to stop, I see someone pulling in the driveway, so I guess I'll go put on my happy-happy house selling face and tell them what a great place this is (if you don't mind a little water in the basement). Say hello to Wanda for me.

Love, Mom.

Mom and Dad having problems? I wondered what kind? Disagreeing over place-mat designs? And Dad actually changed jobs? *That* was extreme. I had thought the story was that he was transferred. As for the coming-back part, though, I was sure he just got bored not having my mom around so he could gripe about his eggs being too runny. I guess I was glad they Did It All for Me, but, you know, I could've used just a little more enthusiasm.

I guess that's harsh. I know they aren't bad people. After growing up with them, stuff I'd see on TV that people in families did to each other—even what happened to Diana—always seemed so *fake,* the arguing and anguish and fights and the teary scenes where everyone makes up and gets all warm and woolly with each other. I mean, I know TV isn't exactly reality, but nothing like that ever happened at our house. Of course, I didn't have a brother—after five, anyway—or a sister to compete with. And my parents were like, "We don't want to tell you what to do with your life or interfere as long as you stay out of trouble," which was fine with me. And I *did* learn to be self-reliant—they always seemed to be so occupied and all—which was also fine with me. In fact, what made me angry was that I kept my part of the bargain. I stayed out of trouble. It just came and bit me on the ass. I mean, was it my fault school was so screwed up—would any *adult* put up with that?—or that the chimney on Wanda's old house didn't work? But they never seemed to realize that. To them it was all the same thing.

I guessed I probably should write back or call or something now, since they'd gone and made the first moves. Maybe I'd go down to the library and send them an e-mail.

I DIDN'T HAVE TO WORK that night and was just lying around the cabin when late that afternoon I heard a racket on the Green. When I looked out, I saw that the tables were being dragged together. I ran outside to help Deke with his, and he told me everyone was getting ready for a special annual celebration that Loosie Starshine had brought with her from Ireland, which she spelled

"Lughnasa," pronounced "Loon-assa," and which everybody else called "Lunacy." Deke showed me the invitation in Loosie's rock-poster-style melted lettering.

When I cornered her, she told me that in the old country it was a celebration of the first grain harvest at the time of year when everyone was kind of loony from (a) being hungry and (b) eating bread made from last year's old grain, which was often covered with a kind of mold that got them high. (Don't try this at home, kids.)

What this had to do with everyone getting all dressed in drapes and sheets, pink plastic wrap, and old pieces of furnace ductwork, crowns of leaves on their heads, me wearing a secondhand bathrobe with fake six-shooters for pockets on the sides that Wanda bought me so I'd be decent in the mornings—what all this had to do with this celebration, I don't know.

Someone dragged out one of those cornucopia things made out of a rusted tin chimney, and a bunch of lumber, old chairs, pallets, and logs were piled between Wanda's cabin and the wishing well for a bonfire. (Wanda was still sulking; maybe they could lure her out yet.) Rode Kool patched and wired up the old stereo and got it cranking again.

Thankfully the mambo record got broken in the last air attack, but Jolly Roger seemed to have a whole trunkful of others like it, and as soon as it started to get dark, he put on an album of love songs that drooped like an old pair of undershorts, sung by a once-popular and still-not-dead-yet singer. Everyone booed until Roger cranked the speed up so the guy sounded like a chipmunk on espresso, and the party was on its way.

People did all kinds of strange made-up dances to this for a while, and then Roger switched to gypsy accordion music and people really got flying.

Meantime they were digging into the pile of fruit that spilled from the tin cornucopia—Roger running around with an apple in his mouth—the grills were going, long skewers with chunks of corn on the cob, tomatoes, onions, potatoes, and the occasional mango sputtering away.

As it got darker—a little earlier these days—the bonfire was set, and soon everyone had joined hands and was swooping around it in big circles, a few jumping through it, Loosie beating out the flames on the edges of the smoldering bedsheet she wore.

Wanda wasn't anywhere to be seen, though. I told her through her bedroom door what was going on, but she either was sleeping and didn't hear me—hard to believe with all the noise—or deliberately ignored me. Every once in a while, a knot of people would gather around her front door and chant: "We want Wanda! We want Wanda!" but it seemed to do no good, so they soon would go back to dancing.

It got darker and darker, and one time as I whooshed around the big circle, I saw a woman standing just outside the light wearing a familiar plastic tablecloth with a sash of morning glory vines and a man's fedora hat with flowers stuck in it, and it hit me with a shock that it was Wanda!

The circle opened and pulled her in, and soon she was whipping around with all the rest of us, not her usual whooping self, but serious; smiling only from time to time, like when a bunch grabbed one of the big old chairs and carried it around, Deke on top, wearing a crown carved from a watermelon rind, pulling tissues from a box and throwing them in his path. They set the chair down next to Wanda and, through persuading and pushing, got her to sit in another and stuck a similar watermelon crown on her head, right on top of the hat she already wore.

They paraded both of them around the place—some big music that sounded like it wore a helmet with horns on it scratching away in the background, everybody cheering, someone throwing marshmallows at them, Deke expertly catching each in his mouth. Soon Wanda, who had looked troubled balancing on the shaky chair, was laughing and wiping stray watermelon pits off her forehead.

They carried the chairs around the great heart-shaped path that went past the front door of each cabin and finally set them down in front of the wishing well, backlit by the bonfire. Roger gave each of them a pad of paper and a silver wooden pencil; Wanda and Deke wrote something, and each gave a page to Roger. Without reading them, he folded them in quarters, solemnly dropped them in the gilded coffee-can bucket in the well, and tossed in a flaming stick from the bonfire.

A flame—baby to the big fire behind it—burned, and a snake of smoke drifted out of the can, and everyone cheered and picked up the chairs again, but just at that moment, something big crashed into one of the tables.

"Oh, no!" shouted Loosie. Deke and Wanda were dumped, and everyone scrambled for cover wherever they could.

It looked like the bad boys were going for blood this time. Instead of friendly water balloons, reeking wet bed pillows, or rotten fruit, hard stuff was falling from the sky: rocks, bottles, car parts.

One of the missiles clanged into the sign over the entrance, and another—we later found out it was an old motorcycle battery—landed smash into the bonfire, causing an atomic mushroom cloud of tiny flaming pieces of wood to plume up to the height of the top of the cabins and land in a wide circle, starting dozens of other little fires on the surrounding tabletops, piles of junk, and dead grass and weeds.

Everyone now ducked out of their make-do bomb shelters and started stomping on the flames and throwing pails of ice water. I ripped off my robe and ran around in my boxers flapping at the flaming dead weeds around Wanda's cabin—guess I wouldn't have to cut them now—the big music from the record still leaping in the background through all of this.

Meantime other stuff was flying in, amazingly enough not hitting anyone, although Mysterious Willie's pants got drenched when a brick hit a pitcher of beer at the table where he was sitting like nothing was going on. Clat reappeared from his cabin wearing a football helmet and pads to wheel off the barbecue grills.

Deke had taken off almost immediately for his truck, determined this time to catch the Stoners in the act.

In the midst of it all, I remember seeing Jane Juan, who had somehow got hold of her old paintball gun, leaping through the firelight, furiously plugging away.

And then it all stopped. When all of the screams and crashes died down, I could hear the faint sound of an engine—Deke's truck, its high-pitched whine getting fainter and fainter as it got farther and farther away—and then only the highly amped *scratch-click, scratch-click, scratch-click* of the stereo needle in the blank groove at the end of the record.

Everyone gradually drifted out of hiding to stamp out the few remaining flames and pick up the wreckage and throw it in a wheelbarrow that Rode was pushing around. A few slumped at the tables, shaking their heads and mumbling. Rode wanted to get a vigilante party up to go trash a few homes in Stone Coach Woods, but people were not coherent enough or just plain not interested enough. "And whose houses would you hit anyway? And with what? Eggs?" Loosie snuffed. "Darryl wouldn't like that."

So everyone drifted back to their cabins. Wanda, her crowned hat on crooked, kissed me on the forehead and said, "Don't wait up. Deke's going to be pretty upset when he comes back," and instead of coming home, went to his cabin.

But I was too cranked to sleep, so I walked. Quickly dumping my bathrobe in the house and pulling on a pair of shorts and a shirt, I went out into the night, which was warm and full of stars once I got away from the lights.

I walked well off the road, since I didn't want some yahoo running me down and since I'd happened to put on dark clothes without thinking and also because of the flowers Loosie had drawn on my face in marker. There was no moon, and every once in a while, I tripped over a clump of grass or a guy wire to a telephone pole, but the air was so sweet and it felt so good getting away from the Far and its troubles that I just kept going.

I walked for a while alone on the road and then, all of a sudden I heard, way back in the distance, a car or truck. As it got louder and louder, along with the usual hum of its engine I could hear another higher squealing sound, like the loose belt I'd heard weeks ago when the locals had tried to steal the wishing well.

I ducked into the woods. Almost immediately, a pickup truck sped by—one with a lightning bolt on the side. In the light from its dashboard, I caught a glimpse of a passenger in the front. It was a girl, trailing her hand out the window and laughing. Her eyes glinted violet. I doubted she saw me.

As the truck faded into the distance, someone sitting in the back flipped a lit cigarette over the tailgate, and it sparked along the black asphalt. Then I was left with the crickets chirping and other small rustling sounds around me in the woods. I stepped back out.

After that, I didn't feel like walking anymore, and I set off back toward the Far. As I got closer, I could see a glow in the sky above the place. I thought maybe some hardy partyers got the bonfire going again. Might be nice to sit quietly around and cook some marshmallows. But as I got closer, I could hear people shouting and then a siren off in the distance.

When I walked under the entry sign, I could see that something was seriously wrong. A thick cloud of smoke was pouring from the far side of the Green, flames lighting it from underneath. I could see black cutouts of people running back and forth in front of this lurid light, one holding the skinny line of a garden hose, a pitiful stream of black water dribbling out of it, that he was flinging on the flames coming from—*It was Wanda's cabin!*

Fast forward: I break into a run, a leaden blob in my stomach, frantically searching the blackened weeds for something I can use to put out the flames, but there's nothing, and I begin pulling up clods of scorched grass and pounding them on the flaming wood, Deke and Wanda and Loosie and Roger all throwing pails of ice water and beating on the flames with old shirts, rubber dishpans, wet feathered boas, anything they can find, as Rode whips the fire with the water from the garden hose that he's pulled from the cabin window, the siren getting louder and louder but never any closer until finally in an explosion of howls and flashing lights a fire truck blasts through the entryway of the Far, barrels across the grass, dodges the picnic tables and other junk and—MYSTERIOUS WILLIE JUMPS IN FRONT OF IT, WAVING HIS HANDS BECAUSE HIS HAT IS ON FIRE!—and it swerves to miss him, knocking the wishing well to splinters as booted, helmeted firefighters of all shapes and sizes from the local volunteer foundation soakers leap out and blitz Willie with extinguishers, then bash through the cabin door with axes while the hose is run out to the street and hooked to a hydrant, finally loosing a big calming arc of water on the flames, filling the air with clouds of hissing steam and the burned newspaper smell of wet, charred wood.

"What happened?" I said to Rode as the sheriff's cruiser pulled up behind the fire truck, a glaring Sheriff Darryl behind the wheel. "Who did this?"

"It just started," Rode said. "We didn't see anyone out here. Probably from when the bonfire got hit."

"I thought it was all out," I said.

"We did, too," said Rode. He said that Tiny, one of the firemen, thought it started in the weeds in front of the house. "A live coal or something. Guess we didn't stomp it out good enough," said Rode.

I looked around. Everyone was smeared with dirt and ashes, wearing grubby, torn robes and blankets, crooked crowns, turbans, and helmets. Willie, covered in white extinguisher foam, wandered like a ghost, the remains of his burned hat jammed back on his head. Lit by the final dim flames of the fire, the scene was like one of those pictures you see in a history book of people in the Middle Ages who have survived the plague.

"Good thing she wasn't inside." Rode nodded toward where Deke was hugging Wanda, who had her head down on his shoulder and her back turned to the whole mess.

Rode finally set down his dribbling hose and began picking around in the busted remains of the wishing well. Soon he seemed to find what he was looking for. He held it up in the flashing bubble lights of the fire truck and the sheriff's cruiser. I could see it was the golden bucket—smashed flat where the truck had run over it.

"Looks like a bad night for wishes," he said to no one in particular.

chapter 22

foot notes

I told you how people are always trying to pick me up
when I'm out walking? Sometimes it's people I know, or
like back where I grew up, friends of my parents. ("Aren't
you *Sid's* boy? What're you doin' way the hell out here? You
want a ride? Come on, get in.")

I always turn them down. I'm sure they don't always get
it, especially if I'm standing there in a downpour like an
idiot, water sheeting off my poncho. But how can I begin to
explain the obvious?

Walking is *walking*! If I wanted to get rides, then I'd be
hitching, and that's something I'm not the least bit
interested in.

Oh, yeah, I tried it. I read my Kerouac: wild rides with
colorful strangers who pour out their innermost unique
short-story hearts; rich older women in limos cruising for
young studs. Despite the carsickness, I had to see what it
was all about. Do hangovers keep people from drinking?

Now I see why even Kerouac wound up taking the bus.

First of all, if you're hitching, people think you're
weird—like walking but more so—and the average person
won't stop. Sometimes you still get these old, bearded
1960s guys driving VW microbuses, but I guarantee they'll
hit you up for gas money every time.

Usually what you get, though, are perverts: mouth-
breathing pasty-faced chubbos who try to give you a beer

from a backseat cooler—stocked with the body parts of other hitchhikers—and then pat their hand on your thigh like they're just being all friendly-like.

Once, before I knew better, I took a ride with this guy, and when he stopped for gas, I thought I'd go take a pee. I guess he saw me looking for the handle, 'cause he quickly ran around and opened the door.

As I stood at the urinal in the grubby gas station restroom, something suddenly clicked.

There *was* no handle.

I was wearing my pack—I always kept it with me—and when I was through, I took the dirt path behind the gas station, walked a few miles into the bush, and camped out. I stayed away from all roads for a day or so.

Or you get religious fruits twisting quotes from the Bible at you like it was theirs alone. Don't get me wrong. I have lots of respect for religious people who do what they believe and keep it to themselves, but it's the ones who sound like an infomercial for a Sinbuster™ that I have trouble with: "But wait! That's not all! Believe today, and we'll include at no extra cost the healing of boils!"

One guy did this whole riff about how he always picked up hitchhikers because his preacher said they were the Lord in disguise. He didn't even crack a smile when I started scratching all over and said, "Thanks. You don't know how itchy this human suit gets after a while."

Same guy told me that where he came from, people handled rattlesnakes to test God's will, but when the Spirit seized *him*, he would drive at cars or trucks in the opposite lane to see if God would pull either of them away in time. He pointed to where his sideview mirror was hanging by a wire and said an eighteen-wheeler clean near sheared it off the other day, but He Was Saved! Hallelujah!

So now if anyone stops and asks if I want a ride— anyone but Diana, of course—without even looking, I give them the *opposite* of the hitching handsign: fist out, thumb pointing down. Most of the time, they pick up on it right away, say an unkind word or two, and peel off.

I can live with that.

chapter 23

AFTER THE FIRE WANDA *REALLY* BOTTOMED OUT.
She didn't want any part of checking out the damage, though I'm sure she couldn't miss seeing all the crud tossed in the stubbly burned grass in front of the cabin: the sofa with all its guts yanked out, a couple of chairs with busted legs, the kitchen table with char marks on it like barbecued chicken, a reeking pile of soaked rugs and torn window screens, busted lamps, shards of mirror and its empty frame, and a whole world of smashed bits of stuff.

Inside, it smelled like burned wood, wire and plastic, wet dogs, and even bleach. There was water all over the place, pooled on top of an end table, bulging out of the ceiling—pouring out and splattering over the already soaked carpeting when Deke poked it with a broom handle.

"Not as bad as it might be," said Deke the next morning after looking around for a while. "Looks like most of it was in the living room here."

In fact, as we stepped over a mound of plaster, more pieces of mirror winking out at us, we could see into the sunny kitchen, where a pot sat on a stove burner and dishes were piled in the sink, the doorway framing it all like a picture hung on the sooty wall.

Likewise, the bedroom and bathroom—although they smelled rank—were untouched, except where water had flowed in and soaked the rugs.

I tried to tell Wanda I was sorry—that it wouldn't have happened if I'd chopped down the dead weeds and grass like she'd long ago asked—but she waved me away. "It's not your fault," she said. "Forget it, I don't even want to talk about it."

Deke tried to sell her on the idea that it wasn't so bad, but she wasn't buying. She sat at the picnic table on the far side of Deke's cabin so she couldn't even see the mess, smoking cigarettes—Deke wouldn't let her smoke inside—mostly staring off to where the pieces of the wishing well were all spread out over the center of the Green like a bomb had gone off inside it.

"Stay with us in my cabin until we get Wanda's place back in shape," Deke told me the night before, and although he didn't stress the "us," it was clear that something unspoken had happened between him and Wanda.

Deke moved some stuff out to the backyard of his cabin and put a tarp over it. In the space he created inside, he put down an old wire bedframe and laid a canvas, down-filled sleeping bag on it for me. Although it smelled like mildew, it was as comfortable as being swallowed up in a warm, cooked marshmallow.

After our tour of Wanda's and making arrangements for me to move in that afternoon, Deke had to go off to work, leaving me to start digging into the mess.

"But what do I *do?* Where do I *start?*" I asked, panicky, as he packed his lunchbox and headed out to his truck.

"When you're facing a complete disaster," he told me as he hefted his toolbox out of the truck for me to use, "what you do is start *somewhere.* You pick one small corner of it. You clean up that little piece—make sense of it—and then go on to the next thing. I know you got the skills; I've seen you in action. Gotta go," he said, and he got in his truck and was gone.

Well, gosh, *thanks*, Deke.

I tried to follow his advice and, starting somewhere, picked the front yard, further breaking up the chairs and table and piling them on the sofa and raking up all the other stuff and dumping it in cardboard boxes.

Then I basically did the same thing inside, closing the door to the bedroom and bathroom and tacking plastic up over the kitchen doorway, knocking down loose plaster, tossing out any burned stuff into the yard, peeling up and dragging out the soggy, stained carpeting. After a while a couple of the others—old Jane Juan, Red Branstool, Clat, and Jolly Roger, hung over though he was—joined me. Loosie and Rode put out some lunch at one of the tables and we ate, and afterward I got so into it, I forgot how late it was until Deke drove up.

"Whew," he said, shaking his head and grinning at the neat piles of stuff in front of Wanda's house. "You guys really tore into it."

After dinner, I helped him load the pickup and tried to get a couple of hours' sleep before work. I must've knocked right off, since before I knew it, my alarm buzzed and I eased myself out of the sleeping bag, splashed some water on my face, brushed my teeth, and took off for the doughnut mine.

Wanda had offered to let me drive her fire-breathing behemoth, but I didn't want to leave her without wheels for the morning. Besides, the quiet middle of the night was usually my favorite time to walk.

But this night, as I set out along the narrow footpath glowing white in the dark grass on the side of the road, I was too troubled to enjoy it. The air had a rotten smell in it—something run over and cooking on the highway all day. The stars, which usually filled me with such awe, reminded me of the splatters of toothpaste on Deke's bathroom mirror.

What was it with Diana? I knew she liked me. What else could I make of our times together in the dark open houses? But why did she hang out with that crew? What did she get out of harassing people—us—in the Far? Shooting all that heavy stuff in on our heads and burning somebody's house wasn't a game. She was smart enough to know this. She must've known these people meant something to me—at least Wanda. And yes, the others, too—Jolly Roger, Jane Juan, Loosie, O. K., the Branstools, Clatoo, and Deke, of course—they had all started to become part of . . . Well, I don't know how to say it. They were there at all the right times, I guess. I thought I'd told her how important they had become to me. Maybe she was jealous.

Or maybe it was the same with girls as what my mom said about houses. You never get the one you want; it's a myth. But I thought I had something—someone—good to hold onto this time. Shows that maybe I was right all along to check out of relationships before they checked out on me.

I dreamed my way through my chores at the Donut Works that night. While she did the bookwork and ordering, Bert had started working me out at the counter in the mornings after I'd finished my cleanup. I was so disconnected that day, though, that I did at least two things that easily could've caused serious bodily harm: I put a too-big lid on someone's to-go coffee and gave someone else bran muffins instead of jelly doughnuts. Luckily both customers came back without injury, and I was able to fix things without Bert knowing.

Walking home later that morning—car exhaust reaming out my sinuses, the sun cutting into my eyes, and cicadas screeching me deaf—seemed like a bad idea compared to walking to work the night before, but I didn't want to call Wanda to come get me, so I began to trudge. I hadn't gotten very far when Diana pulled up.

"Cool tattoo," she said. All smiles. Loosie must've used permanent markers when she drew the flowers on my face at the party the night before, since the roughest scrubbing I could stand still hadn't removed the faded remains.

"Thanks," I said flatly. I couldn't believe she had the nerve to stop.

"Heading home?"

"Yep," I said. I made no move to get in. "Saw you out the other night."

Her smile weakened. "Oh?"

"It was pretty late."

"Past my bedtime?"

"You were with some guys driving around. In a truck."

"And?"

"What were you guys doing?" I had to hear her say it.

"I was out with some friends, if that's a crime." She frowned up at me from the low-slung car.

"Thought you didn't get along with those guys."

"Not all of them. Not *all* the time." She wore sunglasses, so I couldn't see her eyes. "What's this burr you've got up your butt all of a sudden?"

I don't do arguing. At home, if you were pissed at someone, you basically squelched it so's not to disturb the ghost of Donnie past with any strong emotion. And, anyway, if she wouldn't admit to it . . .

"Forget it," I said, and turned and walked away.

"I will," she said, and I heard her peel off behind me.

I plodded along, more glum than ever. Maybe she was a different person than I thought: the shoplifting, the way she didn't seem to care about my friends at the Far, the date-rape thing, and who knows, maybe the whole molesting thing with her father, too. Could she be some psycho—making it all up, jerking me around?

I was about to turn down a path that was a shortcut to the Far when I heard another car stop next to me. I got ready to flip the thumbs-down sign but saw it was Wanda.

"Just went for some coffin nails," she said. I saw a fresh pack on the dashboard. At least it was one of the filtered ones. "Give you a lift?" She was trying to look a little cheerier, but it wasn't working.

"Thanks, Wanda," I told her. "But I need to walk something out."

"Okay," she said, allowing a small smile to cross her lips. "See you in a while then."

"'Bye," I said, and took off down the path. Once away from the noise of the traffic, I was alone again. All I could see were trees and brush and high grass. It would have looked exactly the same to someone walking here a thousand years ago.

chapter 24

GETTING WANDA'S CABIN BACK IN SHAPE went quicker than I expected, especially when I remembered the scene with everyone running around, dark against the flames, like on the TV news where some city is being bombed.

From a distance, Wanda's house looked like someone had shot it with an asteroid-sized black paintball smack on the left front corner. This was where the fire had mostly burned, dark and inky on the corner, fading to brownish soot as it fanned out.

The next Saturday, using a two-by-four and a marker, Deke drew lines down the front and side of the house, right past where the wood had been charred. Then with his electric saw, he cut along each line right through the outside siding boards. When he was done, a bunch of us attacked the burned corner with crowbars and hammers, ripping off all the black wood in a manner of minutes. Rode, shirtless and hairy-legged in a kilt up on the roof, tore off melted shingles and flung them in time to the house-smashing music he blasted from the sound system.

Soon the frame of the house stood bare in the corner where it had burned. The studs underneath were charred but sturdy. In some places, where the plaster had been busted off on the inside, you could see all the way through to the living room.

Wanda came out of Deke's cabin, took one look at the bared, blackened bones of her cabin and the piled-up stuff we had ripped off, and ducked right back in.

"Kind of scary, ain't it," said Roger, "when you see that's all there is to it."

Next Deke, who had driven away when we started the tear-off, reappeared, the back of his truck stacked with new plastic siding.

"It wasn't being used" was all the explanation he gave about where it came from.

In an hour or so, with Red Branstool's help, he had the new stuff in place. Didn't seem to bother anyone that where the old wood siding was painted a peeling red—with multicolored splats, of course—this new plastic stuff was a bright, clean blue. Deke finished off the job by adding a couple of strips to cover the gaps where the two colors of siding met.

"Jane," said Rode, pointing to the blue corner, "get Red to give you back your paintball gun so you can make it match the rest of the house."

"You can't see it from inside anyway," said Red, nervous about the gun being brought up, especially after old Jane had gotten hold of it again the night of the fire. The judge had let her off easy the first time—a fine and some picking up trash on the highway—and Red was anxious that word would get out she'd been at it again.

Over the weekend Deke hauled the burned remains away, load by load, and contributed stuff from his collection to furnish the place, even a front door to replace the one smashed by the fire-fighters.

You know the circus act where this tiny car drives up and fifteen clowns get out? Deke's place was the clown cabin of furniture. He brought out a sofa—which smelled only a little of cat pee—a lamp, a big overstuffed chair covered in plastic, a rug that was perfectly fine when you put the chair right on top of the stain that looked like the outline of Australia, a coffee table, a dining room outfit, and all sorts of umbrella stands, hall tables, book-shelves, and hat racks. Funny thing was that afterward his place looked just as packed as when he started.

Since all that was left was to cover the holes in the walls inside and paint, I expected Wanda would want to have the water and electric turned on and move back in. But she showed no interest in any such thing. It was beginning to look like getting Wanda patched back up wouldn't be anywhere near as easy as patching up the cabin had been.

Like I said, I have this talent for knowing *before* I'm not wanted, and I thought they might like it better if I wasn't camped underfoot in the small space Deke had cleared in his living room. So with Wanda's permission, that night I hauled the old sleeping bag over to her cabin and set it out on the cat-pee sofa.

I used an old kerosene lamp and a camp stove Deke gave me and showered at his place. In spite of all this, and the lingering burned smell, it felt good living at Wanda's again. Like I'd come home.

But lying alone in the dark cabin, deeply dug in the sleeping bag against the cool of the night, my face buried in the soft give of the canvas, I couldn't help but remember how good it felt to have my face buried in Diana's neck as she pressed next to me in the dark rec room of our old open house.

Since I'd snubbed her the night after the fire last week, I kept wishing that I'd run into her at the Donut Works, or at the roadside store where I first saw her, or *anywhere*, but I didn't even see her car. Losing her, I realized, lost me one of the big reasons I wanted to stay here. Maybe I *could* learn to live with Millstone. Watching TV in a closet couldn't be any worse than watching it lying in the tub in the bathroom, that is, if Wanda ever did decide to get the power back on.

At work the next morning I could barely push the broom, tired as I was after the weekend of heavy lifting and too few hours of troubled sleep. I was keeping one ear open, since in addition to sweeping the kitchen, I was supposed to be minding the store. The bell on the front door jingled, and when I went up front, there were these three guys goofing on the names of the doughnuts ("Filled Straights" and "Jelly Balls"—don't blame me; I didn't name them) and punching each other in the shoulders.

I recognized them from Stone Coach Woods—the runt with the goatee and his two droogs, the ones who had harassed me. They kept grab-assing around, shoving each other into the cases, and either didn't recognize me or pretended not to.

"Ain't nobody can get her," the runty guy was saying as he looked in the case, ignoring me. "She thinks like she's the queen of something—the Ice Queen—"

"Jason says he got in her pants," said the guy with the backward hat. "Gimme a couple of those," he said to me, pointing to the chocolate with sprinkles. I bagged them up and put them on the counter.

"Jace?" The runt stopped looking in the case and stared at him. "The Face? He's a lecher in his own mind. Remember that 'model' he went out with? He can't get in his own pants if his mother don't help him with the zipper."

"*Tell* him," said the guy with the hat to the skater guy.

"Face says it's contacts make her eyes like that—that purple color," said the skater guy.

Suddenly I was listening.

"So he's like her optometrist or something?" said the runt. "Who didn't know that?"

Me?

"He said he went over her pool," said the skater. He looked at the guy with the hat and shrugged.

"Was *she* there?"

The two guys looked at each other.

"All I know is, he came on to her the other night," said El Runto, "when we picked her up after we bombed the hippies? He was like high or something, and you know how he's like with that tired 'I'll satisfy your wildest fantasy' crap, and she's like 'You mean you're going to leave?' Laughed right in his face. You got more of those?"

"I got some in back," I said. "How many you want?"

He told me, and as I went through the swinging door to the kitchen, I heard him say, "She's *cold*. If he went over to her pool, I guarantee it was to clean it."

Bert was lost in the numbers on the computer screen and never looked up as I took a couple of doughnuts off the rack, dropped them on the floor, and kicked them around through the pile of dirt I'd been sweeping before putting them in the bag.

"Anything else?" I asked as I handed it over out front.

"Nope." They paid and left, bumping shoulders through the door, slamming it behind them.

When they were gone, it was very quiet.

chapter 25

I'M SURE I was a regular roadside attraction, muttering and whacking myself upside the head as I walked home later that morning after hearing those guys in the doughnut shop.

> SEE! THE WORLD'S BIGGEST DUMBASS!
> ONLY 12 MI. AHEAD!
> CLEAN RESTROOMS!

Whatever made me jump to the conclusion that Diana had a part in the last bombing of the Far? Had I spent all that time watching cop-and-lawyer shows for nothing? Forgotten the thousand scenes where the judge looks over the top of his little half glasses and says, "Appears to me like all you got here is a buncha half-baked cir-cum-stantial evidence. Case dismissed!"?

When I got back to Wanda's cabin, of course I couldn't sleep. I kept looking at her partly melted phone—the only thing in the house still working. I even picked it up a couple of times and started to punch in Diana's number but quickly put it back down. What if I got one of her parents? Worse. What if I got *her?*

I paced in circles in the cabin for—I don't know—must've been an hour, finally ending one of these expeditions around the sofa by heading out the front door.

On the road again.

One foot in front of the other again.

Left!

Left!

Left, right, left!

The rhythm of the road, soles on the sidewalk, hitting the street, taking the air, on my way to who knows where?

Watching the tips of my shoes for a hint.

Making my exit before someone told me I wasn't wanted.

A little late, since at least one person let me in on it already. Me.

But for once it wasn't doing it for me. I felt like I was gliding along on one of those long conveyor belts like you stand on at the airport. Numb. I couldn't find the place in my mind where I could get lost in the comfort of it all.

After an hour or so, I looked up to find myself standing in front of our old open house. It was still empty; still for sale, the word "Reduced" tacked on the sign, meaning they cut the price and still nobody wanted it.

It suddenly reminded me of a painting I'd seen once in a book. It showed a house all by itself along the side of a road behind a couple of trees, no one around, the road stretching empty off into the distance.

My throat was dusty and scratchy, and it hit me how tired I was from working all night and walking all morning. And since all this walking wasn't doing it for me anyway, I thought I'd stop in for a few minutes and get off my feet.

Inside, everything was untouched from the first time we'd gone there; everything in its place. This was one of the other things I liked about open houses—nobody around to screw things up.

I found a glass under the sink—right where I'd left it—and turned on the water to rinse it out. The pipes clanged and banged; a brown snot of rust bubbled out, and it took a minute to clear before I could fill the glass. As I drank, I looked out the window over the sink. Leaves and pieces of newspaper blew through the backyard; flowers in a pot hanging on the garage were all brown and drooped over. The light over the garage door hung by a wire. No wonder they cut the price.

I used the bathroom and got another glass of water from the sink. Then I sat on the sofa in the living room, setting the water on the end table and staring at the closed blinds.

Did it make *any* sense to jump to the conclusion that just because Diana was riding around in a truck, she was responsible for everywhere that particular truck had been and for everything that its driver and other passengers had ever done? I should've known she was not the kind of person who would have a part in something that would cause anyone harm.

Later it clouded up and started raining. The room darkened; I even thought I caught a whiff of chlorine and coconut oil. We'd been here enough; maybe the walls were saturated with Diana, breathing her out. I could almost feel what it was like to have her soft mouth on mine—to be out in that place where her mouth took me, a place farther out than where I'd been on any of my longest lost walks. How if I peeked when we were joined like that, even though *I* was gone, I could always see *her* looking—eyes wide open as she kissed—there in the moment, not wanting to give any of it up.

Daydreaming on this and tired as I was, next I knew, *I'm in my big old familiar maddening dream house again, Diana with me this time, worried about her sisters lost somewhere in one of the rooms. I'm about to say I'm unsure of my way around, but as I begin to tell Diana, it dawns on me: "Wait a minute," I say. "I have a room here right through that door." But then I open it, and it's just another hall. I see Diana is disappointed and move faster and faster, pulling her on and on through halls and doors and rooms, around and around again, finally hearing a strange clatter and chunk*—and I snapped to.

It was the front door! And I was shooting upright from where I was slumped on the couch, grabbing for the half-empty glass of water—they'd see it and know something was up—knocking it over in the half dark, the rug cushioning the noise, keeping it from breaking, but now there was that big wet spot. Too late to do anything about that. I scooped up the glass and started toward the door to the garage, but I could already hear the key in the lock. Dammit! I was *positive* I took the key out of the keybox—how did they get it so fast? And I realized I wouldn't make it, so I changed direction and walked as softly as I could down the hallway to the back bedrooms. This was all I needed: get caught breaking in here and deported in handcuffs and leg irons directly to Millstone, where I'd be thrown in the brine or off the brink or whatever they call it.

From behind the bedroom door, I could hear whoever it was come through the house and to the doorway to the garage, then I heard the garage door open and a car drive in. Getting it in out of the rain.

Maybe they would go down the basement or upstairs to the second floor, and I could make it out the front door. Otherwise what could I do? Hide in a closet? Nope, checking for pole—what my mom calls closet space—was one of the main things people did. Out the window? I could see it was one of those things with screens and slide-down glass on the outside, and I'd make a terrible racket. But what else *could* I do? As I was trying to open the inside window, pushing up on the sash—the thing must've been painted shut—I heard kids giggling.

"Quiet, you two."

Diana and the girls! I finally thought to check my pocket: sure enough, I had two keys—my spare and the one I took from the box to hold for insurance. Diana had used hers; that's how she got in so quick.

I heard them come through the living room and into the kitchen and then go down the basement stairs. A switch clicked.

I came back down the still-dark hall. When I stepped into the light in the kitchen doorway, Diana, one strap of a backpack over her shoulder, looked around and saw me. "I thought you might be here," she said coldly. "Don't let us bother you."

She turned and walked down the stairs.

I followed.

"Hi, Nick," the girls said, like seeing me there was the most normal thing in the world. I nodded to them.

"Diana," I said, following her around the back of the wet bar. She bent over, taking a six-pack of soda and a plastic bag full of grapes out of the pack and putting them in the half-size refrigerator. She closed the door, a couple of sodas in her hand, and turned to face me. I flashed on the first time I ever got close to her in the store.

"I need to talk to you," I said.

"About what?" she said. She wasn't going to make it easy.

I glanced at the girls, who were plugging a video game into the TV.

"Alone," I said.

"We were alone enough the other day." She popped the tops on two of the sodas and gave them to the girls.

"I just wanted to tell you that I'm sorry," I said.

"For what?"

"You're going to make me say it?" I said.

"I'm not a mind reader. You obviously have some problem."

I was silent for a few seconds, trying to collect my thoughts.

"It was when I saw you—in the truck," I said.

"The truck?"

"The night Wanda's cabin burned. Did you know?"

"I heard the sirens, but how could I know? Badly? Anybody hurt?"

"No, nobody; we pretty much fixed it already," I said.

"And what does this have to do with me?"

"Well, I saw you in the truck after we got bombed, and—"

"The truck? By 'the truck,' you mean—"

"It was the one I saw you in—with the lightning bolt—way back when you guys tried to stea—move the wishing well? I was out walking the night before, and I saw you in it with some other people."

"Yes. The truck again. You got me. I cannot deny it. I went for a ride with my friends in a truck last week."

"Well—it was a mistake on my part—I thought you were in on it. The bombing at the Far. We had a party, and they shot stuff in, but this time it was heavier, and there was a fire, partly because I didn't cut the weeds down." I was babbling.

"I'm still not getting it." She turned and reached in the refrigerator for a soda of her own. She didn't offer me one.

"It was heavy stuff. Like what we talked about before with the slingshot but—well, it was like you told me with the wishing well. I thought you were in on it."

"Look, like I told you, whatever I did was a game—for fun." She popped the top and took a drink.

"But they shot bricks and stuff. It was dangerous. Someone could have gotten hurt. Me," I said.

"Yes, it was. And when I saw they had a couple of boxes with all this heavy crap in them, I told them I wasn't interested."

"I'm sorry."

It was the only thing I could think to say.

"You keep saying that," she said. "I want to hear why."

"For thinking that you would."

"Would?"

"Do something like that. I mean I was . . ." I trailed off.

"Afterward they picked me up. Is that a crime? They were like, 'We bombed the hippies,' and I was like, 'So?' I didn't want to hear about it. I can't control what people do." She took a drink of the soda and stared level at me.

"I didn't know."

"How about *asking*?" she said. "You could have asked."

"I know I should have," I said.

"But it's worse than that," she said. "You didn't trust me."

"It's not that," I said, automatically.

"Then what *is* it?"

"I—" But I couldn't put it into words. "Never mind," I said, and I turned and started for the stairs.

"You know," she said in a low voice, waiting until I was halfway up, "that's your problem." I stopped. "If you're mad or put off by someone or something they did, or that you *imagine* they did—instead of just coming out and *saying* what it is that's bothering you, you keep it to yourself; you never let on. I don't know if you even let on to yourself. Instead, you walk." I turned to see her come out from behind the counter. "You were so willing to blame," she said. Her voice was strained like she was going to cry.

Where had I heard that before? Of course—my old girlfriend, Sam—Samantha—accusing me of playing "the blame game," where I was always finding someone to stick it on when things went wrong and never telling them. Of course I then blamed *her*, for not being sensitive to what was paining me: my brother dying, my parents being so distant, my teachers not understanding my witty genius. Waah! Waah! Waah!

Never told *her*, of course.

I stood halfway up the stairs, all this stuff boiling around inside me, stuck on whether to walk or not, thinking about what Diana had said, listening to her talking with the girls about what they were doing tomorrow. School was going to start in a month, and she was trying to find out if they needed shoes and stuff. They were only paying attention in between setting the game up.

And then, as I stood there listening to her voice, it suddenly hit me what I was doing—what I *had* been doing all along: Here was someone who had let me get close—the closest I'd ever been to anyone—someone who really understood me. And yet I was so absorbed in my own stuck-up eagerness to be out ahead of her, to catch her failing me—I was so intent at finding a fault, a flaw, a glitch that would expose her for not liking me (like all the others before her who had screwed me over—poor me). I was so *focused* on being wary and watchful in my relationship with her. I was doing all this *so that I could get there first.* Beat her to the punch. Cut her cold before she had half a chance to cut me. If there was any rejection to be done, *I* was the one who was going to do it.

I'd show *her.*

I'd show *them.*

Messed-up thinking, I know. And all of it keeping me from seeing who *she really was,* and probably not helping me much with anyone else either—my parents, my teachers, Wanda, my old girl-friend—line 'em up and check 'em off.

Diana sat on the sofa reading a magazine; the girls were sprawled on the floor in front of the TV. By this time they had the game working; its music, punctuated by bloops and bleeps, filled the basement until Diana told them to turn it down, and then it got quiet.

"Hell," I said, and turned around and went back down.

The girls, intent on their game, ignored me as I walked over to the sofa and sat next to Diana.

She was snapping the pages of her magazine too quickly to be reading.

"Would it help to say that I'm sorry?" I said.

"I don't know, since you haven't." She kept snapping the pages.

"What I mean to say is, I *am* sorry."

"You think that's all it takes?" she said.

"What else can I do?" I said.

She set the magazine on her lap. "You know, if you're going to be with someone, you have to trust them."

"I'm learning," I said.

"And trust—that's one thing that is *not* a game. If you lose it, it's about the hardest thing to get back."

I nodded.

"It has to be earned all over again," she said. "You almost have to start from the beginning."

"I am truly sorry," I said.

"You have to mean it."

"I *do*."

We were both quiet.

"Come with me for a moment." She stood, pulled me up off the sofa, and led me by the hand through a set of swinging doors into the laundry room.

As soon as we got through the doors, while they were still flapping back and forth, she put her arms around me and backed me up against the washing machine in the darkened room. We kissed, her leaning up against me.

"I missed you," I said.

"I missed you, too," she said.

We kept kissing for a while, but I could tell something was wrong. She seemed distracted, like when we first got together.

"What is it?" I said, worried that it would be a long road back.

"It's only—" she said. "It's not you. It's him. He's at it again," she said.

"With you?" I said. I felt the anger quickly well up in me. "I thought you said—"

"No. No. No," she said, shaking her head. "He knows better than that. It's the girls."

"What did he do?"

"Nothing; not yet, anyway. But I can tell. He's been trying to get one or another of them alone. I've told them to stay together, but they don't understand; they're too young to . . . I can't . . . That's why I brought them over here."

She leaned her head against my shoulder, her arms around me, as if we were dancing.

"I have to do something," she said as if to herself.

"I can help," I said.

"No. I don't want you—"

"Diana."

"This is my problem," she said. "I don't want to drag you into it."

"Diana," I said. "I'm *already* in it."

"I don't know," she said, burrowing her head into my chest. "I don't know."

chapter 26

"But I got a *letter* from Mom," I told my dad, "and I was going to write her back." I winced when I heard the words coming out of my mouth, hoping he wouldn't say it: "The road to hell is paved with 'wuz gonnas.'" Maybe if he mixed it up a little for once: "Satan's nostrils are clogged with 'wuz gonnas'"?

Didn't he know that things went from those I *was going* to do to those I *wuz gonna* do only because he told me to do them in the first place?

But strangely, he didn't say it. Maybe he forgot?

I'd picked up the phone on the first ring, expecting Diana, and here was my father again. Telling me that *Mom* was still worried (as far as *he* was concerned, I'm a bucket of warm drool?) and they hadn't heard from me lately. But I knew what he was really after.

"I *will*," I said. "Write back."

"I'll tell her," was all he said. "I know she'll be happy to get it. And I do too."

"What?" I said, not following him.

"Miss you."

"Oh, yeah, I know," I said. "Mom told me."

"Look—" he started to say.

"I know, I know," I said. "Millstone. But it doesn't start until September."

"Except for the orientation."

"Right," I said. I really did forget about that.

"Which is the weekend before. It really would be good if you—"

"I know, Dad."

We were both silent for a moment.

"How's Wanda doing?" he said. "With the doughnuts?"

"Fine, fine." How could I begin to tell him? Not only didn't she own the business to begin with, but now she'd been fired from it and was puffing away the last few dollars of her inheritance—from him and Mom—on cheap gas-station cigarettes?

"You're still working there?"

"Yeah," I said.

"How's that going?"

"Fine," I said.

"They pay you enough?"

"Yeah," I said.

"It's quiet around here without you."

"Mom said—in her letter."

"What about your stuff?"

"My stuff?" I said.

"That you'll need at Millstone," he said. "Your socks and clothes and things."

"Maybe you and Mom could put them in a suitcase and ship it to me?" I said.

"I guess we could," he said. He was quiet for a while then. "I guess I thought we'd see you before."

"Yeah, well," I said. I wasn't going to commit to going home, not right now, not with everything in the state it was in.

"Well, I'll tell Allen, then," he said.

"Allen?"

"Mr. Salter."

Uh-oh. On a first name basis with old Al, are we?

"Well . . . ," he said. "You know, your mother and I were talking . . ."

I waited.

"We were thinking we might just get in the car one weekend and come out there and see—"

"Dad," I said. "Wanda's place is kind of small, and—" I hoped he wasn't serious.

"We could stay in a motel or something."

"Dad."

"We were just thinking."

"I don't know, Dad," I said. It would be a disaster.

He was quiet for a few seconds.

"Don't worry," I said, "I'll keep in touch."

"Okay," he said.

"And I won't forget," I said. "The letter."

"Right," he said. " 'Bye."

" 'Bye."

A COUPLE OF NIGHTS LATER, when I met Diana and the girls at the open house, she looked all cool and resolved.

"You have to work tomorrow night?" she asked.

"No," I said. "Why?"

"Good," she said. "The timing will be perfect."

"For what?" I said.

"I've finally decided to do something about him."

"Him, your father?" I said. "What?"

"I don't want to talk about it," she said, nodding toward the girls: Kit watching TV, Kat reading a paperback.

"Come upstairs for a minute, then, would you?" I said.

"I *don't* want to talk about it."

"Why?"

"I'm afraid I might talk myself out of it."

So what *was* this plan that was so terrible she was afraid to talk about? Cut the brake lines on his car? Spike his prune juice with rat poison? Sprinkle his jock strap with itching powder? Tie his shoelaces together?

All she would tell me is that I should be at home the following night, and she would call and tell me where to meet her. I gave her the cabin number—the phone being the one thing that still worked. She also said that I would need to bring my aunt's car, making sure the license plate had mud on it or something—which, of course, was no problem.

Wanda was still up and down. In the week or so since the fire, she had some good days when she was out in the garden and funny and her old self and bad ones when she stayed in bed all day and looked like she'd been whacked in the face with a bag of ice cubes.

Deke had suddenly been putting in extra time on Old Vic. He said that colder weather would be here before you knew it, making it harder to work, but I think he was feeling it was time to get the big old place finished and do whatever it was he planned to do with it. So it had become my job alone to continue work on Wanda's cabin, trying to get it back into the condition it was before.

One whole wall was so full of holes that Deke said it was best just to cover it with drywall—that stuff like plaster that comes in a big sheet? You nailed it on, and then to finish it, you had to put this tape where the pieces came together and smear this goopy stuff from a bucket over it and also over the tops of the nails. Once that was dry, you sanded it smooth with this thing that looked like a piece of window screen attached to a block of wood.

It seemed if my hair and clothes weren't white from the flour at the Works, they were white from the plaster dust I was kicking up in Wanda's cabin. One time as I finished for the day, I happened to glance in the chunk of mirror I'd propped on the mantelpiece. All covered in white dust as I was, standing against the new white wall, it was as if I'd disappeared. With all this stuff coming down, I found myself fantasizing how great it would be to blend into the woodwork like that—to be invisible, like when I was out on the road.

Old thinking dies hard.

On top of it all, Bert—one eye on the calendar—had started nagging me about how much longer I planned to stay working at the shop.

I wished I knew.

The next night I paced around the cabin, waiting for Diana's call. I pulled the old TV out of the closet and tried to unscramble its ghosts for a while, then gave that up and made some coffee. It got later and later, and finally I thought I'd just walk around the Far a few times. The moment I got out the door, however, the phone rang, and I ran in and picked it up.

"Now," said Diana. "At my parent's house."

Wanda left me a spare key to her car, since she wasn't going much of anywhere these days, and in the gathering dark, I slid on over to the parking lot. After thumping on the hood as quietly as I could to scare off Yasgur, I took off.

Driving into Stone Coach Woods, I couldn't help thinking of the unfriendly reception I got there the last time. Then I remembered that driving this big, paint-splattered rhinoceros of a car, I'd attract a whole lot less attention than when I was (of all things) *walking*.

I rolled through the dim streets, deserted as usual, pulled up the curving drive to Diana's house, and like she told me, took the turnoff that went to the side entrance, starting to think maybe I'd imagined the call, since there were no lights on and the place looked abandoned. But as soon as I pulled up, Diana appeared, carrying a fat, black trash bag, and hissed at me to kill the headlights.

"I have to leave it running, though," I told her. "It doesn't always start."

She shook her head and dumped the bag in the vast back of Wanda's car, where it looked like a bean in a bushel basket, and told me to follow her into the house.

The girls hardly said hi, as they ran back and forth in the ghostly light that filtered in through the windows, pulling things out of closets and stuffing them in bags like the one Diana had carried.

"What's going on?" I said.

"We can't get this open." She jammed an olive-green metal box in my hands. "It has like the bankbooks and everything in it. Can you get it?"

"Diana!" I said. "I can't—"

"I knew I couldn't get anybody around *here* to help," she said, "but I thought—"

"They'll put me away for good if I get caught in this," I said. "I don't know if—"

"Look," she said, "don't worry. We're only taking what's ours, and then me and the girls are getting out."

"Getting *out?*" I said. "To where?"

"To out of harm's way," she said. "Are you with us or not?" She reached to take the box back.

"You got a screwdriver?"

"There's one in the junk drawer in the kitchen by the sink," she said. "Hurry."

It was one of these stupid short ones with a wooden handle, and I pried and twisted at the lid before finally popping the lock.

"Here." I brought it to her.

She took out the booklets and documents one by one and held them up to the weak light, then stuffed a half dozen or so into her jacket pocket, leaving the rest in the busted box, which she stuck in one of the kitchen cabinets.

"Can't we put on a light?" I said.

"Help the girls," she said.

The girls were busy dumping drawerfuls of clothes out on their beds and grabbing handfuls of socks or underwear or T-shirts and stuffing them in bags. They already had two bags full, which I carried out to the car.

After that there wasn't much of anything—a couple of small lamps, their sleeping bags, a box with some kitchen stuff.

"We're almost there," she said, hauling a suitcase and another plastic bag of her own things to the car.

"Come on, girls. Time to go." She spoke into the dark open doorway of the house.

"We only have a half-hour window or so," she said to me. "Smitty usually takes a break about now." I remembered the pimply-faced guard who had stopped me the last time I was here and who I'm sure would have pepper-sprayed me if Diana hadn't come between us.

Even though it was still summer, the girls came out wearing winter coats. "We almost forgot these," said Kat, and they bundled into the back seat of the car.

"Get that bag on the washing machine and close the door, will you?" Diana said to me.

I picked it up and took a last look around the darkened laundry room. A T-shirt with the dancing skeleton logo of an old rock band was draped over the edge of a laundry basket on a shelf next to the dryer. The skeleton glowed in the dark. I quietly closed the door.

"Let's go," said Diana.

"Where?" I said.

"Just get us out of here, and I'll tell you."

"Wait!" said Kit, and before Diana could stop her, she was out of the car and back in the house. After what seemed like an hour—

Diana got out of the car and hissed at her from the door—she came back, a pink blanket balled up under her arm.

As soon as she slammed the car door, I began backing out, but before I could get to the street, a car pulled up across the drive, blocking us.

"Damn!" I said, when I saw reflected in my backup lights the golden shield of the local G-man.

"Smitty," I said to Diana as I saw him step out of the car and start walking up the driveway.

"Let me take care of this," said Diana.

I have to hand it to Smitty, he had the act down good. Standing slightly behind me, shining the flashlight into the car.

"What do you think you're doing?" said Diana, stepping on his opening line, which he delivered anyway.

"Everything okay here, ma'am?"

"Yes. Everything is okay, ma'am," said Diana, leaning and talking across me. "Now would you please get out of our way?"

He looked at the stuff in the back and the girls in their winter coats.

"Is there a problem?" he asked them.

They looked at Diana.

"What does it look like?" said Diana. "The damn power's out." She looked in the direction of the completely dark house.

Smitty looked around. The lights were on in the house across the street.

"Call it in for you?" he said.

"No, thanks," she said. "I said the *power*, not the phone. We already called. We're meeting my parents at a hotel."

He looked at me for the first time. If he recognized me, he didn't let on.

"Okay, sorry," he said. "Just like to keep an eye on things."

"Thanks, Smitty," she said. "I'll make sure the Congressional

Medal of Honor people hear about it. Now will you *please* get out of our way?"

It wasn't until we drove out of the gates of the place that I could feel the tension in the car finally begin to slack.

We stopped to pick up her car, which she'd parked in a vacant lot next to the small grocery—the idea being that one car would attract less attention.

Before long the girls were giggling and chattering in the back seat as I followed Diana. She still wouldn't tell me where we were going, but turned here or there, taking backroads routes that I recognized from my walks. After a while I thought I knew where she was headed. I flashed the lights and pulled up next to her.

"What?" she said, looking up at me out of the driver's window.

"Diana, you aren't thinking—" I said.

"Nick, just drive, will you?" she said, pulling ahead.

And sure enough, after a while we were bumping down the deserted road, and soon the little house in the high grass was coming up.

She turned in the driveway and hopped out, and in another moment or two, opened the garage door.

I drove the big car into the empty garage next to her little one.

"I don't have a good feeling about this," I said. "I told you; it's been open too long; it's getting stale."

"It will have to do for now," she said. "Help me get this stuff inside."

chapter 27

DIANA'S PLAN WAS TO LIE LOW with the girls until "something comes up." Yes, she had a few dollars, but she refused to stay in a motel, even the kind where the clerk is in a bulletproof booth. "And, besides, a motel is the first place they'll check," she said.

I hoped she meant her parents and not the FBI.

So she scoured the paper, trying to connect with some cheap apartment, meantime setting up housekeeping at the open house. "It's only for a few days, and my sisters are going through so much already with all this, I want a real home for them," is how she explained it.

I would have offered to put her up at Wanda's cabin, but the small issue of Diana being a Stoner, added to the problem that Wanda's place still had no water or electricity, ruled it out. And besides, even though I didn't ask, I was sure Diana had no interest at all in bunking at the Happy Hippie Farm.

Luckily Diana had enough cash to live on for a while, since she'd put together a good-size stash from advances on her credit card and jewelry she'd hocked (hers and her mom's), not to mention the cleaned-out bank accounts.

She would have put away more, but she had been trying to convince herself that her father had changed, reformed. Maybe she was even beginning to believe her mother's claim that she had imagined the whole thing. But then one weekend he was suddenly all interested in her sisters "having their own space," and painted an unused guest room to be Kat's. And he really hadn't done anything. Then she caught him prowling the halls late one night checking to "see if the girls were okay." It was all so innocent and fatherly. And he really hadn't done anything. And then one day she came home from shopping to find him back from work, Kit sitting on his lap on the sofa. She snapped at Kit and sent her off crying and confronted him, and of course he really hadn't done anything, but it was all Diana needed to convince herself. That very evening she called me and told me to be ready.

I have to admit, even after she told me this, I still had the slightest tinge of doubt that maybe she was blowing it all out of proportion; that maybe her mother was right. Of course, I didn't say anything. As Diana said, trust is the most important thing in a relationship.

After I dropped her and the girls off at the open house, Diana waited until she figured her mom would be back from her bridge game, then called from a pay phone and told her point-blank that she and her sisters were gone and were not coming back.

Her mother continued to play deaf, dumb, and blind, threatened to call the cops, and finally called her father, getting him to cut short a business trip. When Diana called back the next day— "just to make sure they weren't planning anything stupid"—the father was all bluff and bluster, telling her that she was crazy; that it was her word against his, reminding her of her earlier scrape; and—slipping a card from the bottom of the deck—claiming that she never understood simple affection anyway. She hung up on him.

But she had heard all she needed: no direct threat to call the cops; enough sputtering and hesitation in his voice to be sure, for the time being, anyway, that he wasn't going to *do* anything. Diana knew her mom was afraid of losing everything—daughters, husband, house, pedicures, bridge games, late-afternoon gin-and-tonics—so she'd be even *less* likely to act.

For the next couple of days, in the mornings after work or in the evenings before, I'd stop to visit Diana and the girls. Wanda was still distracted, and Deke was wall-to-wall occupied with his job at the shingle factory and fixing up his huge, decrepit house, so neither of them noticed I was gone longer than usual.

In spite of all my worries about how stale the place was, it was so isolated, I had no trouble turning unnoticed into the driveway. If someone was behind me or coming the other way, I'd just go on past and after a while drive back.

The one time someone *did* happen to come up when I was in the driveway and even slowed like they were looking, I got out of the car, walked to the For Sale sign, straightened it up, then got back in and drove off.

I'd usually show up at the house with a bag of groceries—soda and milk and frozen pizzas and stuff. Diana and the girls used the microwave to cook nearly everything, and the small basement refrigerator was big enough for food for a day or two.

After we ate and cleaned up—we used paper and plastic for everything, and I threw it all in the trash at work—I'd take her and the girls off to some neighboring town to look at some dump or two she'd circled in the paper, and then we'd go out for ice cream.

The places we looked at were always too small, too big and drafty, too unsafe, with bad fuses and plumbing, too overrun with mice and bugs, in bad neighborhoods where people might want to climb in your window and check out your cash, or in good neighborhoods where people might want to come in your door and check *you* out. "I don't want to bring them just anywhere," said Diana, and so they stayed where they were.

Diana made sure to get the girls out of the house during the day to the mall or the movies or wherever—shoving most of their stuff into a basement storage room in case someone should come along. At night, to make up for the extra power use and avoid a spike in the electric bill that might draw attention, they turned off the heat and snuggled all together in a pile in their sleeping bags.

And after the first couple of days of this, something strange began to happen. I would find myself at the house, sitting on the sofa, my arm around Diana, the kids sprawled on the floor, eating popcorn, laughing along with them about some dumb TV show, and I'd get a feeling inside that—well, I don't know exactly *what* it was.

It was kind of like the feelings of peace and calm I used to get when I was a little kid with my mother at an open house, playing in a pool of warm sun on a polished wood floor. A fresh place, different from the house where I grew up with the pencil marks measuring Donnie's growth on the door frame, his empty bed next to mine, the black hole of his absence sucking all the light and joy out of the place.

In *this* house, it was like Diana and the girls filled up that big empty place. I felt a lightness, a weightlessness even, being out of its supergravity pull. It was a feeling that stayed with me as I drove off into the night and saw the dark outline of the house in the rearview mirror of Wanda's big car.

Diana herself was less moody and restless. She and I both knew that staying here was temporary. But, like the other things crammed into the shrinking rational part of our brains—how to divide fractions, the date of the Magna Carta, the parts of a cell—after a while it became easy to forget. That is, except for one nagging worry. Maybe Diana and the girls weren't always aware of it, but I knew that every day we stayed there, we were in deeper risk of getting caught. And as happens with dangerous stuff you get familiar with, we got more and more careless: leaving blinds open, stuff out on the counters—a can opener, some matches in the kitchen, a toothbrush and deodorant in the bathroom—switching too many lights on at night, walking around by the windows where everybody could see.

The moment you realized you were at all comfortable in an open house? That was the exact moment you needed to move on.

Even though it was hard to find evidence of it, I knew it was possible I could learn from my mistakes. And I should have listened to the warning sirens going off in my head before real life came along and grabbed us by our collars and the seats of our pants and tossed us out in the street.

One day, a week into staying at the house, we were all out in the Wandamobile in a nearby college town. It was only an hour's drive, but the town was a whole other world, full of coffeehouses with people sitting at outdoor tables and lying on the grass in front of big formal college buildings that looked like churches, playing guitars, one guy leading an iguana on a leash. This was exactly what we needed. Somewhere else.

We were scouting apartments as usual, this time striking out for new territory, but with the number of college kids living in the place, and the fact that the school year would start in a couple of weeks, rentals were few and expensive, so we were coming back once again beat and discouraged.

When we swung around the bend to the house, I knew right away that something was different. As we got closer, I could see that the grass had been cut, and there was a new sign from a different real estate company in the yard.

I drove past.

"What are you doing?" said Diana. "The girls have to go to the bathroom."

"Just a minute," I said. I swung the car around and made another pass before I got out and checked the door. At least they hadn't changed the key.

I pulled the car into the garage next to Diana's and closed the door.

"What was all that about?" said Diana after I sent the girls down to the basement to pack away the few groceries we'd picked up.

I pointed out the changes to her and explained they probably meant there was new interest in the place. She got quiet and didn't say anything. We tried to settle down for the evening, but every time we heard a car go by, Diana and I looked at each other, ready to bolt.

When I left to go to work that night, Diana had finally settled down, especially after I convinced her that nobody would be looking at a house that late at night.

"We've *got* to find a place," Diana said.

Meantime, my aunt, who was depressed but not stupid, was starting to pick up that something was going on.

She was never so uncool as to try the Is-there-something-you-want-to-talk-with-me-about? thing, but you could tell by the silences and the looks as we ate dinner at Deke's that she would have *liked* to.

"How's things?" she'd ask.

"Fine," I'd say.

"Everything okay at work?"

"Yup."

It was starting to sound like my answering-machine conversations with my parents.

Finally it came to this:

A couple of nights after the new sign went up, Diana and the girls and me were in the house, sitting at the card table in the basement. It was dark and late and we were so wrapped up in a noisy card game the girls had picked up at camp one summer we didn't notice when a car pulled in the driveway until Kit said "What's that?"

We all froze, our faces lit by the battery-powered camp lantern in the middle, the cards fanned out in our hands.

Maybe it was only someone lost and turning around. This happened every once in a while.

But then there was the bump and rattle at the front door. I quickly checked my pockets: I found my spare on its ring right away, but a frantic pat of all my other pockets told me we'd already paid one of the costs of getting too comfortable: I'd left the original key in the lock box on the door. I put my finger to my lips.

Diana and I exchanged looks. The girls gaped, eyes wide. I set down my cards and tiptoed across the floor and up the creaky stairs, where I checked to make sure the bolt was slid in place. I crept back down.

The front door opened, and we could hear whoever it was talking more clearly now, but still only picked up an occasional word. The floor creaked as they walked around upstairs for a while; then the basement door rattled, and there was more muffled talk—and steps going away.

It got a little quieter.

"Where did they go?" Diana whispered.

"I don't know, probably upstairs," I said. "This would be a good time for us to get out. Come on," I said, and just like in the drill I'd insisted we practice every night, we went for the old coal cellar and the back stairs.

But just then, I heard the front door open again.

"Wait," I hissed. I knew from my mother's routine they *had* to see the basement and wouldn't give up so easily. "They're going out the front and around. They'll be coming in the back way."

So we changed direction, and I sneaked up the stairs again, gently slid back the bolt, and opened the door to the kitchen.

No one.

I waved for Diana and the girls to come up and hustled them out through the door off the kitchen leading to the garage. The garage door itself was still down, so they probably hadn't seen our cars yet.

"Don't start your car until I open the door," I said.

Diana nodded, and she and the girls got in her little car.

With the door to the Wandamobile open and the key in the ignition, I hit the garage door button, leaped in, and cranked the engine. I heard Diana's car start right up. Maybe I was giving it too much gas or something, but Wanda's car picked this exact moment to have one of its fits.

Ruh-RUH-rer-ra-ruh-RAH-rur-ra-ruh (cough, cough).

Ruh-ruh-RER-ra-ruh-rah-RUR-ra-ruh (Aaaack!)

The garage door began its long, grinding rise. It always worked fast enough before, but this time . . . I remembered this ancient philosopher we studied in school, who asked how an arrow could ever hit its target if it went half the distance to it, then half *that* distance, then half *that* distance, then half the ever tinier and tinier distances. If he'd been around now, he would have asked how this garage door would ever open far enough for us to get out. It went up one foot, then half a foot, then half that, then half *that*. I expected any second for the agent and the lookers to pop up in my rearview mirror in the barely opening gap between the garage floor and the door.

Ruh-RUH-rer-ra-ruh-RAH-rur-ra-ruh (cough, cough).

Ruh-ruh-RER-ra-ruh-rah-RUR-ra-ruh (Aaaack!).

Wanda's car hocked and stalled. I took a panicky look at Diana, who had already begun to back out. This time, for luck, I said the same bad word that Wanda used, and when I turned the key, the car exploded to life, excreting a buttload of smelly blue smoke into the small space.

Luckily the agent's car wasn't pulled all the way up, and the lookers' car was behind hers, so by turfing our way backward through the side yard, we had barely enough room to get around them, making it out onto the road right as I saw the agent peek around the house, just as we took off thundering down the road—lights off—in a cloud of smoke and dust.

"*Damn*, that was close," I said to myself, looking in my rearview mirror as much as out the windshield. Nobody seemed to be following.

After a while, I switched on the headlights and flashed them and got Diana to pull into a church parking lot up ahead.

"You okay?" I said.

She nodded, but instead of grinning like she usually did when we nearly got nailed—something all too familiar lately—she looked scared.

"What about all our stuff?" she said.

"They'll leave it," I said. "Nobody will do anything until tomorrow."

And much later that night, when I was sure the agent had gone and any deputies checking the place were long since dreaming in their cruiser out by the river, we snuck back and grabbed what we could, sweeping the cards off the table into a bag along with everything else and making another escape into the night.

It was late, and they were so exhausted, Diana and the girls slept in Wanda's car out behind the Donut Works while I did my shift.

Later next morning, bleary-eyed and grubby, fortified with a bag of rejects and coffee, we looked for another place.

I'd kept my eyes open—just in case—and I steered us to another open house, also out by itself, but with other places about a quarter mile down the road each way. There was no handy basement apartment either, although the family room and kitchen were in the back.

"You know, Diana," I said as we pulled the girls' things out and hauled them in, "we can't keep doing this forever."

"You think I don't know that?" she said, her eyes all flashy. "The girls will be starting school in a couple of weeks. We'll get something by then."

Somehow I knew there'd be no snuggling on the sofa that night.

chapter 28

I GOT BACK TO THE CABIN and slept for a while after getting Diana and the girls settled in the new place, but this flicking noise kept waking me up, and when I propped myself up on an elbow to see what it was, who do you think I should find sitting at the table playing with a pack of cigarettes?

"Wanda?" I said. "What're you—"

"Well, it *is* my house," she said. An unlit cigarette hung from her lips like a would-be suicide who isn't sure he wants to let go. I noticed the ashtray was clean.

I dragged myself past her to the bathroom and splashed water on my face from the plastic bucket on the toilet seat before I remembered that the water and electricity were back on.

The inspector had been by, and after Deke performed some electrical voodoo and Loosie sicced a big lunch on him, complete with mashed potatoes and a pie, he declared the cabin once again fit for human habitation, or at least for us. But Wanda said she would stay on at Deke's anyway, and that's why I was so surprised to see her.

"Hungry?" she said.

"I guess," I said.

"There's coffee and some frozen waffles."

This I took as a good sign—bringing groceries to the old place. The fact that she was up and out at this hour was also good.

I took the box out of the freezer and popped a couple of the waffles in the toaster, poured a cup of coffee for myself, and took out a plate.

"No syrup, though," she said.

"It's okay," I said. "Butter and sugar are fine."

"Or butter."

She sat there, fiddling with the cigarette pack, watching me.

I stood next to the toaster, peeking in every once in a while, getting my eyebrows singed.

It popped, and I jumped.

She was still looking at me when I sat down and started knifing up the waffles.

"There's something you're not telling me," she said.

I choked down the dry wad of waffles in my mouth and drank a swallow of coffee.

"What?" I said.

"I don't know what."

We sat there silently as I took the next bite.

"We've always talked about things," she said. "It feels funny when we don't."

I didn't say anything.

"You know, it's not going to bother me," she said. "Whatever it is. Unless you killed somebody," she said and paused. "And left fingerprints," she added.

"I wore gloves," I said.

"That's my sister's boy," she said. "Anybody I know?"

"*Used* to," I said.

We were both silent again.

"So why aren't we talking?" she said.

I could feel the blood rising in my face. I took a long draw on my coffee, washing down the rest of waffle one. "You haven't been around much to talk to," I said.

"I know, I know." She set down the cigarette pack and took a wooden kitchen match from the box on the table. "This whole thing . . . well . . . you know," she said.

"I guess, I don't know if I do."

She gave me a tilted-puppy-head look. "Look," she said. "I guess I shouldn't expect—"

She stopped and sighed and started again.

"When you get older, sometimes you realize that in spite of your best efforts, you don't change. You can't always live yourself down. It gets to be the same old stuff, and you get tired of it." She broke the match, leaving a sliver connecting the two pieces.

"Stuff?" I said.

"It's not only losing my job and the fire. . . . You didn't know when you were younger, and it wasn't something I could talk with you about"—she took another match from the box—"but you should have realized by now that Madel—your mom, and your dad, weren't entirely wrong about me."

I didn't say anything, but continued carefully eating the remaining waffle, one small piece at a time.

"I realize I am kind of . . . flighty, I guess is the word. I'm not always responsible. I just *do* things."

"You didn't think that was so bad before," I said.

"I said that?" By now she had snapped three or four matchsticks, leaving the halves connected, and was playing with them on the tabletop.

"You used to say that people are too careful with their lives, like they're going to break or something," I said, "and that's why you said you went in the Peace Corps, for instance. That wasn't so bad."

"Oh, for telling *others* what to do, I'm great, and besides, down there, you didn't have a lot of room for mistakes. I mean, it wasn't like, 'What should I do with my life?' You didn't have any choices; you had to hoe the beans or connect up the water pipe, or you wouldn't get to eat for the next couple of months."

"And it's not like that here?" I said, meaning the Far, meaning it part as a joke.

"Well, even here the garden is nice, but if it failed, you could go to the supermarket. Nobody's going to starve. You could do one thing or another or nothing. But my point is, I feel I let people down. Like you."

"Oh, Wanda," I said.

"Yeah," she said, "say what you want, but you don't know."

"Then tell me," I said.

She looked up at me. There was a seriousness in her eyes I didn't ever remember seeing before.

"You really want to know?" she said.

No, I thought.

"Yes," I said.

She picked up one of the broken matches and held it at eye level and twirled it, seeming to talk to it instead of me.

"You may have wondered how with all those boyfriends, I never got pregnant?"

"You told me once," I said. "You couldn't."

"Well, the fact is, I could and I did. Down there in Brazil with one of the local organizers. But he was some big important guy and . . . it was best, they all thought, if I left." She kept twirling. "Not only did I get pregnant, but I had the child. A boy. Your mom insisted, though, that I was too young—hell, I was only a couple of years older than you, nineteen—and that I should give him up for adoption. I did get to see him first, though. He was dark-haired and serious. He never smiled the whole time I held him. They said smiling comes later anyway. But I liked that seriousness. That was how he was. I thought, I guess, that if I could keep him, he would be able to help me. That some of it might rub off. That's how selfish I was then. But I had agreed, and I had no money, and there was nothing—you didn't have all the things you have now to help—there was nothing I could do."

The broken end of the matchstick flew off onto the floor. She didn't even look to see where it went.

"What happened to him?"

"He went with a family—a young couple, they told me—down there. I never found out who they were or where. That's all I knew. That was part of it; they didn't tell you then. He would be your age. Maybe a year older. He must be out there somewhere, but I've never heard—"

"You never tried to find him?" I said.

"I've called a couple of times and written some letters, but the agency down there is gone, and the records—well, they didn't keep such good ones to begin with. But I was so sad after that. It was years before I remember even laughing. I promised I would never leave someone who I cared for that much again, but then . . ." She looked at me and let it hang.

I remembered when I discovered her house was empty; it left a feeling inside of me like I'd sucked down a couple of cold, raw eggs.

"So I don't know what I'm going to do with myself, now," she said.

She arranged the broken matches on the tabletop to form a star, missing a piece where the half of one had flown off.

"Wanda," I said. "I don't know about what happened before. I do know that I came all the way out here to find you. And that you took me in." I stood and walked over to her side of the table and hugged her from behind where she was sitting.

"Thanks, Nicky," she said, kissing my cheek. "You're sweet to say that, but I—"

"And I know you were going to . . . you *would* have called me when everything was solid."

She didn't say anything.

"And you *would* have," I said. Her hair smelled good. "You

haven't been smoking," I said, seeing the cigarette up close and suddenly realizing it still wasn't lit.

"I'm trying," she said. "Deke doesn't care for it."

I let her go and got a couple more waffles out of the box and stood over the toaster, watching as they cooked.

"So what about it?" she said.

"What?" I said.

"You tell *me*," she said, tamping the cigarette on the table.

And then I knew I was going to talk. Maybe say some things I shouldn't. But it *was* Wanda. The same Wanda who, back when she was in the Corps, snuck into some big-bucks resort and mooned people in a restaurant through an underwater window in the hotel swimming pool.

"What if I told you a story about something that happened to someone?" I said.

"Go ahead," she said, "I'm a field of corn." She leaned forward on her elbows.

"Well, it involves a girl—"

"Of course," she said, the unlit cigarette bobbing on her lips again.

"And she was having troubles at home," I said.

"Troubles? What kind of troubles?"

"Oh, all kinds. She wanted to go out on dates, and her parents kept telling her to be home at like eight-thirty. And there were clothes she wanted they wouldn't buy for her. And her dad was trying to fool around with her. And she wasn't doing well in school." I dug into the second batch of waffles, shoving a big piece of one in my mouth.

"Go back to the part about the fooling around," my aunt said.

It took me a few seconds to swallow.

"He had been since she was little and she didn't know any better," I said.

"I mean, we're talking *sex* here?" she said.

I nodded, holding up my finger until I could get some more waffle down. "Yes," I said. "And so she finally decided she was going to do something about it."

"Like kill the bastard?"

"Wanda, she was maybe ten or twelve when it started."

"Like tell her mother?"

"She tried that, and her mother didn't believe her."

"Like call the police?"

"Except," I said, "except by that time she already had run-ins with the police and she knew they wouldn't believe her." I popped another piece of waffle in my mouth.

"So what *did* she do?" said Wanda. "Hurry up and chew!" I knew I had her now.

"What she did was kidnap them," I said through a mouthful. *"Them?"*

"I forgot to tell you. She had four little sisters, and she was worried the father was going to try something with them. In fact, he had already started making moves."

Wanda's eyebrows rose, and she pursed her lips so her cigarette stuck out straight.

"And she couldn't do it alone—kidnap them—so she got a guy to help, a guy she knew. They snuck in there one time late at night when the father and mother were away and got the kids out with their clothes and stuff and whatever they could carry."

"And where did they go?"

"Well, there's the problem. Where *could* they go? They found some empty houses that they sort of camped in for a while."

"'Empty'? You mean abandoned?"

"No, like For Sale, but nobody was in them."

"Don't tell me they caught one on fire."

"No. No. No." I said. "They just stayed in them."

"And they weren't caught?"

"Nope. Well, almost, once. They were careful, and of course they knew it was temporary."

"Let's go back to the kidnap part for a second. The police didn't come after them? Didn't the parents want them back?"

"I guess she made the parents think she might tell the police about the fooling around—even though she couldn't. She basically bluffed them into thinking it would be *Film at Eleven* if they made a stink about it, so they pretty much left them alone."

"She blackmailed them?"

"No. Not really. She didn't want anything from them. She and the kids cleaned out their own bank accounts, but they didn't have enough for very long, and they had to leave one place fast. They almost got caught, like I said. They couldn't be camping out in these places forever." I suddenly saw where I was going with this.

"So they had to find somewhere," said Wanda.

"Yep. Somewhere they wouldn't be found—in case the parents had second thoughts—and also somewhere cheap. So this guy had this woman friend—actually his mother's sister—who happened to have a house nearby. It was small and wasn't in such great shape—lately—but she wasn't using it."

Wanda leaned back in her chair.

"And what he did," I continued, "was he set them up there—since she wasn't using it anyway—and they lived there."

"Happily forever after?" said Wanda.

"Happily for a while. It wouldn't be permanent either, but just a place to stay while things cooled down."

"And then what?"

"And then, I don't know what. That's as far as the story goes."

She thought for a while.

"If the parents won't come after them, why hide them any-where to begin with?"

"Well, like I said, it's not likely, but not guaranteed either, and if the father decides to force the girl's hand, and she has to try to turn the father in . . . Well, her record isn't so good, and there's a chance the kids could be taken back."

"Couldn't this guy's mother's sister get her butt in a sling for hiding them out in her house—harboring fugitives or some-thing?"

"Not if the police never came after them and if the girl had the goods on the father, and he was some big honcho and it wouldn't help his company any if—"

"Back to that again. And this guy was *sure* the father did it? That she wouldn't be making it all up?"

"No, no chance. The guy knew her—" I put the last of the second waffle in my mouth to end the sentence. The less I said about this, the less Wanda would pick up on any of my doubts.

"It's like betting on a good bluffer with a weak hand." Wanda took the unlit cigarette out of her mouth and looked at it.

"So?" I said.

"So? What 'so'?" she said. "What's wrong with a little bet now and then? I think the mother's sister would say, 'Bring 'em on.' How many did you say there were? Five?"

"Only three. The girl—and two sisters. Oh, and there's one more thing you should know." I brought my sticky dish over to the sink and began rinsing it off.

She waited.

"What if the girl was a Stoner?" I looked back over my shoulder.

"And what if," Wanda said, "this guy's grandmother's daughter's sister felt she owed him one?" She broke the cigarette in half and put the pieces in the ashtray.

And that settled that.

NEXT MISSION was to break the offer to Diana. Would she want to live in Wanda's cabin on the Happy Hippie Farm?

"Why not?" she said, not looking too cheerful or too upset about the idea. "But I'll have to pay her," she said.

"She won't take much, but she *is* short these days," I said, knowing Wanda wouldn't take a cent.

So, later that day, I cleared Diana and her sisters out of the place they'd been holing up in and drove them around back of the Far to the parking lot. I used a piece of plywood for a ramp and had Diana drive her sports car up in the back of the old bread truck that Deke still hadn't put the wheels on. The fact that the blocks had sunk into the ground made it even easier for her to get up in it.

Nobody was around, which I was grateful for. I didn't know how the girls might react if Mysterious Willie showed up with his burned hat, playing his bagpipes, or if Jolly Roger rode across the Green on a unicycle wearing the tutu with the flashing lights.

We unloaded their stuff into Wanda's tiny cabin, and I set them all up in Wanda's bedroom. Diana let the girls have the big bed, and she took the rug on the floor at the foot of it. I made some peanut butter sandwiches for Diana and the girls; all they'd had that day was some dry cereal they'd managed to take with them.

I sat with them, although I wasn't feeling well enough to eat, and just had coffee. Every once in a while, there'd be a creak or a clunk as the cabin got used to shouldering its new weight, and I'd jump.

"What's the matter, Nick?" said Kit, who had been studying

me as she ate. Kat and Diana were keeping their heads down and trying to make as if everything was normal.

"Nothing," I said. "Just haven't had much sleep yet," I said. "I'll be okay."

Finally there was a knock on the door, and I jumped again, trying to cover by getting up and answering it. It was Wanda.

"It's your house," I said. "You don't have to knock."

"I want you to feel you have some privacy," she said. "You must be Diana."

Diana was standing there by the table. The girls stayed seated, but looked up curiously. This was their first Hippie up close, and I think they expected her to come floating in on a cloud of incense, wearing a big floppy tie-dyed Earth Mother dress, playing finger cymbals. In fact, she wore jeans and one of Deke's old snot-colored sweaters.

"Hi," said Diana, shaking the hand that Wanda had offered. "These are my sisters. Caitlin and Katherine, say hello to Miss—"

"Wanda is fine," she said.

They stood and shyly shook hands as well.

Then nobody seemed to know what to do.

"I want you to feel safe and comfortable here," said Wanda, finally breaking the silence. "If you need anything, let Nicholas know, or tell *me* if he's neglecting you." She put her hand on my shoulder. "Oh, and don't worry about anyone here. All of us know how to keep our peace. It might be best, though, if you stay mainly in back of the cabins when you go out so no one can see you from the street."

"Thanks," said Diana. "Thank you," said the girls in unison.

"Nick," said Wanda, "come on over to Deke's with me for a minute and help me carry over a couple of things."

"How's everything?" said Wanda when we got outside and out of earshot.

"So far, so good," I said. "Diana is kind of quiet, though."

"She just needs to get used to it," said Wanda. "Moving here is a big step for her."

In the evening, we all went to bed early—I had to get up for my job, and the girls and Diana were all exhausted. I lay on the sofa, not hearing so much as a squeak from the bedroom. Much later—I must've fallen asleep—I woke to something brushing my forehead. I started to sit up, nearly bonking Diana in the nose with my head.

"Easy," she said, her hands on my shoulders, gently pushing me down. She sat on the edge of the sofa, leaning over me. She ran her hand through my hair.

"Thank you," she said, and her hand still on the side of my head, she leaned and put her mouth to mine. I reached my arms around her—it seemed very natural—and pulled her down until she was warm next to me. She didn't resist. We kissed in the close, full darkness of this house we both lived in.

At least for now.

chapter 29

IT WAS LIKE I fell naked from the sky straight down into a pair of Big Dad, rivet-reinforced, "Can't Bust 'Em" leather-butt overalls, their suspenders sproinging me up and down. SPROING! And I'm dangling in the middle of arguments between the girls over who wore the other one's sweater because the other one used the other one's deodorant, and:
SPROING! I'm sitting at the table with Diana, filling out all the girls' health forms and deciding how far she wants to run up her credit card to get them new shoes for school, and:
SPROING! I'm crouched in front of a kitchen cabinet, screwdriver in hand, fixing a door that fell off, and:
Later that night, the kids off snoozing in the bedroom—SPROING! I land on the sofa next to Diana, the whole place—the living room, anyway—*really* to ourselves, with no worry about someone barging in the door, but before we get too far:
SPROING! and I'm off again doing doughnuts till late next morning.
At least for a couple more weeks.
At least until the summer vacation runs out.
At least until Diana's parents have me dragged away in chains to jail.
At least until *my* parents have me dragged away in chains to Millstone.
Speaking of which, my father is working the phone again.
"Who is that I hear in the background?" is the first thing he says after "Hello, Nick?"
"Someone Wanda has in to clean up." I look over at Diana,

thinking maybe this isn't such a good thing to say, but she actually is, at this exact moment, using the vacuum to suck a dust tyrannosaur out from under the bed and can't hear me anyway.

"She has someone come *in* to do that?"

"Well, with both of us working and everything—" I say.

Silence.

"How are you?" he finally says.

"Fine, fine," I say. "How is everything there?"

"Good," he says. "I hope you like blue."

"Blue is good," I say. "Unless you're talking about leftover chicken."

"Chicken?" he says. "Oh. Heh, heh, heh." He actually gets it!

"No," he says, "paint. Your mom is having your room painted. She says you need some cheering up, and blue is just the color."

"Yeah," I say. "That sounds great." Hard to beat the miraculous cheering power of blue. Are they planning on renting out my room?

"But that's not the main reason I'm calling," he says. "I want to let you know to be looking out for a check."

"A check?" I say. "For what? I'm doing okay." I don't want the strings.

"Your mother and I wanted you to have something—a little something—to get started."

At first I'm confused. How does he know about my moving in here with Diana and her sisters? But I quickly realize he's talking about getting started at Millstone, of course.

"I'm okay, Dad," I say.

"I know, I know," he says. "We just wanted you to have something."

We're both quiet.

"Dad, what if I told you I wanted to go to school *here*?" Blurt, blurt.

"There?" he says.

"Yeah, the high school around here. I know some kids who go." At least one. "Wanda could be my legal guardian, sign the papers."

"You know the score," he says. "We promised the judge."

"Yeah, but he didn't say I'd have to go to *military* school; to *Millstone.*"

"Right, right. But you know, if you should get in some kind of . . . If something else happens, it could be worse. Remember what the judge said about juvenile detention."

"Well, with Millstone and the school where I went, they *expect* I'm going to do something. They'll be waiting. But if I went here, it would be different. I'm different."

"Different?"

Yep, I'm the Can't-Bust-'Em temp-Dad of kidnapped kids hiding from the law with their sexually abused sister in a half-burned cabin surrounded by a bunch of hippie lunatics.

"With the job and all," I say. "I've saved money and everything, and I haven't been in *any* trouble since I've been here."

None that I've been caught at. Yet.

"Nick," he says. "I don't know. We put down a deposit at Millstone."

"You can always get it back. Look," I say. "The object of the place is to teach you what? I remember Salter—*Colonel* Salter—saying that it was 'self-reliance.' How can I better show self-reliance than by relying on myself?"

That seemed clear.

"Nicholahhhhs," he says, not wasting a breath by forming my name entirely from a sigh.

Clear to me, anyway.

"Please at least talk it over with Mom," I say. "I know Wanda will let me do it . . . stay with her."

"You haven't even *asked* her yet?"

"Don't worry about Wanda," I say. "I'll talk with her. You'll see; it will be fine. She could be responsible for me." I wince. Using "responsible" and "Wanda" in the same sentence? This is like waving a balloon in front of a kid holding a pin.

But he says nothing.

"It will be great," I say.

"Nick. I have to go. I just wanted to tell you about the check."

"Will you think about it?" I say.

"Your mother and I will talk."

"Okay," I say.

"Okay," he says.

"We love you, son," he says.

"We love you too," I say, whoever "we" may be.

AT FIRST I tried sleeping in my usual spot on the couch during the day, but when I saw how impossible it was with three other people around, with Diana's permission, I moved to the bedroom, rolling out my sleeping bag on top of the made-up bed. Lying there with tiny shrunk-up panty hose hanging off the bedstead, bottles and cans and jars of lotions and creams and gels and sprays on the dresser, I felt . . . contented?

Where this came from, I do not know. Remember me? The guy who didn't need much of anyone to get by? The guy who walked if a room got stuffy?

How did I wind up sitting here in my Can't Bust 'Em's making decisions about such things as where to put a lamp and what kind of air freshener to buy for the bathroom? What could have brought this on? What was next? Things were not as automatically clear as I thought they'd be just because Diana and I and the girls had finally settled somewhere.

What *was* my role in all this? This dad act was a good summer replacement program, but in spite of its ratings, I didn't think I wanted it in the regular prime-time lineup.

So, later that day, the phone call from my dad giving all these questions new urgency, I thought I'd ask Deke about it.

"Dunno," he said. "Gimme another sheet over, would you?" He talked out of one side of his mouth, since he was squeezing three or four nails between his lips on the other.

I was working with him in Old Vic's kitchen. He had pulled up half the floor where water had pooled and warped it and was kneeling down nailing in pieces of plywood. On top of these would go new floorboards.

I tilted a four-by-eight-foot sheet of the wood off the stack leaning against the wall in the living room and slid it across the exposed floor beams between us. With the floor open, you could see down into the dungeon where stacks of rotted screens were kept. This is probably as much light as had been down there in a hundred years, and all kinds of things were scurrying around.

"I mean, how do you feel about it with Wanda?" I asked. "With her living in your cabin now and all?"

He nicked a nail with the hammer, sending it ringing across the room.

"Well, that's just it." He started another. "With Wanda, you never know. She might get up one morning, shake herself, and be gone." He picked another nail out of his lips. After a half-dozen more hammer blows, he added, "I don't know you can base anything on us."

"But don't you feel like—I mean, I know you don't have kids or anything—but like you have a place to *be* in, to come home to?"

He paused and sat back on his legs. "Me?" he said. "I missed all that homey stuff when my pap ran out. Never really learned the lingo, I guess. And, like I said, Wanda is an unusual person."

"But I don't even know what I *am*, living there with Diana and the girls," I went on. "I mean, I'm her boyfriend, I guess, but Diana, she's kind of like Wanda. You know. Independent."

"Yeah," said Deke. "Wanda always used to get prickly if you tried to take care of her. But now that you mention it . . ." He trailed off.

"What?" I said.

"Well, with all the bad luck she's had lately, she's . . ." He took the nails out of his mouth. "I think she's decided I'm not so bad after all. I may not be as wild as some of the other men she lived with, or as pretty, but something's shifted inside her."

"I've noticed, too," I said.

"I think the whole thing with getting canned from the dough-nut place?" said Deke, "and the fire and her coming over to my place—it's been better. Good, even. It's like she's more *there*, more focused. It's like it's got her thinking." He smiled and put the nails back in his mouth and started hammering again.

"She's cut down on her smoking."

"I know," said Deke. "She promised she'll be giving it up. And that's what's been weird in this whole thing. For once with Wanda, it's like she's ready to let somebody take care of her for a while. I don't know how long it will last."

"That's what I wonder, too, with me and Diana," I said. "It's like we each have plans for our own lives, so we're not going to get settled down or anything. And as far as the girls . . . I don't know what I am—an uncle or a big brother or something. And I sort of feel like a *father*. I mean, how weird is that?"

Deke kind of shrugged. "I can't really tell you," he mumbled, "not having much experience in it myself. Another."

I got another sheet and slid it over, and he tapped it flush with the one he'd just nailed. The gap in the floor between us was narrowing. Over his hammering, I said, "What do *you* think

about Diana? Her being a Stoner and all?" Maybe come at it another way.

"Well, it goes to show there's problems everywhere, I guess. I
used to envy folks like that, nice house and all—living in the beat
old places I have—but just 'cause you live in a pretty house—" He
hammered for a while, then: "And I don't know that all of them—
Stoners—are so bad. Sometimes I think it's karma."

"Karma?"

"What goes around, comes around. I told you I raised some
hell myself. Maybe it's kind of a payback. 'You sow what you reap,'
'You butter your bread and lie in it.'" He grinned a naily grin.

"Be careful you don't swallow those," I said. "And what about
Wanda? How does she feel about it?"

"Why don't you ask her?" said Deke.

But I didn't have to.

Wanda was coming over every day for something, and she and
Diana had clearly hit it off. Wanda helping her get the girls ready for
school—organizing their clothes, seeing what they were missing,
suggesting what to get to fill in the blanks. Wanda giving Diana a
couple of her blouses. Wanda showing up with a casserole—for
once no oat and herbs but some tuna and macaroni thing the girls
actually liked.

They were kind of alike in many ways, Wanda and Diana.
Wanda never thought the same way as everyone else about
things; she ran away from home and had family problems—not
the same sort of problems, of course. And both of them put up
with some foolishness, which is probably why they tolerated
Deke and me so well.

In the end, it seemed that watching out for us—me and Diana
and the girls—seemed to be just the thing to lift Wanda out of her
own funk.

The day after Diana and her sisters arrived, an invitation had been shoved under the door for a party to welcome them to the 'hood. It was a big valentiny heart thing with ants drawn in all around the edge. Given the bad luck with outdoor parties, this would be a "Heart Hobble," where the whole rowdy gang would crowd in cabin after cabin, eating meal after meal and drinking drink after drink, until they'd staggered all the way around.

The day of the party, Wanda helped us dress in our second-hand-clothing-store best—Diana looking great in a kind of old prom dress with fake fur around the neck and armholes and hem, Kat with a poodle skirt that instead of a poodle had the outline of a tractor on it, and Kit with pajama bottoms with fire engines and a shirt and clip-on bow tie on top. I wore a velvet jacket with satin lapels over a T-shirt that read "Eat More Fish!" and a baggy pair of green bathing trunks—not wanting to be too conspicuous.

It took all the rest of the day to work our way around. The last cabin we stopped at was Deke's. To make room inside, he'd moved a bunch of his stuff out on the lawn, laying rugs on the grass and arranging his collection of old sofas and chairs, lamps and tables, like it was a room, complete with a stuffed moose head on the Big Tree and a chandelier hung from a wire stretched between the Tree and his house, although with the fear of being bombed, we all crowded in his cabin anyway.

But it seemed impossible to have a party at the Far without *something* coming down. And sure enough, everything was in full swing at Deke's—Jolly Roger in his full roller-rink glory—when there was a pounding at the door. Wanda peeked out and motioned for Diana and the girls to get in the bedroom.

Everyone did their best to ignore Sheriff Darryl standing out front, wearing his usual hangdog look, hat held by its brim in front of his crotch.

"We makin' too much noise, Darryl?" Wanda shouted over the

blare of the music, which Rode had punched up to the mega-decibel range.

He shook his head and signaled for her to step outside. She looked back in at Deke and shrugged, then left, taking Darryl by the arm, wearing a big smile.

When she came back in, the smile looked about as lasting as an icicle that you take inside in the winter.

"What did he want?" we all wanted to know.

"Just Darryl exercising his authority," said Wanda. "It's gettin' kinda flabby, you know. He wants us to quiet down some, is all."

Later, when Darryl had gone and the other residents had finally drifted homeward, we sat around Wanda's eating leftover pie, drapes drawn, lights low.

"Darryl says your father was down to visit," Wanda quietly told Diana. "He told Darryl you were missing and that you'd taken your sisters with you. He didn't say he wanted to file charges; he only wanted the sheriff to keep his eyes open. He told him he was getting ready to get a lawyer and would rather not go through all that if he could find you and, as he put it, talk sense to you. Darryl's feeling is that if your father ain't pushing, he's not shoving—for now, anyway. But who knows when that will change."

Diana looked grim. "The bastard," she said in a low voice. "You didn't tell him—"

"That's not how we do things here at the Far," Wanda said. "But I don't know how much longer you should stay. I'm sure Darryl knows. I'm sure he thinks of our little talk there as kind of a wink to the wise. If your father does decide to press charges, and Darryl has to get a warrant—"

"Damn him!" said Diana. I doubted she was talking about Sheriff Darryl.

chapter 30

I'M GETTING THAT DÉJÀ VU THING.

It's like we're back in the old open house—pulled drapes, low lights; stay away from the window; don't go out till dark; make sure you have plenty of batteries, bottled water, crackers, bandages, splints, life preservers, a shortwave radio.

"I don't know if I can take this," Diana says. The kids are all whiny and tired of playing cards and watching the old black-and-white TV. I've got her alone during the day, which means we're up in the treehouse—the only place where we can really have any privacy.

"And what are we going to do when school starts? I'm sure he knows where we are; he's waiting, playing us out."

"Why?" I ask. "Why doesn't he just have the cops come in?"

"I don't *know*," she says. "Maybe he doesn't want to upset them—the girls—look like the bad guy. Maybe he wants to get them alone and convince them I'm crazy. Tell them the whole ugly story about the trouble I was in with the cops and those guys. I never told them anything about it; they were only little kids. They're confused enough by this whole thing already. They keep asking, When can we go home? They don't understand, and I can't really give them all the gruesome details of what he—"

The "he" being, of course, her father, who she can't bring herself to name even by title or finish sentences where he's the subject.

"We've got to do something," she says, getting that fierce-eyed look she gets when you shake her from some desperately bad dream and you're to blame for all of it, including the waking-up part. Now I know exactly what Deke meant when he said Wanda could be "prickly." Dealing with Diana was becoming all of a sudden like puckering up to some spiny cactus.

But then the next afternoon, when I stumble out of the bedroom after my usual too few hours of sleep, I see her and the girls going through their school supplies. She looks relieved and happy. She says that she and Wanda had gone out alone that morning and had a long talk.

"I figured it all out," she said once she sent the girls off to stash everything away in the bedroom.

"Yes?" I said, waiting.

"We're going back in."

"We?" I said. "Where?" I hoped it wasn't where I thought she meant.

"To my parents'," she said.

It was.

"There's something I need," she said.

"Diana," I said. "I can lend you a few dollars if it's something important." I felt sick to my stomach. "What is it, anyway?" I said, sitting down at the table.

"I'll tell you later," she said, nodding at the girls, who were a few feet away in the other room, pretending they didn't hear a thing, when I knew they were soaking it all up like soda on dry sand. "On the way. Let's go."

"Now?" I said, standing in my flour-splotched, crusty clothes, which I'd pulled on from the pile I'd left next to the bed earlier that morning.

She just looked at me. "Wanda said it was okay to use her car."

I didn't know that a daylight raid on Diana's parents' house was such a good idea, and I told her so. But Diana explained that in the daytime there would be even less suspicion and that her mother usually went to get her hair done about now, and with the girls here, her father should be at work.

I gulped some cereal, went into the bathroom, and started brushing my teeth. "They'll be watching, no?" I said through a mouthful of foam.

"Who?" she said. "And what for? We're already *gone*, as far as they're concerned, and it's the last place they expect us to be, anyway," she said.

"That fits, since it's the last place I want to be," I said, wiping my face as I walked back into the living room. I knew this was cold, but I didn't get it. Why go back? It nagged me that maybe this was some sort of weird mental thing with her. I read in a magazine at the dentist's about people who secretly wanted to be punished for stuff. Did she *want* us (me!) to get caught? Was this some kind of pattern, like the fake date-rape thing?

"Grab that blanket," she said.

"Hey, that's mine," said Kit. It was her baby blanket.

"It's okay," said Diana. "We'll bring it right back."

I wadded it up and stuck it under my arm.

"You girls keep busy now and stay out of trouble. If there's anything you need, call Wanda." She kissed them both on the forehead.

THIS WAS TOO MUCH. It was like all those dumb horror movies where the babysitter hears noises in some creaky old house—an ax killer, chopping up corpses in the basement—and heads right for the stairs to investigate in spite of how loud you scream at the screen, "Don't go down there, you moron!"

"Stop squirming, will you?" Diana said as we sat at a stoplight. "You're making me nervous." I felt like we were on some cop show helicopter video where they put the arrow on the screen pointing to the car that says "Suspected Kidnappers." I wished it was a longer distance to go.

"So tell me why—" I started to say.

"Turn," she said.

All of a sudden, here we were rolling past the deep, wide lawns of Stone Coach Woods again.

As we got closer, I could hear and then see a truck from a tree-trimming company that was parked across from Diana's parents' house. A couple of guys in uniforms were cutting down a tree in the front yard across the street. The place had so few trees as it was, but it looked like this one had died. They had this chipper thing on a trailer roaring away, and every once in a while one of them would pick up some branches and feed them in and it would suck them up with an extra-loud roar.

"Diana," I tried to shout over the noise.

"Come on," she shouted back and leaped out.

Once around the side of the house, I thought we'd be out of sight like the last time, but some of the leaves on the thick bushes in front had started to turn orange and drop off, and you could begin to see through them to the street.

"Did you bring the blanket?" she said.

I showed it to her, although I still didn't know what she planned to do with it—throw it over her father when he came in and beat the living crap out of him with a broomstick?

I thought maybe they would have changed the keys or something, but Diana didn't even get to try hers. She just turned the knob, and the door swung open. It was too easy. And we found ourselves back in my nightmare, walking through the laundry room, blinds closed against the sun. At least the T-shirt with the dancing skeleton was gone.

Even though I'd been there only once, the layout was sharp in my brain as if it was grooved in by a jackknife, and I saw that Diana was headed for the bedrooms. She shot past hers and her parents' and sisters' to the one farthest in the back, one we hadn't gone in the last time.

"His study," she said, trying the knob. It was locked.

Without missing a beat, she grabbed a hanger from the hall closet, unbent its hook, stuck this straightened piece of wire in the hole in the middle of the doorknob, and popped the door.

The room was piled with junk: a couple of scratched file cabinets—one gray, one green—an exercise bicycle, cardboard boxes, and an old desk and chair. On the desk—looking out of place, all shiny and new—was a computer.

Diana dove under the desk and started ripping out cables. "Help me," she said from underneath.

"Diana!" I said. "What *is* this all about? Couldn't you use the ones at the library or something?"

"I *need* this," she said.

So I crowded in next to her—she had a sharp sweaty smell on her I'd never noticed before—and pulled out the plugs behind the machine.

"Take out the monitor," she said. And I picked it up, being careful there weren't any stray cables still holding it, and carried it out. The tree chipper out front was pumping out such blasts of noise I felt I could hide in it.

When I got back she had the bottom part of the computer disconnected. "Here," she said. "Wrap this up in the blanket. I want to make sure it doesn't get broken."

"Diana," I said. "Would you—"

"Don't argue," she snapped, "just take it," and with a couple of cables and the keyboard tucked under her arm, she stormed out.

I put the trailing cables on top of the thing and carefully

wrapped it in Kit's pink kiddie blanket. It was heavier than it should have been, and I just wanted to get it in the car and be gone. When I stepped out the back door of the house, however, I froze.

There was the local guard, hand on his hip near his gun, calmly chewing his cud and standing between Diana and the passenger door of the car.

"I don't have time for this, Smitty," she was saying.

"What's the problem?" I said, imagining how I looked in my rumpled, flour-stained clothing from the night before.

"You again?" he said, eying the bundle in my arms. "Josh, is it? You in on this too?"

"On what?" I said.

"This is none of your business," Diana said to him, trying to get by. He put his hand up, as if he was halting traffic for a family of ducks crossing the road.

"I think it *is*," he said. "Your father said to keep an eye on things. He said you took off; that you might come back." As he moved to block her, I noticed the holster guards were open on his gun as well as the pepper spray.

"Come back and get my own stuff?" she said. "Is that a new one around here?"

The tree grinder across the street roared, and Smitty waited until it finished eating the limb it was chewing on to reply.

"He said you don't live here anymore, and if I saw you taking anything, I should treat you like any other thief."

"And you believe he was *serious*?" said Diana.

This seemed to throw him off.

I started to walk to the driver's-side door, but he took a few steps in front of the car to stop me and my pink bundle.

"I'm going to have to ask you to put that back," he said, the one hand still up, the other still near his gun.

"Or what?" said Diana. "You're going to shoot him?"

Great! Give him ideas.

With Smitty no longer in her way, she opened the passenger door.

"Diana," I said. "Do we really—"

She got in, set the keyboard and cables in the back seat, and slid through the car, coming out the driver's door so she stood behind Smitty.

"Nick," she said. "Just put it in the car. Smitty will let you by."

I took a step forward.

Smitty had other ideas. He stood his ground, staring levelly at me, actually putting his free hand on his gun butt. His mouth looked dry as he chewed his gum.

"Damn it, Smitty," said Diana. "Let him by!"

"I don't think so," he said. There was a slight waver in his voice, as if he wasn't a hundred percent sure.

The bundle was feeling heavier and heavier in my arms, and the blanket made it slippery and hard to hold.

"What have you—" he waited for the tree grinder to finish— "got there anyways," said Smitty, "that's so important?"

"None of your business," said Diana. "Nick!" she said.

I moved forward, but Smitty was there. We were eye to eye, only the frilly pink package between us. I could smell the fruity gum on his breath.

We might have stood there the rest of the day if another car hadn't pulled up behind Smitty's cruiser. It was some big, black land barge with gold-tone wheel covers and trim.

An older woman, dressed in a skirt and boots—gray hair molded in a helmet on her head—got out, a small silver purse bouncing at her hip.

"Diana!" she said. "What's going on here?"

"We're leaving," said Diana. "That is, if Smitty ever gets out of the way."

"Hello, Mrs. Lawson," Smitty said without taking his eyes off me. "Mr. Lawson told me to—" The noise of the tree grinder blotted out everything else he said.

Diana's mother—that's who it had to be—held her hands over her ears.

"Where have you been?" she said to Diana when the noise level dropped again. "Where have you taken Kit and Kat? You know we've been very, *very* worried." Smitty and I stayed butting eyeballs as she ignored us both.

"Don't worry, Mom," said Diana. "Like I told you on the phone, I'm okay, and they're okay, too."

"Why are you doing this to us?" Her voice was shaking. "Your father is about to call the police."

"Tell him to go ahead," said Diana.

"You know that won't help anyone," she said. "Why don't you just come home?"

"Home?" said Diana as if the word were some big ugly insect that had crawled into her mouth and died. "I think you know."

The woman locked eyes with her for a moment or two, but then wavered and looked away.

"You just won't admit it," Diana said. And, after a pause: "He was moving in on the girls."

"Diana," said her mother, shooting a glance at Smitty. "He's your *father*."

The machine tore into another tree limb as they both stood staring at each other.

"I know that he tells you I'm lying." Diana raised her voice, cutting through the whine of the machine. "That it's my word against his."

"You can't just . . . leave," her mother shouted right as the machine shut down entirely, the last word loud in the silence that followed.

"I already have," said Diana quietly.

"We won't let you," said her mother. "Who is this?" She suddenly noticed me, standing there with what looked like a wrapped up baby in my arms.

"This is a friend. A good friend of mine," said Diana.

"What have you got there?" her mother said to me.

"Dad's computer," said Diana before I could answer.

"What are you doing with it?" said her mother.

"I'm taking it," said Diana.

"His *computer*?" said her mom.

The quiet after the machine stopped was almost painful.

"I'm trying to even things out, Mom," said Diana.

"But, Diana—" she said.

"Please don't get in my way on this."

The woman just looked at her. She didn't say anything.

"I need your help with *something*," said Diana, close to tears. "Just let us go."

Her mother, standing up straight this whole time, finally slumped so that her purse slipped off her shoulder and plopped on the driveway. She leaned against the rear fender of the Wandamobile, one hand spread on her stomach, the other cradling her head. She said nothing.

Diana nodded at me, and I took a half step around Smitty.

"Mrs. Lawson?" said the guard, who hadn't moved as he waited for things to play out. "Mr. Lawson said—"

"This is my house, too," said Diana's mother, so softly I barely heard her. "Let him go." She looked down to where her purse was lying, like a dead silver fish.

Smitty frowned, shook his head, and stood aside. Diana opened the back door of the car. Brushing past her mother, I bent over and eased the bundle into the back seat next to the other stuff piled there.

"This must be the boy you were telling me about on the phone," Diana's mother said as I straightened up.

"This is Nick," said Diana.

The mother smiled weakly at me. "Take care of her, will you?" she said, reaching her hand out as if to shake mine, but placing it on my shoulder instead.

"Diana?" I said, truly puzzled for a second; thinking maybe she was talking about one of the kids.

"I guess that was a foolish thing to say, wasn't it?"

I smiled at her, and she nearly smiled back.

Smitty, still shaking his head, walked back to his cruiser and stood waiting outside its open door.

I got in the car and turned the key. Thankfully, it started on the first crank.

"I love you, Diana," said her mother. "And the girls. Give them a kiss for me, would you?"

Then Diana and her mother hugged. When they separated, Diana picked up the purse and handed it to the woman, kissing her on the cheek as she did so. Then she walked around the car and slid in next to me.

In the rearview mirror, I could see the two cars lined up behind us, their doors open. Then, as if on cue, Smitty got in his and Mrs. Lawson in hers, and they shut the doors, started the engines, and backed out into the street next to the tree cutters' truck.

As we drove by their cars, tight in the narrow space left on the street, Smitty sat looking straight ahead—bored, as if this was something he'd seen a thousand times. Mrs. Lawson gave us a weak smile, and we were gone.

Diana stared grimly ahead until we drove out past the gates of the development, then she suddenly put her hands to her face and sobbed.

chapter 31

As it turned out, Diana wanted her father's computer for more than just the kids' schoolwork.

"I hope this was worth nearly getting shot," I said when we got it back to the cabin and set it up on the old library table Wanda used for a desk.

"You'll see," said Diana as I left her to hook it up and play around with it. After a while she said, "Come over here."

What was on the hard drive was some of the saddest, sleaziest, sickest kiddie porn you've ever had the bad luck to see. Hundreds and hundreds of images. They were worse than looking at those gross car accidents they show in driver's ed. It was the kind of thing that if it was about food, you would never want to eat again.

Also on the drive were yard-long slime trails of chat-room talk, mostly on the same theme as the pictures.

"See this 'LilGifGuy'? That's him." She still couldn't bring herself to say "my father."

"He left it on one night, and I saw the glow coming from his study and went in to turn it off and saw this crap." She shook her head as she paged through screen after screen of dialogue.

"He got on-line with all these other perverts and *talked* about this stuff and exchanged these pictures and names of girls and things." She scrolled down the screen. "Here's even one from a couple of days ago where he was trying to get this—it must be some young girl—to meet him. I hope it was an FBI agent posing. He is *so* sick."

I could tell it was torture, but she made herself read it. Then she burned a couple of copies of all of it—the pictures and everything—onto CDs. One she mailed to him—no letter, no nothing, only the CD with a piece of bubble wrap around it. The other she hid somewhere she wouldn't even tell me. "Insurance," she said.

After this we seemed to drop off Sheriff Darryl's radar, and we never heard any more of the bluff and bluster about having the law come down on us, or anything from her father for that matter, except how sorry he was, and this through Diana's mother, who Diana continued to call.

"I feel kind of sorry for *her*," Diana said later. "When you think about it, she did have a lot to lose. If she blew the whistle on him, then it would have *all* come apart, *all* of us would be gone, and she would be alone, and she would have been the one who did it. Life as she knows it would be over." When I heard Diana talking like this, worrying about her mom, I knew it was starting to come back together for her—starting to make sense, at least in some jumpy, spliced-together way.

And as for me? Right now I felt like I was in the middle of a slow-motion train wreck. The only way everything would come back together would be if they ran the film backward.

First of all, there was the small matter that I'd mistrusted Diana *again*. Luckily I never confessed my crazy idea that she really wanted to get caught going back for the computer and all; luckily she must have racked up my wariness to plain old wimpiness. But it was hard living with myself. I remembered all the stuff she said about how important trust was to her.

Like Wanda, I started to wonder if I could ever change.

Next there was the bigger matter that it was only a week before I had to go to Millstone and their "Orientation On-Demand," as they called it in the crumpled pamphlet I fished out of my pack.

Meanwhile, marking time, I ducked Bert's questions at the

Donut Works about staying or leaving. Deke and Wanda didn't bother me, since they seemed to have enough troubles of their own—Deke with his job shucking shingles and his life's work restoring the old house, Wanda still licking her wounds, although I did start to find the paper open to the classified ads in the mornings. Maybe she was looking for another job? I had no trouble figuring what Diana wanted as, with the kids in bed, she drew me close in the cool darkness of the cabin.

That Sunday evening Wanda said she had something important to tell us, and she and Deke came over just as Diana and me and the girls were finishing an early dinner of burgers from the grill out back.

"I want to come right to the point," Wanda said as they sat on the sofa with us around them on the floor. She paused and looked at Deke. He was deliberately looking off over our heads.

"You're going to have to leave," she said.

"Wanda!" I said.

"Not right away," she quickly added. "You'll have time to find another place."

"Isn't there something we can—"

"I'm planning on selling," she said. "I'm afraid I need the money to get me through till I find work."

Who could argue with this?

Diana was silent. The girls looked down at the floor. I had the feeling like when I put my sweatshirt hood up and could see only that small circle of the world immediately in front of me. I knew we weren't going to be here forever, but to have to move again so soon—

"What about the Far?" I said, dumbly. "I mean Loosie and the Branstools and all. It's like you can't just *go*."

"They'll understand," she said. "I'm sure they will. They know all about keeping on the move."

"But they helped you out before, maybe they can—"

"Exactly," said Wanda. "I've been on the dole enough around here. Besides, I don't think I can take unraveling another Cheerios wreath, or more of that cheapo shampoo you've been slipping in on me." She combed her fingers through her hair, and it stayed stuck out.

She was silent for a moment, letting it all sink in.

"In the meantime," she continued, "Deke and I found a place we thought Diana and the girls should look at."

That explained the classifieds.

"It seems nice, and the rent is cheap. The neighborhood isn't great, but it's coming up," she said.

"Okay," I said, "I guess." Diana didn't say anything but only stared out the window. I could tell she was thinking that it was more of the same: another betrayal in a line that by now stretched back as far as she could see.

"Come on," said Wanda, "we wanted to show you."

"Now?" I said. "Where?"

"I thought you said Diana liked surprises," said Wanda.

Diana's face was blank. The girls looked at her, but she said nothing.

"Let's," said Wanda.

We rode in the Wandamobile like in a one-car funeral procession, everyone looking out their own window, all of us lost in our own thoughts, even the kids quietly sitting back in the cargo area.

I sat behind Deke, who was driving, and tried to catch his eye in the rearview mirror, but he continued to dodge me, looking straight ahead.

Soon we were in a halfway familiar neighborhood.

"I haven't been around here in a long time," Diana said, in a daydreamy voice. "I had a friend used to live over here. I remember the high front steps and the sidewalks and all."

Pretty soon, the neighborhood got *very* familiar.

"It's near Old Vic?" I said, but Deke still wouldn't catch my eye. "You know—I told you about it—the house that Deke is fixing up?" I said this to Diana, trying to cheer her up. She didn't turn from her window.

"In fact, there it is," I said, as we turned a corner.

Then we slowed as we got close to it.

Then we pulled in its gravel driveway and rolled up to the side entrance, through the pillars and fancy woodwork into the open garage.

"What's up?" I said, when we stopped.

"This is the place we wanted you to look at," said Deke, his eyes in the mirror finally catching mine and lighting into a smile.

"Old Vic?" I said.

"Come on in," he said, opening the car door.

We went on up the steps and into what Deke had told me was the parlor. He'd stripped it all out so it was now a big open room. But he led us through it into the living room, which in a radically non-Deke style was also nearly empty, with only a couple of big comfy chairs and an old pink sofa that I remembered being at the bottom of a pile of stuff in his cabin. The kids stopped to admire the strange murals that he still hadn't painted over.

At the stairs Diana smoothed her hand over the foot of the polished wood statue of some woman holding a bow and arrow with a dog next to her.

Upstairs looked like a hotel, with doors lined up on each side of a hall. Deke opened one, and it led to a stairway up to the third floor.

"We thought you and the girls might like it up here," Wanda said to Diana. The big, cobwebby ballroom awed the girls, but off through a door on one side of it was a whole other set of rooms.

"These were maid's quarters back when," said Deke, "and

there's everything you need up here—a couple of bedrooms, a bathroom, a kitchen. You could have it all to yourselves."

The living room had wide windows that swung out into the middle of a huge tree right outside, now bright with red-and-yellow leaves.

"This is great," said Diana. "But you know we can't pay much."

"Not to worry," said Deke. "The place is paid for, so we don't need much, if anything."

"We *will* chip in," said Diana. "I'm looking for part-time work, and Kat could do some baby-sitting."

"Every little bit helps," said Deke. "But we'll be able to get on for a while from what we get for the cabins."

"You're selling yours too, Deke?" I said.

It all of a sudden hit me how much I'd miss the Far.

"'Fraid so," he said. "Can't afford a city house *and* a country house. Want to see your room?"

"Me?" I said.

"Well, if, like Deke says, you're going to school here," said Wanda, "you'll need somewhere to live."

I looked at Deke. "No such thing as a secret," he said.

We went back down to the second floor and through one of the doors into a big square room with windows on three sides—already set up with an old iron bedstead and a dresser and a braided oval rug on the floor. The room had its own fireplace and was full of light from all the windows.

"Great!" I said, bouncing on the squeaky bed.

Deke and Wanda stood, arms around each others' waists, and smiled.

"It's much closer to downtown, too," I said. "I could walk to work."

"There's a bus that stops down the corner. . . . It's a ride, but it goes over past your old schools," said Wanda to Diana and the girls. Wanda explained that the Branstools would let us use their address at the Far, which, being next to Stone Coach, was in their old school district.

We went downstairs, leaving the girls to explore. As the four of us stood in the fading light in the kitchen, Deke got us out a couple of cans of soda. We could hear them upstairs whooping and hollering, chasing each other in and out of all the rooms.

MY FATHER had never called back since the time I'd blurted out my plan about staying here. Since I hadn't heard from him, I'd convinced myself that he'd chucked it as another one of my idiotic ideas that, like TV commercials, if you ignored them, would go away. And he did have the law on his side. If I dug in my heels and he wanted to make an issue of it, the judge would back him.

I was due to report to Millstone this coming Saturday, so it was time for me to start fishing or get off the pot, or however you say it. And so one afternoon when Diana and the girls were out with Wanda shopping for school clothes at secondhand shops, I saw my opportunity. Sitting on a box of books in Wanda's cabin, I picked up her old telephone and punched in the familiar number, thinking I'd leave my plea or demand—or whatever came out—on the answering machine.

I got my mom.

"Yes, dear?" she said, as if I had been in the other room and had come in to talk with her as she was going over her listings.

"I don't want to go to Millstone," I said. Might as well get right to the point, hey?

"Your father said you didn't," said my mother.

"I'm *not* going," I repeated.

"Oh," she said.

I didn't say anything.

"Nicholas?"

"And I'm thinking of staying."

"There?" she said.

"Wanda is moving to this new place." I wanted to get it all out quickly. "It's bigger than the one she was in—and she says I can stay—I'm welcome to. I want to get her and Deke—that's her boyfriend—"

"A *new* boyfriend?"

"It isn't like that," I said. "Deke is a nice guy. I like him. *You* would like him."

"Deke," she repeated.

"It's his real name," I said, not going into the "Deacon" thing. "I want to get her and Deke listed as my guardians so I can get enrolled here in school."

"Your father said that you wanted to stay with Wanda," she said.

Then, after a pause she said, "Wanda," all dreamy, like it was a name she was thinking of calling a baby or something.

Then she was quiet again.

"I'd miss you," she suddenly said.

"I'd miss you, too, Mom," I said quickly. "But they need me here."

"Isn't it something?" she said. "The ones who are always messing up—"

"What?" I said.

"They always get all the attention."

"Mom, did you ever think it's because they need it?"

She was quiet.

"I mean," I said, "you guys can take care of yourself pretty good. Dad and you have been married a long time now. You have the house—"

"It's not like it's been easy," she said. Silence on the line. She may have been crying. With my mom it was sometimes hard to tell even if you were there.

"We had some bad times, you know, your father and I," she continued after a while, her voice kind of shaky. "It isn't always all roses, but you have to stay with it. And you know how I hate real estate."

"You *do?*" I said. This was news. "Since when?"

"You saw me. At the open houses. I guess you were too small to notice."

I only remembered playing in those big, empty houses, my mom somewhere showing off the rooms.

"And your father—you know how he moved out for a while right after it happened—when you started school?"

Another chanting of the ancient family saga around the smoky peat fire in the great hall. It was like that old joke where guys in prison get to know each other's stories so well they call them by their numbers.

"Yes, the other job—the 'opportunity'—after Donnie died. He thought it might work out better." All the same code words. I wondered where this was going.

"It was a trial separation," my mother said.

"Separation?" I said.

"It does terrible things to you, something like that. I mean, we're not some kind of special beings just because we're parents. You start blaming, and they—the other person—always reminds you, even if they never say anything. I went back to work to take my mind off it, and I guess I always connected it with that time."

"Mom," I said, "why didn't you ever tell me this?" I was mad; she couldn't go changing the saga after I'd learned it by heart.

"You were too little to talk about it when it happened, and . . . Well, how do you bring that up?"

"What happened?"

"It was a trial, like I said. It was a job with another company—oh, maybe a couple of hours upstate. Had an apartment there and everything, but after a while . . . He was worried about you. Leaving you without a father."

I said nothing, letting this all sink in.

"So he came back. It was hard for him. He was depressed."

Hard to believe Dad having such a fashionable illness.

"He blamed himself for Donnie, you know."

"Mom," I said. "It was an accident."

"People don't always think that way."

"He turned, the other car came out of nowhere, it was speeding." The traditional verse.

"But he thought he had the turn signal," my mom said.

"Turn signal?" She was messing with things again.

"Like at home—the green arrow where we get on the thruway," she said.

"And he didn't?"

"There never was one."

I was quiet for a while, trying to figure out where this new tale went. It was sort of like finding out your parents—these familiar people you lived with all these years—were adopted.

"He couldn't get his old job back, and he had to get another," she went on. "We barely got along. We both lived under the same roof, but that was about it. One time we even agreed, when you grew up and moved out—"

"You and Dad?" I said. I couldn't believe what I was hearing.

"—we would go our separate ways. But something happened. We kept at it, and something happened. It's like we learned all over again. And meanwhile I kept working real estate—walking houses."

"Why?" I said "If you hated it so much?"

"I don't know," she said. "I just did. I needed the money to be independent at first, just in case. I didn't know if he would stay.

Then, after a while, I realized it made me feel good. People always have such hope right then when they get a house. It was like I knew *somebody* had a chance for getting things to go right. So it kept me going."

"Mom," I said. "I need my chance."

"I know you do, Nick," she said. "Your father and I . . . You got us back together, and I guess we were kind of worried that if you left—"

"It's not like I'm dying or something." It came out before I fully realized what I said. "I'm sorry," I said. "I didn't mean—"

"It's all right," she said. "It's been a long time."

The line popped and clicked.

"I just wanted you to know this," she finally said. "Why he is like he is sometimes. I'll talk with him."

"Thanks, Mom," I said, relieved.

"I'm sure I can bring him around. He didn't know what to do next. He knew you were unhappy. We both knew it. But we couldn't seem to do anything for you. Are you sure you'll be all right?"

"I'll be fine."

"And how *is* Wanda?"

"Wanda is fine."

And as I said good-bye to my mother, I found myself crossing my fingers that she would work her magic on my father. It suddenly struck me that this was one of my mother's obnoxious habits. When she had some client on the phone who was hot to buy a house, she would hold her fingers up, crossed, the whole time.

I held my crossed fingers up and looked at them closely. I wondered why I had found it so annoying.

chapter 32

foot notes

"Walkin' to Missouri," my father always said with a laugh whenever we drove past someone walking out in the middle of nowhere—a line from an old song, I guess.

I've started to think that maybe he made fun of them because they *scared* him. Here he had spent so much time and effort building a career, paying for a house, saving up money, getting insurance and sturdy eyeglass frames, only to have it all come crashing down in the flick of a steering wheel.

Maybe it scared him how easy it would be to let it all just drop; to leave work one day and keep on walking, following the railroad tracks to Missouri or wherever.

In some strange way it makes me admire him that he never did; that he stayed.

For *me*, as it turns out.

chapter 33

RODE KOOL had rigged a spotlight that shone on the mysterious project he'd been working on since the day after the fire. Draped with burlap as it was, it looked like a mound of bears sleeping out in the middle of the Green, where the old splintered wishing well had stood. Everyone stood around, called there to witness its unveiling.

After a bagpipe flourish played by Willie and a tug of the rope by Loosie, the burlap split into two neat halves and slid to the ground.

There, bathed in the eerie blue light, was a sparkling new well. It looked like the old one, but when Loosie christened it with a bottle of Yoo-hoo, it clanged like a flagpole hit with a baseball bat.

"Solid steel," said Rode. "Welded it myself."

In it he'd hung a new bucket, this one made out of Loosie's old tin chamber pot, handed down by her grandmother and painted the traditional gold.

Everyone scribbled on scraps of paper and dropped them in. Roger squirted the sacred lighter fluid and tossed in a match and everyone stood kind of sad-looking in the light of the tiny flame of their burning wishes—barely a wink in the gathering cold and dark.

Then Rode fired up the record player, and everyone danced late into the night, for once unmolested by flying water balloons, road kill, or batteries.

Turns out that Sheriff Darryl, motivated by Wanda's cabin burning (she must've been right about his feelings for her), had done more than the usual shrugging and hand-wringing. Poking around Stone Coach Woods, he found a particular pickup truck—lightning bolt on the side—that had suspicious splotches of yellow paint in its wheel wells and other tight places where its owner couldn't get it off on short notice.

Wearing out some more leather on the soles of his fancy hand-tooled boots, he found out that old Jane Juan had mail-ordered a batch of yellow paintballs, which she smuggled past Red Dog and Fawn. This was the ammo she was shooting off the night of the fire, some of which she'd fired in the direction of a fleeing pickup. If her aim was as good as Red insisted, it's possible some found their mark.

At least, that was Sheriff Darryl's theory. He mentioned it around Stone Coach Woods and let it be known that if such an attack were to occur again, he'd be more seriously committed to following up on it.

So it wasn't like the Stoners got all warm and fuzzy all of a sudden; it was more like they knew if they tried any more stunts, they'd be eating fried baloney in the sheriff's lockup.

Diana and the girls stayed out late partying at the ceremony, but I had to shower up for work. Since I hadn't heard from my parents yet, my plan was to call them before I took off for the night. If I was to be leaving for Millstone, I'd have to get things together after work tomorrow morning.

But as I rinsed the shampoo out of my hair, I heard the phone ring and the answering machine pick up. I turned off the water to listen better: It was my father's voice.

"Hello? Hello, Nick," he was saying. "Are you there? Please answer if you are."

I jumped out of the shower, toweled off the leftover suds, and struggled to pull my jeans over my wet legs. Meanwhile, my dad went on.

"Nick. Your mother and I have talked. We think it's okay—" he said.

"Yes!" I said, finally shoving my feet out the bottom of the jeans.

"—what you want to do. Stay there with Wanda; go to school." Towel around my neck, jerking up the jeans as I went, I finally got out to the phone. Dad had paused as if he was waiting for me.

"Mom had a heart-to-heart with Wanda," he said. "She thinks it's what you need."

Wanda hadn't said anything to me about this. I stood there looking at the answering machine, deciding if I wanted to pick up. We had communicated like this for years, and here he was, giving me all the news I needed. Why upset things now?

"I've already called Colonel Salter," he went on, "and I told him you wouldn't be coming. He said he was disappointed. He knows you would have made a fine student. I hope you know that we'd love to have you home here, but we know there are things you have to do—want to do."

My hand hovered over the phone.

"You're getting older now, and you have to have your own life. Mom thinks—"

"Dad?" I said, picking up.

"—that's what was getting to you. . . . Nick?"

"Yes, Dad. It's me. I was in the bathroom."

"Well, we just called to tell you that it's okay that—"

"I heard. Thanks, Dad. That's great news."

"—you can stay. We'll send your stuff like you wanted."

I heard a click and then another voice. "You'd better send us a list."

"Hi, Mom," I said. She was on the other line. "I don't need a lot of stuff, just some shirts and things." I realized how little of my former self I needed.

"And we'll have your class records and all sent to your new school," said my dad. "You'll have to give me the address."

Good old organized Dad. I imagined him with his clipboard and checklist, calling Salter, calling my old school, following Mom around from room to room gathering up my socks and shirts. For some reason this image made me sad.

"Okay," I said. "This is great. Mom, Dad," I said, "I won't let you guys down." I hoped I wasn't lying. "I promise."

"That's what made your father and I decide," said my mom. "We didn't think you would."

"Thanks. Both of you," I said. "I hope you know staying here has nothing to do with you guys." I was feeling more and more like this was true and like I didn't want to hurt them. Like Mom said, they weren't some kind of special beings. They were only doing what they knew. Maybe it was my stint as Can't Bust 'Em Dad that gave me a feel for what that was like. "And it's not like I'm going away forever, or anything," I quickly added.

"You know you're always welcome home," said my mom. "No questions, any time. We just finished your room. It came out great."

"I'll come," I said. I wasn't ready to commit to exactly when yet. We were all quiet for an awkward second or two.

"Mom, Dad," I said. And then I blurted it all out: "I guess I need to tell you I really am sorry for all the trouble I've caused you lately, and I love you guys." And I meant it.

After they got me to promise to call regularly, we said our good-byes and hung up.

And this is how Diana found me, sitting there on the sofa in splotchy wet jeans, towel around my neck.

"What's happening?" she said, sitting on my lap. "You're all wet," she suddenly said, trying to squirm away as I put my arms around her.

"They're going to let me stay," I said, holding her even more tightly.

Funny, but that feeling I usually had when I was all full of something—happiness, sadness, gas, whatever—that feeling that made me want to get out and walk it through?—it just wasn't there. I felt happy to be sitting for once, Diana in my lap. The old dead feelings of resentment, anger, hurt, that I usually needed to slough off after dealing with my parents were gone. I felt hugely lighter for it. Once school starts, I'd call. I'd like to get back there by Thanksgiving, at least. I wondered if I could get Diana to go with me.

All that was left was to pack up and move out. The morning of the day we were going to leave, I had to take one last look over everything from the Big Tree. I scrambled up the gray slats, almost as quickly as Deke, in total trust they would hold. The Far was quiet, as it had been that first morning, the cabins still rough around the edges, the river winking like a dented soda can as it poured past the junkers in the parking lot. I could see the new wishing well already shooting off heat waves from its sheet metal as it sat out in the sun.

As I sat with my back to the huge trunk of the tree, I thought of the story Mysterious Willie told as lore of the Far, which matched up with the sketchy information Deke had given me about the treehouse's builder:

The Chinese farmer who built Happiness Farm had a brother from the old country who started acting up one night after a junk satellite skipped flaming through the skies. He'd taken to climbing to the top of the tallest ginkgo in town and wouldn't come down. Thinking that a change of sky might help, relatives packed him off to his rich brother in the States. Although their hearts may have been in the right place, they were kind of foggy on their astronomy, since the night sky, give or take a few hours, was pretty much the same. On his brother's farm he built the tree house in the Big Tree—big even then—and pretty much lived up there until one Fourth of July, when the wild flashes from the town fireworks show tripped his circuit breakers. His brother found him up there, dead, next morning. When he built the cabins, the brother couldn't bring himself to cut down the tree or demolish its platform.

It seemed about right that one of the earliest structures on Happiness Far was built by someone who was searching for the chariots in the sky that he knew would swing low and carry him off sometime soon.

For now, though no chariots were in sight. Things had become all too predictable.

It was time to go.

And so a few days later a small group of the inmates surrounded Deke and Wanda and me—Diana and the girls having gone on ahead—as we loaded the Wandamobile for the last time. O. K. Sunbeam took time off from her morning calls, and Jolly Roger and Rode Kool, Loosie, Clat, Willie, and the Branstools were all there, along with Jane. There were tears all around and housewarming gifts for the new place: some fireworks from O. K., a Big Bag o' Sweat Socks (one size fits all) from Loosie, a special mix of tunes from Rode, and a shovel from the Branstools. Roger gave us his lucky fruitcake which he said he'd had since he was a boy; Willie, the old wishing-well can, pounded perfectly flat, which he'd saved. We promised we'd be back—at least for the parties—and I knew we would.

Deke and Wanda got in the front, and I climbed in the back, holding onto the plaster dog that Wanda used for a doorstop, and we drove off.

As we came around and passed by the arch of the entryway to the Far, I broke the Prime Directive. I turned and took one last look at the group gathered there under the sign, all sizes and shapes and dressed all different and all waving, looking like the rejected ideas for a Mardi Gras parade—Roger wiping his eye with the back of his lobster hand puppet.

I had the strangest feeling in my gut. Something I'd never felt leaving anywhere. Like I'd just swallowed the Big Bag o' Sweat Socks.

The next day, Wanda signed me into the local high school—not that much different from where I'd been, with almost the same groups—geeks and freaks and skaters and goths and preps and punks and jocks and nerds and me and Diana. Most of the Stoners went to a private school—the one Diana had left after the date-rape thing—so we didn't have to deal with them. Although she wasn't widely popular, looks take you a long way in any school, and showing up with her beside me gave me a studly status there to begin with.

And life goes on.

Wanda seemed to come back alive in the new place. First of all she apologized for not letting me in on my parents' decision earlier, but they'd made her promise not to tell, and she wanted to start developing a track record—at least with them—of keeping promises.

And it looks like she's finally come off the fence as far as Deke is concerned. She and Deke share the same bedroom, as they'd done at his place since Wanda's cabin burned. "I don't know if she got the wish she made back when we got crowned," said Deke, talking about the Lunacy Festival, "but I do know I got mine." He thinks he may eventually even have some luck in getting her to marry him.

Lately she found a job working in a local greenhouse. I love going in there, especially as the weather gets colder. It's like it's always spring. She must've picked up a talent for growing stuff in the communal garden at the Far. Back in the old house I'd never known her to grow anything more than the mold on dishes left in the sink.

She didn't see me come in one day, and I spied on her from behind a couple of pots of ferns. I flinched when she picked up a pair of snips as she stood on a raised wooden platform, working over a row of potted holly bushes. But she clipped here and there and stuck a bow on each, and when she was done, they looked perfect! All this without a visit to the ER.

Also she can't smoke in there, and she said that smoking was getting in the way of her breathing in all the great smells in the place, anyway. Connect that with her promise to Deke to give up the cancer sticks, and I think that qualifies her as a recovering smokaholic.

On top of this, the greenhouse added a new extension last summer, and she thinks she can get Diana a regular job there, especially with the busy holiday season coming up.

As for me, the end of senior year looks like a long way from here, but if it's anything like freshman, sophomore, and junior years, I know it will be over sooner than I think, and so will high school—forever, which is not long enough. And then . . .

Then, I don't know what.

Diana and I have no long-term plans for *anything*, never mind for "us." It's nice together as we are now, and I know we've got something strong going. But when she talks about it, you can tell it's clear she has her own ideas about what she wants to do after she graduates.

She and her mom have started getting together lately, since her father moved out. He found it more comfortable, for some reason, to be in another faraway town—Diana doesn't want to know where. Her mother said he was getting what she called "professional help" there, which I hope involves someone who is a professional brain surgeon who doesn't believe in anesthetic.

With him out of the house, it looks like Diana's sisters may eventually be able to go back home. This would give Diana some moving-around room. She says she's always wanted to get back out to the West Coast. "You can start fresh there," she told me one day. We were slow-dancing in Old Vic's big dusty ballroom to a tape playing in an automobile tape deck Deke had set up, complete with automobile dashboard.

"West?" I said.

She mentioned the cities she'd lived in as her family shifted from place to place, following her father. "Nobody cares who you are or what you've done or where you're from."

For once, I didn't know if this exactly appealed to me.

"I mean, after I finish school," she added.

"Oh," I said, relieved that I could put off deciding what I wanted to do at least for a year.

You see, I've been rereading that old yellowed newspaper piece that Wanda has faithfully stuck on the refrigerator in Old Vic—the thing about "How to Make a House a Home"? And I'm starting to understand the last rule better: "If you want to live with others, get your own house in order."

I used to think it was the second half of it that I didn't get, but I'm coming to see it's the first.

This place, Old Vic, is kind of—I don't know what you would call it. Sticky? If I ever even *think* of leaving, I get that same strange sock-swallowing feeling I had when we waved good-bye to everyone at the Far. It's not a place I want to walk from. Also, there's only us—no *them*—to blame when things go wrong. So if there's an argument about who has to clean the stove, or take out the garbage, instead of first thinking of taking to the road, I tend to think of how I can change things—often me—so that I can *stay*. How I can work with everyone there. How we can come to agreements on things. How I can be more trusting. In spite of what my mother said, I think I did find exactly the house I wanted.

When I think about it, though, I know that if I ever do leave the place, it won't be like leaving where I grew up with my parents and the Ghost of Donnie Past.

I read somewhere that someone once said, "Home is the place where, when you have to go there, they have to take you in." I think it's also the place that when you have to *leave* there, you have to take it with you; that it has become such a part of you, it's impossible to leave it behind.

So I don't know. Deke says the thing to do when he was young was to backpack around the country. I'm thinking of saving up my doughnut dough and maybe eventually doing just that. And if I found I was walking out west, where Diana is headed, I wouldn't be so surprised.

I do know, though, that no matter where I walk, in the back of my head I'll always hear that dogged drummer. It's a catchy beat he's got going there. One that, maybe you're bedding down for the night having said your prayers, lying between some fresh cool sheets, or slouched on the sofa, remote in your hand, or sitting at the table about to reach for the macaroni and cheese, and it pulls you to your feet, and next you know, you're out the door, your napkin still tucked under your chin, flapping in the breeze as you fall in behind him.

Even if it wasn't for the drum, you'd find him easy to recognize: He's got raggedy clothes and a bloody bandage wrapped around his head; his eyes are fixed to some spot in the far distance, and he wears a big grin on his face.

If you ever do happen to see this guy, look a couple of steps behind. You'll probably see me following him, wearing an equally big grin, hefting my pack, whistling a tune.

Most likely out of step.